IN CONNECTION WITH KILSHAW

Peter Driscoll

SILVERTAIL BOOKS • *London*

Peter Driscoll (1942-2005) was born in London, grew up in South Africa and later moved to Ireland. He was the author of nine complex and intriguing thrillers, the second of which, *The Wilby Conspiracy*, was made into a successful feature film and established his reputation as an international bestselling author. His novels are:

The White Lie Assignment
The Wilby Conspiracy
In Connection With Kilshaw
The Barboza Credentials
Pangolin
Heritage
Spearhead
Secrets of State
Spoils of War

First published in Great Britain by Macdonald and Company
(Publishers) Ltd in 1974
This edition published by Silvertail Books in 2023
www.silvertailbooks.com

*All characters in this publication other than those clearly in the
public domain are fictitious and any resemblance to real persons,
living or dead, is purely coincidental.*

For Hilda, and in memory of Jean

Author's Note

Comparisons with actual political figures in Northern Ireland may be inevitable in the minds of some readers. But there has never been a Kilshaw or a Sullivan or anyone like them, nor are their backgrounds any more than typical of men in the kind of roles I have imagined for them.

The telephone, two feet from his head, woke Finn with a brief, shattering ring. For a moment he was bewildered by the light and then, feeling the cling of stale clothes around him, he realized with bitter familiarity that tiredness had played one of its regular tricks. He'd fallen asleep fully dressed – in the middle of the BBC jazz programme, too. A faint hum came from the bedside rediffusion set.

He rolled on his side, shielding his eyes from the glare of the lamp above, and blinked the dial of his watch into focus. Ten past twelve. Jesus, how he slept nowadays. His mouth was dry and sulphurous-tasting, like the dregs of bad wine.

The phone shrilled again and he stared at it. He could never hear that sound late at night without some slight apprehension, and here the thought of danger was never far from his mind. The curtains of the hotel room, still open, billowed inwards on the breeze. Through the window he looked across a dark huddle of rooftops towards the shipyards and their floodlit steel skeletons. It was quiet outside, unnaturally quiet for the heart of a city, but he was accustomed to it now. Few people went out at night in Belfast; the commuters hurried home to the suburbs and stayed there, leaving the battered streets mostly to the troops and the terrorists.

He picked up the receiver as the phone rang a third time, waited for the burring in the earpiece to stop, and heard the switchboard girl's bright voice.

'Mr Finn? I was about to page you. There's a call.'

He said hello and heard it come out in a dry rasp. But already he had recognized Fortune's soft County Down accent and felt a swift release of tension.

'Harry? I must have woken you?'

'It doesn't matter.'

'Sorry, but I thought we'd better talk. I've made progress, Harry. I've good news and bad news.'

Finn was still thick-headed with sleep. 'You're back from the South then?'

'Since this morning. Could we ever meet for a wee chat?'

He hesitated. He had sensed anxiety in the other man's tone. 'You've been back the whole day. What's so damned urgent?'

'Nothing, only I thought you'd want to know. I've found her, Harry.'

Finn heard himself gasp. 'The girl?'

'The girl,' said Fortune.

'The right one?'

'Och, no doubt of it. But there's more to it, Harry. Bother. We'd better talk. I'm no distance away; couldn't we meet in the usual wee place?'

'Give me five minutes,' said Finn.

He put down the receiver and sat on the edge of the bed for a minute, assimilating the news through a haze of sleepiness and surprise. The girl. Miss Hughes, that was her name. Momentarily he had almost forgotten it, because by now he was used to the idea that they wouldn't find her. He wasn't even sure he had wanted to find her, there was the truth, yet something of the old instinct now had quickened his pulse. But what madness had possessed Fortune?

Bloody Irish, Finn thought irritably. He went through to the bathroom, splashed cold water on his face, shuddered, and glanced up at his reflection in the mirror. Sometimes the sight of his face gave him a shock. It had never been handsome; perhaps once it had had a dark Irish intensity of its own, suggesting restlessness and volatility, hinting at a nature that was energetic, earthy, unorthodox. All that seemed to have gone.

Superficially, at least, the radiotherapy had been more unkind than the disease it had burnt out of him. Between them they had left his face empty and gaunt, the skin patched with dark subcutaneous scars. It would improve in time, but it was still a face that disturbed people; they seemed to sense that it had been close to death.

He tucked in his shirt, straightened his tie, pulled on his overcoat. Better have a glass of water. He'd missed dinner but he wasn't hungry anyway; he still had trouble salivating and the treatment had deadened his sense of taste, so most of the time he ate mechanically to build up his weight and strength. He wondered, seriously for a moment, whether to take the service Browning that was hidden under the mattress of the other twin bed. No. Out on the streets it carried more risk than usefulness, and he'd had enough trouble getting the damned thing into the hotel to start with.

Closing the self-locking door of his room behind him he went downstairs, using the service stairwell instead of the lift. A cold draught was sucked in through windows where panes shattered by the latest bomb blast had not yet been replaced. This was one of the newer and bigger hotels in Belfast, and therefore it was a symbol of confidence that the Irish Republican Army was determined to destroy – even at some risk to its public image, since practically every guest was a journalist. Such were the curious terms on which this war was being fought. Finn stayed here because it was the only place in the city where he could come and go, receive visitors, and make phone calls at any time of the day or night without arousing curiosity. Partington had been right; everyone had assumed that he was a journalist too, and he'd had no trouble acquiring the credentials to prove it.

Most of the press corps were still drinking in the cocktail lounge on the first floor. Finn avoided them, went down to the lobby, out through the revolving doors that were guarded by a porter and a rather conspicuous Special Branch man, and along the pathway of iron hurdles that formed part of the security barrier.

There had been little enough traffic earlier in the raw autumn evening, but now the streets seemed empty and echoing. He walked left and turned into Glengall Street. Just past the bombed-out headquarters of the Ulster Unionist Party, Fortune's Austin 1100 was parked in shadow. Finn waited to be sure he had not been followed before he crossed the street, opened the near-side door, and slid into the passenger seat.

'How are you at all, Harry?'

'All right. You'd better drive somewhere. We don't want to get turned over by a patrol.'

Fortune nodded, fished in his pockets, and lit a villainous cheroot.

'What's the bother?' Finn asked.

'Just... well, I'd better come straight out with it, Harry. I'm dropping out. No more fronting for you.'

He gave Finn a quick, nervous glance.

'I'm sorry. I've never quit in the middle of one before, Partington will tell you that. But I've got to live in this town, so I have. I've got five kids.'

It was so unexpected that it left Finn with nothing to say. He was absently aware that the pain in his ear, a side-effect of the radiation treatment, had started up. Finally he said, 'Why don't we drive?'

Fortune started the car gratefully. The precautions they had always taken were as much for his sake as for Finn's. He was a small, self-contained man with a deep redness in his hair and his complexion. Behind a screen of thoughtful red lashes, his eyes held that striking blue Irish clarity which could easily be mistaken for innocence. He was a Catholic, in a city where a man's religion was written on his face and speech, if not on his soul, so that at some level near the surface of the mind one was always conscious of it. But Fortune also had a chameleon's talent for blending. He was a private detective, probably the best one in Ireland. At one time he had made a living fronting for the military police, tracing army deserters in the Republican ghettos where British uniforms had been unwelcome long before the present troubles. Gradually he had come to the notice of other branches and been entrusted with more delicate jobs. Finn liked him. He admired professionalism, that odd ability to do a thing well even when the heart isn't in it. Finn's heart was hardly in it any longer, but he was a professional too.

They turned left into Great Victoria Street and then down the Grosvenor Road, towards the Catholic wedge of the city that widened out against the flanks of Divis Mountain, faintly out-lined against the clear sky to the west. To an outsider the tribal boundaries of Belfast were invisible, but they were firmly drawn and as rigid as any national frontier.

Fortune said, 'I thought I'd show you where she lives. It's in Andersonstown.'

'So she *is* a Catholic.'

'Sure. Caragh Hughes is the name. She's twenty-seven and a redhead. Quite a looker, so she is.'

'Caragh?'

'It means *beloved* in Irish. Your man has got taste, I'll give him that.'

'Tell me your problem.'

'I can tell you in two words,' Fortune said. 'The IRA.'

'She belongs to the IRA?'

'I doubt that. But the family were always strong Republicans. And her brother, you see, is the Belfast commander of an IRA faction. Sullivan's Volunteers, in fact.'

'Oh, my God,' said Finn flatly.

'Hold on now.'

Fortune was slowing down the car. Ahead, a barrier of hurdles had been set between the cramped rows of terraced houses on either side of the road. Two men of the Royal Ulster Constabulary flagged them down, examined their faces and Finn's press card briefly in the beam of a torch, and diverted them up Leeson Street. Somewhere ahead, they said, a lorry had been hijacked and the tiresome, ritualistic rounds of events had begun: crowd gathered, army went in, stones thrown, CS nausea gas and rubber bullets fired, and finally gunmen from one or another of the squabbling factions that called themselves the IRA had come onto the streets. The sniping was still going on.

They drove off to the right, into the old Catholic working-class heartland of West Belfast, a maze of mean streets which had burgeoned together with the shipyards and linen mills in the nineteenth century and crumbled all too rapidly into slums during the twentieth. On top of the official demolition, three years of bombs, fires, and rioting had left acres of devastation in an area where violence was now practically a way of life. The walls of shattered buildings stood jaggedly in rows like broken teeth, some bearing painted tricolours and shamrocks and slogans that were still legible by the light of infrequent street lamps: UP THE RE-PUBLIC, JOIN THE IRA, and, with grotesque irrelevance, HIGHER FOOD PRICES IN THE COMMON MARKET. Windows had been boarded up; paving stones, ripped out to make barricades or missiles, lay smashed in the gutters with the other debris of sporadic rioting. The city had been tearing itself slowly apart since that summer three years before when the old hatreds had flared up with such violence that thousands of British troops had come in to keep Catholics and Protestants from each other's throats. But this time the sectarian conflict had turned into a prolonged guerrilla war between the security forces and the IRA. The Protestants had waited on the sidelines. The time was rapidly approaching when they would wait no more.

Fortune turned left into the Falls Road. Some way behind they could hear shouting and the occasional clatter of a stone against a perspex riot shield. The detective said, 'It's too late for a real riot. The kids are just getting in some practice.'

'What about the shooting? I thought there was some sort of truce.'

'Truces come and go. Sure, most of the IRA units have been scared into keeping quiet lately. They're afraid of what the Prods may do. Not Sullivan's mob, of course. But things are that hairy now, every fool with a gun is liable to let fly at anything that moves.' He mashed his cheroot into the ashtray and said, 'Con Michael Hughes. Heard of him?'

'His name's been in the papers now and then. Whiz kid, Trotskyite, textbook revolutionary. Pain in the ass too, by the sound of it. On the run, of course. It's a common enough surname. No wonder we didn't connect them.'

'He runs the Belfast end of things for Sullivan, though they say he does pretty much what he's told from Dublin. Got a big thing about identifying with the workers. His great pal is one Billy McGarry – know the name? One-shot Billy, the army lads call him. Right dangerous company, that. Used to be a welder. Now he specializes in shooting soldiers in the head. They want him pretty badly.'

'Nice man to know,' Finn said. 'Where do you get all this stuff, anyway?'

'Connections.' Fortune gave a secretive smile. 'Look, you know the scene here now, Harry. It's a cosy wee war – intimate, domestic. We're informal people; everyone knows everyone. When the IRA comes into it I've got to draw the line. If they even got an inkling that I was working with you, and me a Catholic... it might take five or ten years, but some day there'd be a bullet with my name on it. I'm sorry, Harry. You know what happened to O'Meara.'

'You told me.'

O'Meara had been another detective who worked occasionally for Partington, until the morning last winter when his frozen body had been found on the west bank of the River Lagan. He had been strangled with piano wire, and pinned to his chest had been a scrawled notice: BRITISH SPY.

Finn's earache was getting worse, and he realized he had left his pills at the hotel. He said, 'You know the saying? The English can never remember, the Irish can never forget. I don't blame you.'

'Thanks, Harry. I'll keep my ears open for you, but that's all I can promise. You'd do the same, with five kids.' Fortune paused, wondering whether he'd said the wrong thing. 'Did you ever have kids? In Germany?'

'No,' said Finn.

At some point along the Upper Falls Road they had passed from Victorian surroundings into modern ones, which in their own way were just as forbidding: Ballymurphy, Andersonstown, Turf Lodge, council estates with rows of bleak, featureless houses in pale brick reaching up to the lower slopes of the encircling hills. But somewhere in the middle of all this Fortune swung left, past a traffic roundabout adorned with the shell of a burnt-out bus, into a curious little enclave of suburban affluence. The houses, set well back behind lawns, were large, modern, individually built – ranch-style bungalows alternating with two-storeyed villas – but sharing a tendency towards half-timbered gables, picture windows, and other assertions of middle-class owner-occupancy. It might have been a comfortably off suburb anywhere in the British Isles except for an odd profusion of estate agents' boards. Half the houses in the street were up for sale.

'This area here is Coolnasilla Park,' said Fortune, drawing up opposite one of the double-storeyed houses. It had French windows, a wide garage, and a rather neglected garden. It too had a FOR SALE notice outside, and like all the others it was in darkness.

'That there was the family house. Only Caragh lives there now. The family are Southerners basically, although both the kids grew up in Belfast. The old man was a bookie. He came up here early in the fifties to cash in on the gambling boom. Died two years ago, and the mother went back South to get away from the troubles. It was from her wee place just outside Dublin that I managed to trace Caragh back here. The idea at the time was for Caragh and Con Michael to sell this house and join their mother. Either they've never succeeded or not tried very hard. This area, of course. These are people who've done all right for themselves; they want no part of the aggro.'

'Except for middle-class revolutionaries like Con Michael Hughes,' Finn said. He stared through the darkness at the house. 'Is it conceivable that the IRA have got what we're looking for?'

'Sounds unlikely. We can't even be sure that Caragh knows anything.'

'How did she get on with her brother?'

'I'm told they were very close. Of course, if he knew about her paramour he'd hardly have approved. A bit prudish, like most of his type. But Caragh's always been an independent one. Headstrong. It was a row with her parents that made her leave home and take that flat in York Street. It might have been a row with lover boy that sent her back.'

'It's almost too good to be true,' Finn said thoughtfully. 'Catholic girl and Loyalist fire-eater. It's a pity permissiveness has turned blackmail into a dying trade.' He paused. 'Do you think they were actually in love?'

'My guess is that your man started off feeling flattered and ended up infatuated. You've seen it happen before. Middle-aged fellow, public figure, position to keep up, never dreamed of being unfaithful, suddenly knocked right off his pedestal by a girl half his age. Realizes what he's been missing, specially with a wife – you've seen her – like an old boot. As for Caragh, the idea probably amused her. A rebel, you see. He was everything she'd been brought up to distrust, despise, fear. She'd have enjoyed that.'

Fortune started the car. 'Now you know everything I do. Sorry to drop you in it, Harry.'

Finn, in his small notebook, jotted the address of the house and the name of the agent offering it for sale. In another minute they were driving back down the Falls, each absorbed in his own thoughts. Finn could not be annoyed with Fortune. He approved the principle of survival, having himself narrowly survived the illness – or so he had no choice but to believe. Still, against the recommended procedure and whatever Partington thought, he would have to take over the fronting himself. There was simply no one else.

The Grosvenor Road was still sealed off. A wavering orange glow above the rooftops suggested that the hijacked lorry had been set alight, though the sounds of stoning had ceased. Fortune continued down the Lower Falls and cut off to the right at Albert Street, following the curve of a long line of gutted houses, their doors and windows sealed with breeze blocks to deny cover to snipers. VOLUNTEERS FOREVER, shouted the wall signs. BRITISH BASTARDS OUT!

They were beginning another right turn to take them back to the hotel. An armoured ambulance, the bray of its siren starting a fraction too late, burst into the intersection, taking the corner at a sharp tilt. Fortune cursed and swung to the left but the ambulance slewed and clipped the rear end of the Austin, bumping it onto the pavement before roaring away up Albert Street.

Two more armoured vehicles had boxed in the car. There was

a swift movement of figures across the street, the doors were jerked open, and Finn was looking down the muzzle of a Sterling sub-machine gun six inches from his face.

'Out!' said the paratrooper corporal.

Another para was covering Fortune, and the rest of the patrol that had erupted from the rear doors of the armoured cars were crouched with their self-loading rifles in whatever surrounding shadow they could find. Fortune began some protest about the damage to his car.

'I said *out*!' yelled the corporal. 'Against the wall!'

They climbed out and were shoved against the wall and frisked efficiently and none too gently, while behind them the car was searched too. When they turned round a tall, authoritative figure stood facing them.

Grudgingly the corporal announced, 'They're clean, sir.'

'But why are they driving about in a cordoned area?' the officer wondered.

'It wasn't cordoned when we –' Fortune began.

'Shut up!' snapped the corporal.

Finn said nothing but watched the officer closely. Through the anonymity of the red beret, the major's crowns, the flak jacket, and the face smeared with blacking grease there was a worrying familiarity. The major stared back at him.

'Well, what's the story?' he demanded.

'I'm a journalist.'

'Identification?'

Finn took out his National Union of Journalists card and handed it over. Suddenly they all flinched back against the wall at the sound of shots – a burst of automatic fire some way off, the distinctive heavy thump of a Thompson gun followed by the hard bang of an army SLR. Now Finn knew why the paras were so edgy.

'You've arrived at the right moment,' said the major, more

polite but still distant. 'One of our men has just been killed. We're going in after the sniper. A man we call One-shot Billy. We think we've got him cornered.'

He looked at the card in his hand, then up again. They had recognized each other at the same moment.

'Good God, Harry Finn!'

Finn swore under his breath.

2

Belfast was an easy city to get to know, a friendly, informal place in spite of everything. The trouble was that it got to know its visitors quickly as well. You sought anonymity and found yourself exposed. You were recognized and greeted by people you hardly knew, didn't want to know – a thing that could never happen in London. Not that Finn often made that comparison. He had been born in London but was almost a stranger to it now. Home had been a dozen different places on three continents. For the past eleven years it had been an apartment in Düsseldorf and a weekend hunting lodge lost on a bleak plateau of the Höhe Eifel, the latter much his favourite of the two. There he spent as much time as he could with cans of soup, his fishing tackle, and his collection of old records. Occasionally with a woman too, though it wasn't a love-nest kind of place, more a sanctuary for a self-sufficient man, its whereabouts known only to a few friends, its very existence guarded from his superiors. His wife, when he'd had a wife, had detested it; he longed to get back. But in the meantime his hotel room in Belfast was at least more comfortable than the cramped little flat in north London where, for the past five months, he had slept, eaten, watched television, mooned about – but mostly slept.

Sleep had been the central experience. He had discovered the difficulty of getting up when there is nothing to get up for, so that on days when he did not have to report to the hospital he would stay in bed, dozing and reading alternately, until two or three in the afternoon. Sometimes he felt too ill to get out of bed at all. When he had forced himself to take some soup and perhaps tidied the flat and done some shopping it would be time to catch the early news on television and have a drink, and the evening would fill itself out with whisky and television until he found himself falling asleep around ten o'clock.

So the shapeless days had flowed into each other. The two mornings of treatment under the infernal machine at the Royal National Hospital gave some texture to the week, and on a Sunday morning he might make the effort to get to a pub where there was live jazz. And then, of course, an element of spontaneity was provided by the pain. It could come at any time. It would begin with a sharp stab at the seat of the tumour in his throat and grow quickly to an agony that consumed his whole being.

In his own mind the beginning had been on a cold spring day when he had walked up from Harley Street into Regent's Park and sat numbly on a bench and for the first time faced the probability of his own death.

He had had suspicions, of course. There'd been the loss of weight, the hoarseness, and then the day on which he'd coughed and stared incredulously at a bright blot of blood, the size of a Deutschmark, on his handkerchief. Even then the truth did not penetrate because he did not want it to. The Royal Army Medical Corps physician at Rhine Army headquarters had peered down his throat through a laryngoscope and muttered, 'I don't know that there's much we can do...' and even this Finn's mind succeeded in misinterpreting. With solicitous haste he was bundled onto a service flight with an appointment to see an ear-nose-and-throat specialist in London, the leading man in his field. It was never explained in so many words, but it was clear that the course of intensive radiotherapy that was to begin the next day was very much a last resort. Surgery was out of the question.

He sat for several hours hunched in his overcoat, watching the water of the lake rippled by a cold wind, until he had accepted the fact as totally as he ever would. Once that had happened it was impossible ever to be quite the same person again.

The massive doses of radiation left him exhausted, depressed, apathetic. For three months there was no way of telling whether he was beating the disease. He continued losing weight, but then he wasn't eating much. The RAMC had recommended a small hotel in Bayswater, full of potted palms and retired colonial police officers, where there was an invalid menu. Finn had preferred to seek out his own graveyard, and when the pains became really severe he was glad to be on his own. He had made self-sufficiency into an obsession. He had learned to hate a whole set of other people's emotions which he lumped together under the heading *pity*. Pity seemed as insidious and destructive as the disease itself.

Three years earlier his marriage had not so much broken up as come apart. Whatever thin adhesive had held them together for eight years had simply ceased to resist the force of her continuing frigidity. Finn took some of the blame himself – he had had affairs, none of any consequence – but there was no real need for blame because the whole thing was settled as dispassionately as a sale of bankrupt assets. At any rate, for all practical purposes he now had no next of kin, and he demanded and got frankness from his doctors. One night, a week before the radiotherapy course was due to end, he had an attack of pain so severe that he did not believe he could survive another. The next morning he dragged himself to Harley Street to demand stronger drugs.

'Can't I persuade you to go into hospital?' asked the eminent man.

'No.'

'The really powerful painkillers ought to be taken under supervision, you see.'

'If I go in I may not come out. I can't take that idea. I've got a nine-millimetre pistol at home. Last night I damn near used it.'

The specialist nodded thoughtfully, reached for his gold fountain pen, and wrote a prescription.

'This is called Brompton's Mixture. Its base is diamorphine and cocaine. It's highly addictive, but that doesn't usually matter because it goes only to terminal patients. You must choose for yourself whether you take it.'

The prescription translated into a bottle of clear liquid. Back at his flat, he sat and stared at it. To drink the stuff was to accept a finality as total as blowing his brains out. He had been given a soft option, a long, easy slide, whether to death or drug addiction could hardly matter in the end. Pity in a subtler guise had been offered to him again.

He resolved not to use the Brompton's Mixture, though it stayed at his bedside. He never knew whether he would have held out because suddenly the pains became less severe. The following week, when the radiation was over, a biopsy proved negative. The tumour had gone; there was no trace of affected cells.

But here finality was more elusive. The specialist said, 'We must wait. You've beaten it, yes, but we must be sure there is no recurrence. You'll be some time convalescing.'

3

The paratroopers had begun moving up both sides of Albert Street towards the shooting, darting like mice from one patch of shadow to the next. Finn and Fortune, escorted by the major, followed. Round a turning fifty yards on, Divis Court came into view, a complex of council flats whose ten-storey tower block was well known for its usefulness to snipers. Around the buildings there was now a murkily lit no-man's-land, with soldiers taking cover behind the vehicles that blocked every street.

'We'll get the sod this time,' said the major. 'He's completely boxed in.'

Finn could not help thinking that if he and Fortune had slipped in through the cordon by accident, One-shot Billy might have found it at least as easy to slip out. But he said nothing and let himself be led to the rear of an armoured car, parked in a narrow entry with a clear view of the flats. Two Scottish squaddies crouching there hastily doused their cigarettes. The major spoke on his Pocketfone walkie-talkie, spreading out his men in readiness for a rush at the building. Then he stood waiting for the platoon commanders to report their positions.

His name was Howarth. They had met at Rhine Army headquarters at Rheindalen a few years ago when Howarth was acting adjutant of his battalion and Finn was asking awkward questions about a leakage of NATO alert codes. It was very low-grade stuff, the kind that could safely be entrusted to the files of battalion HQs; there was a joke about them having their own classification gradings, in which Confidential became *Anyone can read it* and Secret meant *Better pop it in a drawer*. The evidence had quickly pointed to one of Howarth's clerks. Finn had planned to leave him in place, hoping to trap the ring in Cologne that was paying him for the stuff, but Howarth was one of those impatient, impulsive people for whom decision-making was an end in itself and action, any action, was better than doing nothing. Without consulting Finn he ordered the suspect's arrest.

Naturally, there was friction; there was also a short period of intense mutual dislike. At the bottom of it was the regimental soldier's distrust of Staff and a bit of Sandhurst bluster against a parvenu asking pointed questions with the wrong accent. Anyway, it did not seem to have harmed Howarth's career. He was a company commander now while Finn, probably ten years older, had marked time.

'So you're a journalist,' Howarth said. 'Seriously?'

'Freelancing. I work mostly for German magazines.'

'I didn't realize you knew anything about it.'

'Oh, they'll print any old rubbish.'

'What are you writing from here?'

'What do you think? How fifteen thousand of the world's most professional soldiers are being kept on the hop by a few dozen gunmen and bombers. How they and their political masters should never have let this thing become a guerrilla war in the first place.'

'That simply isn't true,' Howarth said stiffly.

'Perhaps it looks more convincing in German.'

'You liked living there, didn't you? Can't think why.'

The air was shattered by another burst of Thompson fire. Nothing moved; the echoes died away among the courtyards of the flats.

'Another thing I've written,' said Finn, 'is that the real power to be feared here is not the Catholics and the IRA, but the Protestant extremists. The Loyalist Vigilantes. Kilshaw.'

'I've a lot of respect for Kilshaw,' Howarth said. 'The Vigilantes are not bad to deal with. They're restrained, disciplined –'

'Until they go on the rampage, which they will pretty soon. Discipline is easy to admire. The problem is that it contains an ultimate threat. Paramilitary movements must have violence sooner or later, else they lose their purpose. We don't seem to have learned from the Brown Shins.'

The radio strapped beneath Howarth's flak jacket crackled incomprehensibly.

'Zero one roger,' he said into the microphone. 'Go in. Go in hard.'

They watched as the first section of paras began an oblique, zigzag approach to the building. Almost at once there was another rattle of gunfire, answered this time by a dozen rounds from soldiers who had spotted movements among the rooftops.

'Enthusiastic amateurs,' muttered Howarth. 'But Billy McGarry is no amateur. Just between us – we don't want the press turning him into a hero – tonight he killed his sixth soldier.'

'What do you know about him?' Finn asked casually. He did not feel casual; his earache had sprung suddenly into a grinding pain.

'He's a psychopathic killer,' Howarth said. 'A natural-born marksman. Until a year ago he was a welder in the shipyards; you need a good eye for that. Last month some damn fool marksman from the Royal Anglians lost his SLR. He panicked when a crowd ran at him and dropped his rifle with its night scope. Needless to say it found its way to the IRA and to Billy. In darkness like this he can see his target almost as clearly as in daylight. He'll wait all night for a target, fire one shot, and melt out of sight. This time, though...'

Under the covering fire of the surrounding troops, the first platoon of paras had now entered the tower block and the amateurs were markedly less enthusiastic. The shot that had lolled the soldier had almost certainly come from the fifth or sixth floor. Howarth's radio buzzed with messages as the suspect flats were entered and searched.

'I'd like to take out every building in this area, room by room,' Howarth said. 'The politicians won't let us, of course, in case we antagonize innocent people. Innocent! There isn't a Mick in there who wouldn't hide him, even the ones who *don't* like the IRA.'

'He's one of their own people. That's the way they see it.'

'I've given up trying to understand them.'

'Perhaps they'd simply rather help him than help you,' Finn suggested. Howarth looked at him suspiciously. The British, believing fundamentally in their own decency, had always had trouble understanding other people's capacity to hate them.

Suddenly there was a babble of voices on the walkie-talkie and Howarth visibly sagged.

'Gone again,' he said. 'Not even in the building.'

The two Scottish soldiers muttered to each other. Fortune, who had been silent and noncommittal, said, 'I could have told you.'

'What?' Howarth demanded.

'That he'd be out of the place altogether. It's their policy never to compromise people whose houses are open to them. That's why they stay open. His escape route was planned beforehand.'

'Who's your clever friend?' Howarth said to Finn.

'Seamus Fortune,' the small man answered for himself. 'Private investigator.'

'Indeed? Well, you stick to your job and leave me to do mine.' Howarth's lips had compressed to an irritable white slit; otherwise his expression was hidden beneath the blacking grease but he was clearly struck by an association of ideas. He said to Finn, casually, 'You resigned your commission to take up this journalism lark?'

'I've been ill. I was warded out.'

'You've lost a lot of weight.'

'It was either this or a desk job at Ashford.'

'Did you stay with Int Corps right to the end?'

'Yes.'

Now that the troops had control of Divis Court, there would be no more shooting. In a couple of minutes Howarth was leading them back to Albert Street.

'We've got to beat these people,' he said, 'and do it damned quickly. Sullivan's Volunteers, I mean. They're not just the usual IRA madmen, they claim to be revolutionaries, part of the whole international war against capitalist society, like the Tupamaros and the Weathermen. They've got to be shown it won't work here. If it comes to choosing between extremists, I prefer Kilshaw. At least he doesn't want to turn us all into blue ants.'

Finn could not be bothered to argue. You could rely on Howarth to utter the conventional wisdom. When they reached the Austin it still stood with its bonnet, boot, and all four doors open and the back seat dragged out. Behind the rear door on the right was a deep dent.

"Who foots the bill for that?' Fortune asked.

'You can try sending it to Brigade HQ. They may decide it comes into the hard-cheese category, of course. You need to drive carefully in this town. Good night.'

Howarth had radioed the men on the nearest roadblock to let them through, and soon they were parked behind the hotel again. Fortune said, 'What annoys me is that my tax is paying that man's salary.'

'He's an idiot,' Finn agreed, 'but a dangerous one. My luck to run into him. Before you go, fill me in on Sullivan's Volunteers.'

'Well, he was right, up to a point, there. They claim to be Marxists or Trots or whatever the current fashion is. Personally I reckon underneath they're old-fashioned Irish nationalists like all the rest. Anyway, they're the most fanatical wing of the IRA.

The others are afraid. Like everyone else, they can see the danger of a Protestant backlash, of pushing Kilshaw's people into civil war. Sullivan's lot reckon on the fighting up North here being only the start of a revolution throughout Ireland. They want an Irish people's republic and until they get it there's to be no compromise, no surrender.'

'It sounds more like a programme for mass suicide,' Finn said. 'Does Con Michael Hughes go along with it?'

'Och, I think he's sincere, Harry, but starry-eyed. A textbook man, like you said. Three years out of University College Dublin and knows it all. He's their political commissar, if you like. Believes in violence as a political weapon – not that he's much of a hand for the dirty work himself, from what I hear.'

'And yet he's their commander in Belfast?'

'That probably suits Sullivan himself. Colin Sullivan, leader of the faction. Runs his war from Dublin and makes sure of running it his own way. Con Michael is young, malleable, an admirer of Sullivan. Most of the older men who'd have been more independent are long after being killed or arrested. Apart from Con Michael the rest are the usual bunch of yobbos. That's the trouble with this kind of setup, that somebody like Billy McGarry without enough brains to fill an eggcup can earn himself a reputation from here to the Bog of Allen. Who'd ever have heard of him otherwise? Oh, well.' Fortune snorted philosophically. 'That's about it.'

'Thanks for everything.'

'I'll keep an ear to the ground. Good luck now, Harry.'

Finn let himself be frisked by an embarrassed young porter, went up to his room, took three of his pills, and lay down. He wouldn't be able to sleep till they took effect. Pains came less frequently nowadays but still brought a trickle of anxiety. They had warned him about pains; it was simply the healthy tissue, destroyed by radiation, replacing itself. He had gained some weight, he felt stronger every day, but still he couldn't help worrying when the pains came.

The central heating was too warm for comfort; he removed his jacket and tie. The tie was chocolate brown and pink with a pattern of meshing gear-wheels. Brightly coloured neckwear, all bought from a snooty but trendy little shop in Jermyn Street, was perhaps his only affectation, and rather a negative one at that. It arose from nothing more than a deep inner need not to conform. For the rest he dressed conventionally and rather badly, with a slack civilian care for comfort, not appearance. He had no 'image'; he had somehow grown out of the need to impress people. Strangely, in the past few months, he seemed to have lost the need for people entirely – for their company, friendship, compassion, interest, whatever set of abstracts made up the currency of ordinary human relationships. More than ever his ties seemed like a reminder of some jauntier lifestyle that he had never had. Though he perceived this only faintly himself, to prepare for death he had put himself through some unconscious process of immunization, a protective deadening of his sensibilities that had left him, still to his astonishment, alive, but with a dead and hollow place inside. It was as if he had pulled out the fuses on his feelings, one by one, and had not found a way to replace them.

4

In the early autumn he had walked through Regent's Park again, this time for his interview with the man called Partington at an office in Gosfield Street.

If the purpose of the meeting was still vague, the identity of the man was now slightly less obscure – but only because Finn had taken the trouble to make some inquiries. He had got home in a quiet fury from his visit to Corps HQ at Ashford the day before and phoned a friend in the Ministry of Defence. When you moved often in unfamiliar territory you learned to make use of friends. A scribbled note had arrived in the post this morning:

Re your gentleman. Top civil servant, rank equivalent Permanent Under-Secretary, formally attached Home Office but duties bafflingly undefined. Ex-phone directory (both int. & ext.), and we both know what that means. Some formal details: Anglo-Irish ancestry, educated Rugby and Cambridge. Civil Service exam 1939 and then exempted armed service and spent much of the war in Dublin. Doing what? Your guess as good as mine. Since become specialist on Irish affairs, author (pseudonymous) of an Irish history. Widower since 1962, no children, Chelsea flat, country cottage. Only reason I know this much is that we once did a PVP when he was to serve on an inter-dept. committee.

Sorry, his current job a complete blank but how's this for a guess? There's supposed to be a new think-tank-type Cabinet committee (all details COSMIC) planning long-range strategy over the Irish question. Strikes me

24

he'd be the ideal linkman for them. OK? Stumm, of course. Cheers,
    Maurice.

What intrigued Finn was Maurice Green's use of two words he had known Finn would recognize. COSMIC was the NATO marking for Top Secret; a linkman was someone who supervised the implementation of secret plans, one of his main functions being to conceal the origin of orders from those who carried them out. He preserved the anonymity of his masters. If Partington was advising and serving a Cabinet committee he was almost certainly one of the most senior intelligence officials in the country, one of half a dozen people in Whitehall known with a charming vagueness as 'unattached' civil servants. They worked in a grey area between the politicians on one hand and the various intelligence services and their offshoots on the other, remaining carefully unconnected with any of them.

Knowing this was perhaps the only thing that persuaded Finn to attend the interview.

Gosfield Street was a quiet backwater behind the elegant façades of Portland Place, in an area partly taken over by the rag trade and partly enmeshed in the tentacles of the BBC octopus that reached northwards from Broadcasting House. Partington had the top floor of a sombre Victorian town house. At ground level there was some section of the BBC to do with overseas syndication; up one flight of creaky stairs an export-import agent, recently departed, had installed a glass door through which a suspicious pile of window envelopes could be seen on the mat. Up some more stairs to a door that said GOSFIELD STORAGE SYSTEMS, PLEASE KNOCK AND ENTER, and a brass doorknob that came off in Finn's hand as he did so. The climb had made him short of breath.

'I've *told* the works people about that,' Partington said portentously, coming forward to meet him. 'I expect I'll end up fixing it myself, it's the only way to get anything done. Come through, come through, sit down. Yes, I find them steep too. Storage Systems, don't you like that? Everything is a *system* these days, and nobody stops to consider what a meaningless word it is.'

He was a plump, florid man of about fifty with a handshake that was damp but hearty. He led Finn from a bare anteroom into an office almost equally Spartan: a desk in one corner with a telephone, a portable scrambler unit, and a blotter stained with teacup rings, a couple of hard chairs, a paraffin heater, a threadbare carpet. Partington seemed instantly out of place. The office had a stale, slightly sour smell suggesting infrequent use, but evidently it was more than just an accommodation address. Behind the desk there was a steel door opening into a third, smaller room. Alarm sensors were built into the solid door-frame. Whatever was kept in there was what 45 Gosfield Street was all about.

'Our little library,' Partington said, following his gaze.

'Not a public library, I take it.'

'Afraid not, no. It doesn't lend, either. There are some rare and priceless... well, a lot of innocuous everyday ones too, but it could be *embarrassing*, you know, to have any go astray. Nothing leaves this room, which is why I had to ask you here. Somewhere more congenial afterwards, perhaps. Of course you have some idea why I asked you?'

'They told me you needed someone for a PVP job.'

'Yes, well... Smoke?'

'Not any more.'

'Of course.'

Partington lit a Gold Flake, lowered himself into the chair behind the desk, and posed for a moment with his fingertips joined while he searched for an opening. He was anything but the crisp senior civil servant, more like a self-indulgent and rather self-satisfied businessman, short on exercise and running shamelessly to fat. His neck overflowed the stiff white collar and the knot of a club tie; his girth strained at the buttons of a grey worsted suit. His hair was colourless and thinning and all his features were small, giving him a babyish appearance to which the eyes were an interesting contrast: small and blue and thoughtful with a cold opaqueness that was slightly worrying. Which was real, the pomposity or the coldness? His speech could only be described as dramatically italicized.

'How *interested* do you think you'd be?'

'Not very, to be frank. It seems I don't have that much choice. You must know I've been sick. I can't seem to make the fools understand that I'm cured. I'm still off the active list; they keep delaying my return to BAOR, saying I'd better stay under medical observation another fortnight. Well, I was down at Ashford yesterday. I'm sure you know all this. I still can't go back to Germany, and in the meantime they want me to take a —'

'A soft number?' Partington enjoyed supplying the missing words. He had a grin that was sudden and startling.

'Sorry to sound peevish,' Finn said. 'PVP is hardly my kind of work. I was —'

'I know, I know.' Partington waved a hand dismissively. 'Field Security, Special Investigations Branch, Counterintelligence. I know all that. But I shouldn't go knocking Positive Vetting Procedure if I were you. In its own small way what I have in mind is very positive.' He shifted to a more comfortable position on the chair. '*Very* positive.'

'They called it a temporary warding-out. I can guess what that means.'

'How familiar are you,' Partington asked, 'with the situation in Northern Ireland?'

'What's that got to do with it?'

'Come, Major Finn.' An indulgent smile now. 'Your naïvete is unconvincing. You'll have taken the trouble to find out what you can about me; I'd be *disappointed* if you hadn't. You know roughly the area of my duties. And you know damned well that I'm not wasting my own time as well as yours talking about some piffling PVP job.'

Finn was reduced to silence.

Partington, after trying once more for a comfortable posture on the chair, abandoned the effort and stood up. He went to the window and stared down into the narrow street. 'Northern Ireland at the moment is closer to civil war than it has been for fifty years, do you realize that? It's been coming for a long time, of course. The committee to which I'm answerable has a single task: to prevent it *happening*. By any and every means. We'd like your help, Finn.' He paused significantly.

Finn cleared his throat. 'What can I do – what can you do, for that matter? – that fifteen thousand troops can't?'

'Fifteen thousand, fifty thousand,' Partington said with a gesture. 'If it comes to the crunch they'll be almost powerless. They can put down riots, they can fight gunmen and bombers in groups, but when it comes to a million Protestants taking up arms against half a million Catholics... have you ever tried to stop a *dogfight*, with dogs running from every direction to join in? You're just a nuisance who's liable to get bitten for his trouble. The ultimate power lies in the hands of a *mob*. It always has, across there.'

He returned to the desk to stub out his cigarette in a chipped Cinzano ashtray. He spoke with confidence, on his own ground conversationally, but his opaque look had returned, a kind of glazing that removed all expression from his eyes.

'Ireland was partitioned fifty years ago because the Protestant majority in the North refused to be incorporated in an autonomous Irish Free State that would be largely Catholic. They backed the refusal with a threat of armed revolt, and the threat worked. They've never forgotten that; they're ready to do it again. It's an open secret that we – our Government – would like to wash our hands of the whole Irish question, but those million Protestants make it impossible. They're determined to stay British, to be British at any price. The source of the conflict is really *tribal,* you see, with religion superimposed on it. Most of the Protestants are descended from Scottish settlers; the Catholics are Celtic-Irish. In temperament the two people are poles apart. *Poles* apart.'

Tired of standing, Partington put himself at the mercy of the chair again. He had suddenly noticed Finn's tie – plain crimson silk – and stared at it with something very like alarm. Finn remained silent.

'After partition we let the Loyalists get on with running the country, and they ran it like a club for Protestants – through gerrymandering by their political leaders in the Unionist Party, through jobs for pals arranged by the Orange Order, through a dozen other subtle forms of discrimination against Catholics. When the crisis came three years ago and we had to resume our responsibilities there, we simply didn't know enough about the situation. We made a lot of mistakes. But things have got steadily worse and we can't afford any more mistakes. My committee, at least, is well informed. I've seen to that. We've collected and evaluated a lot of information. We've had access to all departmental reports and we've also established some sources of our own. *People* – that's what we need to know about. In a volatile situation personalities are the key to events. Hence...' He gave a proprietary wave towards the steel door.

'Personal files?' Finn asked.

'Files on everyone with any political significance at all. The kind of dope that allows us to assess their strengths and weaknesses, perhaps predict their moves, and in some cases – well –'

'To compromise them?' Finn suggested.

'*Influence* is the word I'd prefer.' Partington spoke without embarrassment, his baby face impassive. 'Does politics interest you? It fascinates me. The body politic has its pressure points, like a human corpus. A time may come when we need a man's co-operation, or at least the right excuse to *remove* him. Give me your opinion. Who has more power than anyone else at the moment to influence the course of events in Northern Ireland?'

His manner had begun to be slightly irritating. 'Experts only ask you to guess so they can prove you wrong,' Finn said. 'Tell me.'

'Very well,' said Partington, not at all put out. He opened a drawer, took out a mauve-coloured wallet file, and slid it across the desk. The cover was blank.

Finn opened it and glanced at the biographical data sheet stapled inside.

Surname: KILSHAW
Other names: JAMES CAMPBELL

He looked up. 'Leader of the Loyalist Vigilantes. A Presbyterian Messiah. All right, I can't disagree.'

'Don't bother reading it now. There's nothing negative.'

Finn read farther down the sheet:

Occupation: Solicitor, politician
Date & place of birth: 12/3/26, Belfast
Marital status: Married (1 son)

'Forget what the newspapers say about his being a latter-day Hitler,' said Partington, shifting in his chair again. 'In the context of his society he's a perfectly natural figure. For years he was a legitimate politician, a Cabinet Minister in the provincial parliament at Stormont. But he was also the leader of a hard-line faction that was trying to take over the Unionist Party. Perhaps they had no alternative but to sack him, but they'd mis-judged the amount of support he had from ordinary Protestants. He became a hero overnight. A new Lord Carson, a man who'd lead the glorious cause of Ulster against the Fenian rabble, against the forces of the Crown if they tried to sell the Loyalists out, and through a river of *blood*, if necessary. Their imagery may be lurid, but we all know it could happen. You have only to watch your television screen.'

Finn nodded, recalling the nightly pictures, columns of men in paramilitary uniform and Vigilante armbands marching raggedly but purposefully to some new confrontation with Catholics or the army, the fiery speeches from Kilshaw, the oc-casional ugly sectarian clash. The threat of organized violence had always been implicit in groups like the Vigilantes; it had never been this evident. You could almost smell it.

Partington lit another cigarette. Finn said, 'You're looking for a way of damping him down. Or even removing him. Is that it?'

'A handful of men can decide the future of Ulster,' Partington said. 'Kilshaw is the most important of them. He doesn't *want* civil war any more than anyone else does, it's just that in the state of hysterical tension that's grown up over there, irrespon-sible people get the best hearing. Brinkmanship is the usual form of political behaviour; nobody will be more surprised and indignant than Kilshaw when he goes over the edge with every-one else.

'Besides, Northern Ireland is costing the British taxpayer two hundred million pounds a year in subsidies, *apart* from bomb damage and the cost of keeping the army there. Even without civil war, the Vigilantes can keep us involved up to our necks for years to come. All in all, Kilshaw is a bloody nuisance. He knows it, too. Doing something about him is a different matter. He's not *susceptible* to political pressure because he exercises power without responsibility. Personal pressure? In theory, fine, get a hold on him, but in practice the most exhaustive vetting has shown nothing to get a hold of. And then three days ago, at what you might call *theatrically* the right moment, this arrives.'

He had taken it from the drawer, a sheet of grey Basildon notepaper with the envelope in which it had been posted pinned to the back. Finn picked the letter up; it was neatly typed and headed:

IN CONNECTION WITH JAMES KILSHAW

The text was brief and pseudo-military in style, with numbered paragraphs:

1. I have information which could finish him.
2. I am prepared to make it available to you, provided agreement can be reached on a suitable payment. Patience will be necessary.
3. Signify your interest by being at Victoria Station on the evening of 7th November. Stand in front of the main line indicator board from 1800 to 1815 hours. You will not be approached. You will be further contacted in due course.

There was no signature and no date. The seventh had been two days ago.

'A nutter?' said Finn.

'My dear fellow!' Partington was delighted to catch him out. 'Miss a turn! *Look* again!'

He looked again, this time turning the sheet over and taking the trouble to examine the envelope as well. It had been posted in Belfast. It was addressed to:

Mr Partington,
Gosfield Storage Systems,
45 Gosfield Street,
London W. 1.

Finn felt stupid. He said, 'This is from someone who knows about your setup here.'

'Exactly. And who must have been able to recognize me.'

'So you went to Victoria?'

'But of *course*!'

5

They had lunch at one of the better restaurants round the corner in Charlotte Street. Finn ate an omelette. Partington had oysters, coq au vin, eclairs with cream, and blue Stilton. By the time coffee and brandy arrived his baby face wore a thin film of sweat at which he dabbed occasionally with his napkin. From time to time his gaze went furtively back to Finn's tie.

'I called the timing theatrical,' he said. 'To my mind the whole *thing* is a bit stagey, would you agree? The army style of paragraphing, the wording terse and melodramatic – just what a crackpot imagines is right for that kind of letter. But through all that, by sending it to *me,* and at an address that's supposed to be secret, he's letting me know that he's on to me. He's telling me he means business.'

'You believe he's really got something on Kilshaw?'

'My dear Finn, how can I think *otherwise*?' A bottle of Beaune had made Partington more pompous than ever. 'He's got something and he reckons on our wanting it. Enough to *finish* him? Irish hyperbole, perhaps, but there's something provocative about that letter. He's making us wait. Why?'

'He could be scared.'

'He doesn't sound scared.'

'Then he's playing hard to get.'

'Exactly. The best salesmen don't persuade, they give the customer time to convince himself. I believe he expects us to come looking for him. That way he can also be sure of our interest. It's almost as if he were inviting us to find out the facts for ourselves, facts for which he could then supply the *proof.* So making the proof more tantalizing.'

'And more expensive,' said Finn.

'It's a subtle mind we're dealing with. Cream in your coffee?'

'No. You seem to be assuming there's only one of them.'

'By no means. The letter was posted in Belfast, but someone had to be in London to spot me among the crowd at Victoria the other evening. The same person could do both, of course, but that would be risky if there was any chance of my recognizing him in turn. The spotter could work from a photograph or a description, but I repeat – *someone* involved in this knows me or has known me. And he expects me to look for him. Where would you start looking, Finn?'

'Into your background. Among your acquaintances in Ireland.'

A mischievous smile. 'Don't think I haven't tried. There were hundreds, most of them forgotten by now. Failing that?'

'I'd go to the other end and work on Kilshaw. Someone is offering to sell you information about him, which presumes that the information exists. Dig that out and you might kill the proverbial two birds by learning who else has had access to it.'

'Excellent!' Partington pushed himself back from the table with an air of having accomplished something. Then he wiped his brow. 'That's just what I had in mind. Let's *do* what they expect us to do, at least for now. On the other hand they may contact me again quite soon. In the meantime the worst thing we can do is nothing. Time is short.'

Finn didn't like the use of the plural pronoun. He said, 'Why not start by passing the letter to the Home Office Central Research Establishment? They'd give you a full forensic profile.'

'I don't want too many curious eyes on it. In fact I did have a harmless detail photocopied for their calligraphy people to check. All they can tell me is that the typeface is from a Smith-Corona portable that went out of production fifteen years ago. If you found the actual machine you'd need a sample from it, and you've nowhere to begin looking. The first vetting of

Kilshaw was done by a sound local man. You'll have to liaise with him, go through it all again more thoroughly than before. Perhaps with a new mind on the job, a fresh approach –'

'I didn't say I was taking it,' Finn said.

Partington looked astounded. 'My dear fellow! I've been depending on you.'

'It just isn't my kind of job.'

'Is it your health that worries you?'

'No,' said Finn defensively. He searched the other man's face for the signs of unwelcome pity. There were none.

'It won't be physically taxing, you see; there'll be Fortune to do the legwork.' Partington tried to be earnest, succeeding only in sounding conspiratorial. 'Look, you know what's at stake, don't you? The danger of civil war is real. As long as the IRA keeps shooting and bombing, Kilshaw will gather strength. More of the Catholics turn to the IRA as their only defence against rampaging Protestants, and more of the Protestants join the ranks of the Vigilantes to retaliate against Catholics. The merry-go-round moves faster and faster. *Someone* must try to stop it. We start on Kilshaw because he may be vulnerable. Only we must be careful; people like that have powerful friends.'

He took an epigrammatic swallow of brandy, then lit a Corona cigar which emphasized the smallness of his features. Through a screen of blue smoke Finn caught again the oily opacity of his expression, the hardness inside the flabby *bon viveur*.

'One question,' he said. 'Why me?'

'Oh, I was offered half a dozen other people. I think what decided me was something the Director of Military Intelligence said. He said – disapprovingly, I fear – that in twenty-odd years you'd never learned to think like a *soldier*. That was just what I wanted, you see, not somebody strutting about Belfast in a hacking jacket and chukka boots.' He trembled with sudden merriment at the image. 'They find you slightly odd, Finn.

Looking at your tie, I can understand why. Recreations jazz and angling, hm? Signs of a contemplative loner. The best men in intelligence have always been of a melancholic turn of mind. You're half Irish, too – like me. It may help you get inside the mentality. I suspect a touch of the cynic as well.'

'I still haven't said I'd take it,' Finn said.

But he did take it, if only because it had acquired a kind of inevitability. It gave him something to think about besides the future. Int Corps could continue finding excuses to keep him in England until he succumbed and took that desk job, whereas this way he might just convince them that he was still capable of a day's real work. Anyone would think they hadn't read the specialist's report detailing his recovery. But it was always just possible they knew something that he didn't.

At Demob in 1946, at the age of twenty, with the rank of Intelligence Corps sergeant and two years of war service behind him, Finn had signed on for the regular army for one simple reason: he was earning six pounds a week and would be lucky to get half as much anywhere else. He had no training. A sprawling half-Irish family in East London, an upbringing in the Depression, and a schooling that had stopped at fourteen had not exactly prepared him for a brilliant civilian career. Whatever Finn was the army had made him so and he was grateful to it, but without the familial dependence that other men formed, especially other ORs who had been commissioned and slogged their way up to field rank to stave off a premature retirement. He was too much of what Partington had detected – a loner, an individualist – ever to have felt fully integrated. He enjoyed the work he did for its own sake, for satisfying his own peculiar urge to understand people and the way they acted. He was confident in his judgement of people. That was why Partington made him uneasy. The man simply did not ring true.

6

Most of the information in the file on James Campbell Kilshaw
was public knowledge gleaned from official records and newspaper clippings. The rest, resulting from informal inquiries, was
relatively innocuous anyway, but Finn spent several hours
studying it in the Gosfield Street office the next day before flying
to Belfast. It was a useful insight, not only into the man but into
the situation that had bred him.

In the late nineteen sixties, the comfortable monolith composed of the Unionist Party and the Protestant establishment,
which had ruled Northern Ireland for fifty years, began to crack
under outside pressure. Popular protest movements had taken
up the cause of the Catholic minority, who for the first time had
become militant in their demands for genuine equality. The
British Government, in whose power it lay to abolish the provincial parliament and rule directly from London, began to insist
on reforms. Within the party, reformers and diehards began to
feud. But then, temporarily, events were taken out of their hands
as violence erupted, bringing first the British Army and then the
IRA onto the streets.

Kilshaw had been a Unionist member of the Northern Ireland
Parliament for ten years, for five of them a Cabinet Minister and
not a particularly distinguished one. He was noted for his anti-
Catholic views, which made him a rallying-point for right-wing
Loyalists who thought their government was selling them out.
It was only when he was dismissed from the Cabinet, after a dis-
agreement with the reformist Prime Minister, that anyone
realized the extent of his popular support. It came from the
Protestant working class, for whom the complex symbolism of

religion, history, and the British connection had always been a reassurance of their supremacy. Sympathy for his views had been growing in the parlours of terraced houses and in a thousand bleak little pubs where memories and resentments flowed as readily as the stout, recollections of the outlawed Ulster Volunteer Force and the sectarian B-Special police reserve which had once known how to keep the 'Taigs' in their place. On the day Kilshaw was sacked, shipyard workers went on strike in his support. It was his first taste of untrammelled personal power; the same day the Loyalist Vigilantes were born.

Paramilitary organizations were an old tradition in Ulster. Though technically illegal, in times of crisis they had commanded such mass support that they could not be prevented from operating openly. But the Vigilantes offered a far greater threat than any of their predecessors.

The movement had been formed ostensibly as a small watchkeeping force to guard Protestant streets from the terrorism of the IRA. They had grown quickly, becoming more aggressive as they did so. The stationary guards at street corners became mobile patrols; the truncheons they carried were replaced by pickaxe handles, bayonets, and the occasional gun. They began to set up checkpoints in the streets; groups of them roamed central Belfast and even the less militant Catholic areas, and anyone they challenged who could not show convincing proof that he was not an IRA sympathizer would be lucky to escape with a beating. Their activities were part of the gradual breakdown of law and order that had been gathering momentum for a long time. They fed on fear. There was little that anyone in authority could – or dared – do to stop them.

The Vigilantes were organized like an army, with a general staff, transport, communications and intelligence services, and their own internal discipline. To a condescending English eye which might have found the whole thing faintly comical, it took one of their huge parades or rallies to bring the realization home that this was not just another crowd of men in fancy dress but a powerful and independent political force capable of doing exactly what it pleased. At its centre stood James Kilshaw.

Finn's only initial contact, Seamus Fortune, was at Aldergrove airport to meet him. Finn knew one or two people in the army HQ at Lisburn, near Belfast, but they would hardly be of any use on this kind of job. He settled down to work at once.

There was only one place to start, with Kilshaw himself. There was only one way to work, by going back over the facts unearthed during Fortune's earlier investigation, checking the sources again, searching for new lines of inquiry. And Fortune's research had been very thorough. He made an occasional crack about flogging a dead horse but otherwise worked willingly enough. The legwork was all his; it was clearly inadvisable for Finn to do any fronting – talking to people, greasing the occasional palm – and as far as possible they kept their meetings secret. The written material they collected stayed, when not needed, in a left-luggage locker at Great Victoria Street station. Finn spent a good deal of time in the hotel, reading, waiting, arranging meetings with Fortune, maintaining contact with Partington through one phone call a day to the Gosfield Street office. He too was now equipped with a portable scrambler, a battery-operated Code-Phone with a choice of twenty-five codes, enough to baffle even the army signallers who were said to have a permanent tap on the hotel's telephone lines.

The first task was to read a pile of press clippings more detailed than those available in London, photocopied in the libraries of the *Belfast Telegraph,* the Unionist *News Letter,* and other local papers. They supplied a fairly detailed history of Kilshaw's public life since his election to Stormont. While they added little to what Finn already knew, they were worth studying carefully in case inconsistencies cropped up in other areas of investigation.

Next came financial details. With alarming ease Fortune had obtained copies of statements going back twelve years relating to both of Kilshaw's bank accounts, business and private. They reached him through that network of bank employees who supplement their incomes by supplying figures to the shadier sort of credit-rating agency. These alone were worth three days' close examination. Apart from giving a breakdown of earnings and spending for the whole period, they provided useful information about Kilshaw's investments: standing orders for regular payments to his insurance company and mortgage broker, for instance, and holding fees for share certificates and bonds. The business account was of course more complex, but easily enough understood: a steady, almost daily flow of receipts, running to two and sometimes three figures, and withdrawals matching the routine of a small office, petty cash and wages for his few employees once a week, rent and Kilshaw's personal salary once a month, tax and accountancy fees once a year. The only real pattern to emerge was one of declining earnings since the start of the troubles, as his preoccupation with the Loyalist Vigilantes had led to some neglect of his business. Still, it seemed to tick over healthily enough, and in his role of small-time lawyer he remained moderately prosperous.

There was a separate, subsidiary account through which he made transfers of money to and from trust funds of which he was the sole administrator. Here there were no apparent irregularities either, but Finn had one – not very promising – idea. Kilshaw's professional conduct might have been called into question at some time. After a few phone calls Fortune found a lawyer friend who could introduce him to someone amenable on the staff of the Law Society of Northern Ireland. An arrangement was made to check the records.

There were two other bank accounts to which Kilshaw was a joint signatory. He was chairman of the committee of Shankill Distress Relief, a somewhat informal charity that collected and distributed two or three thousand pounds a week to Protestant families who had suffered from bombings or riots. Their account at the Shankill Road branch of the Ulster Bank had two subsidiaries attached to it, one to provide for the payment of immediate cash grants, the other – in the name of Walter Barnett, a fellow trustee – for money to be invested against long-term needs. All cash received was divided, pound for pound, between these two funds.

The other joint account was that of a small private company called Sydenham Holdings Limited in which Kilshaw was a partner and had invested several thousand pounds of his private capital. Fortune had got the details from the Companies Registration Office of the Ministry of Commerce. There were three other directors besides Kilshaw; one of them was the same Walter Barnett.

'Who is he?' Finn asked.

'He's on the general staff of the Vigilantes. He's also the son of an old friend and business associate who died a few years back. Walter and the other partners set up Sydenham Holdings as a kind of foster-parent company that would raise money for the old man's original firm, Marine Services Limited.'

'What's their racket?'

'They buy small ships – trawlers, coasters, tugs, that class of thing – refit them, and sell at a profit. The work itself is farmed out to Harland and Wolff, the big shipbuilders. Marine Services is strictly a paperwork firm. Very small beer, really.'

'This job needs a chartered accountant, not a detective.'

'They clear a few grand every year,' Fortune said, 'and the books seem to get past the auditors. Seriously, I don't see your man working any small-time fiddles when he's scarcely the time

to mind his own shop, do you? There's too much at stake politically.'

They went on to other things. Fortune's resources were
proving to be phenomenal. He had a friend on the staff of the
Royal Ulster Constabulary headquarters in Knock Road who
had reported, not surprisingly, that Kilshaw had no criminal
record. Nor had he ever come to the attention of the police as a
suspect or even a complainant. Finn suggested a second check;
the only new item on the records was a routine notification to
all divisions from the RUC Special Branch that in future armed
plainclothes bodyguards would be present at Kilshaw's public
appearances. A supplementary note, sent confidentially to hospitals and ambulance services throughout the province, stated
that his blood group was Rh-positive and that he had no chronic
illnesses except mild sinusitis. They were treating him like a
head of state.

Fortune had other friends too, in the Inland Revenue office,
the Department of Health and Social Security, and practically
every other place where records are held on individuals and
their private affairs. This was his bread and butter. But at the
end of a week he had exhausted every routine line of inquiry.
There was still not a single lead to work on.

In a perverse way, Finn discovered that he was almost
pleased. Kilshaw had won a round against the system of which
Finn was a part. Maybe he was the power-crazy bigot that the
London newspapers were calling him by now, but you could
only admire his consistent two-fingering of the establishment –
including the London papers. Finn felt he had got to know the
man, perhaps even that they had things in common, such as a
streak of honest bloody-mindedness. The Ulsterman had done
rather better for himself, of course. A postwar scholarship to St
Andrews University had helped, and so had his membership in
those two organizations that provided the right credentials to

any ambitious Protestant public man, the Orange Order and the B-Specials. He lived these days in a lofty Victorian house in Upper Malone but remained closely in touch with his people. His office was above a shop in Sandy Row, an area so enthusiastically Loyalist that the kerbstones were painted alternately red, white, and blue.

'What now, then?' Fortune asked.

'There's only one way. B and E.'

'His office? You'll have to clear that with Partington.'

'Partington will have to say yes if he wants us to get anywhere,' Finn said. They were sitting in their usual meeting place, Fortune's car, parked behind the hotel. 'Personally I'd be happy to chuck the whole thing in. Do you know a good B and E man?'

'Paddy Keefe, the best in town. Locksmith by trade, nice clean worker. He'll do an easy one for a hundred quid.'

'Discreet?'

'Och, sure, I'd tell him my confession, Harry. He's no form and he wants to keep it that way. A delicate worker; he does a bit in the forgery line as well. There's only two locks, a Yale on the outer door and a deadlock on the safe. It's an old safe, no combination. I got a glimpse of it when I did my routine as a fire-extinguisher salesman. There's no alarm. Paddy and I could be in and out in twenty minutes.'

'Assuming you find something in the safe. You may have to search the office.'

'Sure, the safe is the logical place to start.'

'I'll speak to Partington,' Finn said.

Partington was agreeable, provided every precaution was taken. 'We can't afford a scandal,' he said. With every phone call he had been sounding a little less confidently bumptious, a little more petulant. He had still heard no more from the writer of the letter; he was expecting results from Finn.

They chose a Saturday night. At midnight outside a pub in the Falls Road they picked up Paddy Keefe, the Breaking and Entry man, a gangling, stoop-shouldered youth who wore a knitted fisherman's cap and a trench-coat. Then they drove to Sandy Row.

A few stragglers were on their way home from pubs and parties; otherwise the area seemed deserted. They passed the ground-floor doorway that led up to Kilshaw's office, and a hundred yards beyond it Fortune and Paddy Keefe climbed out of the car. Finn turned the Austin around to park it in a pool of darkness midway between two street lamps, lights and engine switched off. He watched the other two walk back down the pavement, pause at the doorway, and vanish inside.

He expected little if anything to come out of this, partly because he did not believe Kilshaw would leave compromising material of any sort in his office, partly because it became more and more difficult to believe that any such material existed. Surely Partington must find it hard to believe too? It seemed not. What made Partington persevere? Perhaps only his enormous ego, keeping him faithful to his theory in spite of all the evidence – or lack of it.

Sandy Row was a long street and very nearly straight, so the four men approaching through the patches of overhead lighting from behind were visible in Finn's driving mirror long before they reached the car. Their presence didn't worry him; pub-crawlers, probably. Watching them only at intervals in the mirror, he missed their measured, deliberate pace. They were almost level with the car before he spotted the armbands and the clubs. They were Loyalist Vigilantes. Kilshaw's men, patrolling the street.

Fear clutched at him. But incredibly they had drawn abreast of the car and were walking past. Sitting still and in almost total darkness he had been missed; otherwise he would certainly have been challenged, his presence questioned. How stupid they'd been to enter a staunchly Protestant area without taking account of the Vigilantes! But now, as they paced towards the building which housed Kilshaw's office, there was another danger. Fortune and Paddy Keefe had been in there fifteen minutes; it wouldn't be much longer before they came out.

As if by thinking it he had wished it, they emerged at that moment.

Fortune's face appeared cautiously round the edge of the doorway – but not cautiously enough. There was a street light right opposite which picked him out clearly. A challenging shout went up from one of the Vigilantes, and the two intruders broke cover and ran for the next corner.

The men went after them. Finn's mind was impaled by the thought of their being captured, exposed. He started the car, slammed into gear, and swung into the middle of the street. With no lights, with a hand pressed down hard on the horn, he drove at the backs of the Vigilantes.

Their footfalls thundered as they ran. They were still spread out across the narrow street. When they heard the car they glanced back, but instead of separating they bunched together to stop him passing. He could not afford to yield! His speed was up to forty with the gap closing fast, to ten yards, to five... With a terrible certainty he waited for the impact and the sickening bump of wheels over flesh.

At the last moment they lost their nerve and scattered. One man took a glancing blow on the arm. Finn was through them, slewing round the corner behind Fortune and Paddy and then slowing to fifteen miles an hour to travel beside them. He held a rear door open and they dived into the back seat in a tangle of legs and arms. Finn accelerated, hearing the hoarse curses of the Vigilantes follow him.

'Jasus, Harry!' Fortune trembled between drawing lungfuls

of air. 'Now there's something... else... we didn't bargain for at all.'

'Something else?' Finn inquired.

'It's a night for surprises, right enough,' said Paddy.

'What did you find?'

'Nothing.' Fortune looked at him helplessly. 'That is –'

'Don't tell me. You couldn't get into the safe.'

'We got in, all right. It's just that somebody... was there before us.'

Finn jerked round in his seat, almost losing control of the car. Fortune gasped for air between clusters of words.

'Somebody had burned a bloody great... hole in the... back of the safe with an oxyacetylene... cutter. Hole's still there... The safe's been pushed back against the wall where the hole won't show.'

'It's empty,' Paddy Keefe added helpfully.

Finn glanced at him. 'When do you reckon this was done?'

'To judge by the state of the metal,' Paddy said, 'no more than a month ago. Sure, it's a powerful crude way to get into a safe, so it is.'

7

Apart from opening a new area of speculation, the news took them no further, a fact that Finn and Fortune were better able to appreciate in the thin autumn sunlight of the next afternoon. It was a Sunday. They had driven out along the north shore of the Lough and parked in a lay-by overlooking the grey, choppy water.

'We know two things more than we knew yesterday,' Finn said. 'We know Kilshaw's safe was robbed, and we're sure that he never reported it to the police. What does that imply?'

'That something embarrassing was stolen. That whoever stole it is the same person who wrote the letter to Partington.'

'All right. But the evidence is still circumstantial. To me there's another implication. Kilshaw's office staff must have known about the robbery; he trusted them to shut up about it. On the other hand, the burglars must have known there was something worth taking. An inside job, I was idly wondering?'

'Why not a couple of ordinary villains looking for loot? Suddenly they realize the value of whatever they'd found?'

'And they also just happen to know Partington's name and address? No. What villain in his senses takes an oxyacetylene cutter to a small office safe on the off chance of finding a lot of money? They needed advance information. They needed to know that it was an old-fashioned safe with no refractory alloys in its plating. Modern safes just can't be opened that way. There needed to be at least two of them to get the gas cylinders and the rest of the gear upstairs in any sort of reasonable time. And yet it has a slightly amateurish look. Paddy Keefe says the whole outer door has been replaced, meaning they smashed through the door rather than pick the lock. What do we know about Kilshaw's staff?'

'There's his secretary. Middle-aged. Been with him sixteen years, ever since he started up on his own. Two women clerks, been there eight and ten years respectively. A youngster in the second year of his articles. Another wee lad of sixteen who makes the tea and runs errands. They're all respectable, with good Loyalist pedigrees.'

'Any recent sackings or resignations?'

'Not for three years, according to the Social Security records. That was soon after the start of the troubles, when business had begun to go downhill. There was a third woman clerk who was dismissed and never replaced. Nothing there, Harry.'

Finn stared across the Lough and back along the road. There was little traffic; it wasn't the kind of weather to drag families away from their television sets for a Sunday drive. His mind felt blank. He knew he had been slowly running out of ideas.

'Anything else you can tell me?' he asked.

'Only that my contact at the Law Society came through this morning. Nothing on their books either, only a traffic offence.'

'Why was that reported to the Law Society?'

'Some busybody policeman had nothing better to do.'

'Have you got a copy I can read?'

'Here.'

The letter was dated October 1969. It was signed by a chief inspector at RUC headquarters and was sanctimonious in tone. In the best interests of the Society and of their member, Mr J. C. Kilshaw, he thought it appropriate to advise them that Mr Kilshaw's car had had to be towed away from a pedestrian crossing where it had been illegally parked on the morning of 19 September.

Although no proceedings are to be taken [the letter went on] I cannot stress too strongly the serious road safety

hazard involved in this type of offence, for which the
courts usually impose an endorsement of driving licence
as well as a substantial fine.

Perhaps, it concluded, as the professional body to whom Kilshaw was responsible, the Law Society would care to prevail on him not to do it again.

Not unreasonably, the Law Society had ignored the whole thing. But the letter had found its way into their files.

'The only thing that interests me,' said Finn, 'is that they didn't prosecute him.'

'Influence,' Fortune said. 'He'd been a junior Cabinet Minister, and by then he was leader of the Vigilantes. He probably got one of his Orange Order pals in the RUC to tear up the summons.'

'It could be worth looking into.'

'Come on now, Harry, you're clutching at straws, so you are.'

All the same, Fortune checked with his police contact, who was able the next day to look up the records in the Traffic Division. They showed that Kilshaw's Rover had been towed away from a pedestrian crossing at the north end of York Street at 8:50 a.m. on Friday, 19 September 1969. The traffic warden who found it there had duly made out the usual three-part ticket and called in the towing vehicle, but after that signs of a hasty cover-up appeared: a release note addressed to the police pound and a notice of intended prosecution which had been filled out by the ticket office but never delivered. Some explanation for this, with an undue emphasis on technicalities, had been scrawled across the form and signed by a senior officer.

So Fortune was right. Influence had been at work. There was no way of pursuing the subject further, but Finn was left feeling faintly dissatisfied by one thought, that Kilshaw had taken a lot of trouble to avoid paying a small parking fine.

They had been at work twelve days without finding anything that pointed even to the nature of the information they sought, let alone to whoever was now in possession of it. They were haunted by the single isolated fact of a burgled safe.

In desperation Finn decided that they should keep Kilshaw under surveillance for a trial period of one week. It sounded easy enough; in fact it was even more difficult than it was unrewarding. They could not possibly do the job properly on their own, but Partington ruled out reinforcements because of the added risk of detection. Special Branch men were rarely far from Kilshaw's side these days and Vigilante bodyguards were with him all the time; trying to keep a watch on his home would have been asking for trouble. Finn and Fortune confined themselves to plotting his movements away from the house as best they could, searching for an inconsistency, some unexplained action or meeting whose significance might suddenly become clear.

The movements themselves were predictable enough from one day to the next. At nine in the morning he drove to his office, from which most of his political as well as legal business was conducted. These days he was seeing more Loyalist Vigilantes than clients. The organization was growing by the day, becoming bolder and more threatening. In parts of Belfast the men in paramilitary uniform now carried pistols and shotguns in broad daylight, practically challenging the security forces to stop them. Walter Barnett, the zealous lieutenant, was one of Kilshaw's frequent visitors, a pale young man with bright ginger hair, who also turned up during the week at a meeting of the Shankill Distress Relief committee and a board meeting of Sydenham Holdings Limited, both of which Kilshaw managed to attend as well.

Kilshaw was rarely at home in the evenings. These were filled with meetings, conferences, and trips to outlying branches of the movement, but two evenings a week – Monday and Thursday – were set aside for recreation. He would play squash for an hour or two at an Orange Lodge on the Ormeau Road, have dinner there, and chat over drinks with some of the members till eleven or half past. On the odd evening when he did go straight home from the office he stayed there; in common with most people nowadays, he and his wife did not go out much socially. Their only son was married and living in Canada.

'We've learned nothing,' Finn said. 'We may as well face it.'

It was just before nine o'clock in the morning of the last day of the allotted week. They had watched Kilshaw arrive at work and now they drove aimlessly about the city; to avoid being challenged by an army patrol – or even a band of Vigilantes – it was best to keep moving.

Fortune said, 'Don't feel bad now, Harry. We never did have all that much hope.'

'I'm going to tell Partington we've had it.'

'He won't like that.'

'If he thinks he can do better he can come over and try for himself.' Finn reflectively rubbed the discoloured, tight-drawn skin over his cheekbones. 'He's pretty clued up on this country, isn't he?'

'He's specialized in it for a long time. During the war he was posted to Dublin with some security liaison outfit. They worked out of Mountjoy prison, of all places.'

'Liaison? Southern Ireland was supposed to be neutral.'

'Sure it was, but in an Irish sort of a way. The sentiments were clear: lookit how many thousands of them volunteered for the British forces. The airmen who crashed on Irish soil were all interned, Allies and Germans alike, but somehow or other the Allied ones it was who all managed to escape to the North. The only real pro-Germans were the hard cases in the IRA, and that was more on account of being anti-British than anything. Oh, there was co-operation all right, though I've no exact idea where Partington fitted in.'

The car had turned into York Street. Finn recognized the intersection from which Kilshaw's car had been towed away three years earlier. An odd conjecture struck him.

'This place,' he said. 'Could it be the place that was important?'

'What are you on about now, Harry?'

'That parking case. He got the summons stopped and we assumed the obvious – that he wanted to avoid prosecution, a court appearance, a fine. What if it was more circumstantial than that? What if it was the place – here in York Street – that he wanted hushed up? You see, the address would have appeared on the prosecution notice and on the papers before the court. It would probably have got into the newspapers.'

Fortune had stopped the car. 'Are you saying, Harry, that he was doing something around here that he'd no business doing?'

'Maybe.'

'At ten to nine of a Friday morning?'

The case was a thin one, he had to admit. The street was like any other on the fringes of the city centre, a bit run down, part business, part residential, a row of three-storeyed Victorian houses facing a row of shops and a Methodist church.

'It's a possibility,' Finn said. 'A slight one, but the only one we've got. Somebody hereabouts might just remember the incident.'

'Let's ask, then. What's our story?'

'Insurance.'

Finn had known times when weeks of plodding in the wrong direction had suddenly been redeemed, when one line of inquiry had quite unexpectedly crossed another. This was one of those days, when it all fell together without his needing to try.

The shops were not yet open, so they started on the houses. The first bell they rang belonged to a Mrs Downey. She was blind, a tiny wisp of an old woman, alert as a sparrow. She had just brewed up and insisted on leading them through to her kitchen.

Mrs Downey's husband had been dead thirty years, killed by the same German bomb that had blinded her. She had converted the house, lived on the ground floor herself, and let the other two as self-contained flats. Her life was necessarily uneventful; the occasion three years ago was still clear in her mind.

'I'm not sure I can help you gentlemen, mind, for I never knew the man's name at all. Only Miss Hughes could tell you, and she's long gone.'

'Miss Hughes?'

'Why, the girl in the top flat. I can't think where she'd be now. From her accent she was Belfast, but I recall her saying she'd been born in Dublin. Perhaps she went back South. Her it was, you see, who came down and asked to use the telephone and brought him in with never a word about who it was. I heard him telling someone on the phone the police had brought his car away and could something be done? Now I'm not sure I should be saying all this. An insurance claim, is it?'

'There's a claim against the driver of that car. We're trying to trace him.'

'Three years after?' said Mrs Downey suspiciously.

'They sometimes take even longer.' Finn sipped his tea and bit into a slice of Mrs Downey's home-baked soda bread.

'We've got to be sure it's the same man. Did he mention the make of car?'

'Och, I know nothing about cars.'

'A black Rover?'

'That might have been it, a Rover.'

'Had he been here before?'

The old lady hesitated. The bright, unseeing blue eyes could not change expression but her mouth puckered. 'Yes, he'd been before. I don't know what to say about that. Her morals were her own business.'

Finn waited.

'I always said it was her own business. She was a lovely girl, but with him up there twice a week, just for a couple of hours of a Monday and Thursday evening, I knew what that meant.'

'Squash nights,' murmured Fortune.

'I knew what it meant. Married. The same one every Monday and Thursday, I could tell by his tread on the stair. I suppose I should be thankful it was only one. With her a nice Catholic girl, you see, I didn't like it at all. But I never interfered, never mentioned it. Eventually it stopped and she moved away, so there was no need of bitterness. God knows we've enough in these times. I expect this is of no concern to you gentlemen at all. I wouldn't want any trouble for her.'

'Of course not. Thank you. You've been very helpful.'

Outside they stared at each other, half elated, half disbelieving.

Miss Hughes also happened to be the name of Kilshaw's other woman clerk, the one who had been sacked within a month of the incident Mrs Downey had described. It took Fortune another ten days to trace her to her mother's home in Stillorgan Road, Donnybrook, near Dublin, and back to the house at Coolnasilla Park.

8

'She's asking twelve thousand,' said the estate agent. 'Price-wise, it doesn't compete too well at the moment.'

The estate agent was the kind of man who could say 'price-wise' with a straight face. Finn, sitting opposite, looked at him sceptically. He was trying to show the right balance of greed and disdain towards a figure that would have been three times as high in the suburbs of London.

'You might try an offer, but with this particular vendor –'

'In times like these,' Finn said, 'no one can refuse a reasonable offer, surely?'

'Point taken. But it's part of a deceased estate. I don't know that she's highly motivated to selling. There've been offers of ten, ten and a half...'

The estate agent shrugged. He had once had a staff of three, but now he ran the small office in Bridge Street on his own. The only people who wanted houses in Belfast these days were a handful of hard-faced speculators from Dublin and London, gambling on peace and large profits in a couple of years' time. He could not afford to turn away any kind of business.

'Offer-wise, you'd have better luck with a different property. I've got several more in that area.'

'That's the one that interests me,' said Finn. 'It's got all the makings of a good investment, but not at twelve thousand pounds.'

The agent reached for his telephone. 'I'll get you an appointment to view anyway. Perhaps she's changed her mind.'

Miss Caragh Hughes was difficult to pin down, but finally she agreed to see him at three o'clock that afternoon. It was one of those confusing Irish days when the elements milled about in a drunken brawl so that you could be soaked to the skin and warmed by the sun six times in the course of a one-mile walk. There was no distance for Finn to walk once he had asked the taxi driver to wait at the front gate in Coolnasilla Park, but he was caught in a flurry of fine rain and went at a trot up the paved pathway to the door. It opened as he arrived; Caragh Hughes must have been watching through a window.

'Come in.'

'Thanks. How do you cope with this weather?'

'Sure, we manage.'

She stood in the entrance hall, hands on hips, taking stock of him. He had never seen a picture of her; now he realized that his imagination had formed one of its own, and inevitably it was wrong.

Five feet six, red hair, green eyes: that much he had got from Fortune, but what did it convey? The face that looked very directly into his was dramatic rather than beautiful, one of those faces with a luminous vitality that would make it impossible not to pick her out in a crowd. The eyelashes were long, the nose Grecian, the mouth wide and generous but with a hint of temper at the corners. The complexion was Irish cream with a faint underlay of freckles. Her body was strong-limbed and well-proportioned, visibly so even under a tailored tweed trouser suit.

She said, 'I'm surprised you came at all.'

'Why?'

'The agent must have told you I'm not interested in offers under twelve thousand.'

'I thought there was no harm in talking about it, looking around.'

'You can certainly look round. I don't want to hurry you, but I've to drive to Dublin after.'

To see her mother, he supposed. Her manner was distant, not to say unfriendly, and Finn thought he could guess why. He would have to tread warily.

'We may as well start right here. Entrance hall leading into the main living room. Dining room off there with a serving hatch to the kitchen.'

He followed her about the house, not dutifully but with an interested professional eye. The study intrigued him most, not that it was the kind of room in which much studying had ever been done. There were two easy chairs, a bookcase, and a mahogany bureau with a flap that opened to form a writing table. There was a reproduction of an eighteenth-century map of Ireland on the wall. There was also a small desk. On it stood an old, black Smith-Corona portable typewriter.

He stood by the machine, tapped the space bar casually a couple of times, and looked round the room. 'No safe?' he said.

'Did you expect to see one?'

'Just in an idle way. I was told the house used to belong to a bookmaker. He'd need a safe.'

'I moved it out after he died. Ugly great thing.'

'Of course. And having one is just tempting someone to rob it.'

He watched for a reaction. There was none. But there was a tension about her, a disturbing air of restlessness as she moved about the room, that was distinctly sexual. She had that rare quality that provoked an instant physical longing in a man; it was impossible to define.

He examined the bookcase. Besides the *Encyclopaedia Britannica* there were perhaps a hundred of the kind of books accumulated over three years of a social science course, mostly in paperback: readings from Marx, Engels, Hegel, and a lot of interpretive stuff together with some of the modern political prophets: Arendt, Daniel Bell, Marcuse. There were also a few of those books of Republican songs and poems that were no less turgid, for all their being Irish, than any other ideological balladry. Here, probably, were all the strands, emotional and intellectual, that had gone into the making of one minor revolutionary.

He plucked out Sorel's *Reflections on Violence*, blew off the dust, and opened it. *Con Michael Hughes, Pol Sci II, University College Dublin* was scrawled on the title page.

'Those were all my brother's,' said Caragh Hughes. 'He doesn't live here now.'

'I know about your brother.'

'Oh? And you're not nervous?'

'Should I be?'

'He doesn't like your type, Mr Finn.'

'What is my type?'

'Investing in other people's misery, he'd call it. Some buyers were scared off when they heard I was his sister.'

'Afraid of being shot for exploiting the Irish proletariat, were they? Do you agree with him?'

'It doesn't affect me personally. There are people down the Falls who'll do anything to get out. They're selling off their wee houses for seven and eight hundred. You'll realize there's some resentment of English parasites.'

'There are Irish parasites too, I'm told.'

'At least they're not the kind that kill the host.'

The temper he had guessed at was showing. He said, 'That sounds like something you might have learned at the University College. Were you there too?'

She smiled, mollified a little. 'One intellectual in the family was quite enough. Do you want to see the rest of the house?'

'Please.'

He pictured the first-generation graduate with intellectual weight added to his prejudices, impatient of fools, con-descending to his family. But he sensed a deeper bond between

Caragh and Con Michael than her attitude of simple tolerance suggested. The young man was not his immediate concern, however. That typewriter: coincidence, perhaps, but it had shortened the odds considerably on Caragh Hughes having something to do with the Kilshaw letter. A way must be found of taking a sample of the typeface.

He followed her up the stairs, aware once again of that disturbing electricity. She must have been used to her effect on men; when she reached the top she turned and gave him an oddly penetrating look.

'There are four bedrooms,' she said.

Three were unoccupied, including the main south-facing one that had been her parents'. Her own was a small, cheerful room with a frilled bedspread, a silver crucifix on one wall, and two framed photographs among the clutter on the dressing table. He let his glance stray past them. One was a family group taken on the lawn outside when her father had been alive, the other a first communion picture of a small glowering boy with curly black hair.

He stood beside her in the doorway, close enough to smell her perfume. 'Aren't you afraid,' he said, 'living here alone?'

'Sometimes, yes. I often hear shooting.'

'I'm surprised you haven't moved before. The house has been on the market eighteen months.'

'I'm not that desperate to move.'

'In fact you don't want to sell at all, do you?'

That one caught her off guard. Her gaze wavered. She went to the dressing table, searched among the compacts and bottles, found a cigarette, and lit it with a gold Dunhill. Composed again, she looked at him levelly through a stream of smoke. Her tone became scornful.

'What would you know about it, now?'

'Only that you've purposely set too high a price on it. That you refuse to consider offers below that. None of my business. I just can't help wondering why you want to stay in Belfast.'

'And I wonder, Finn, what you want here at all.'

An ambush. He had not trodden warily enough. He said, 'You think that, do you?'

'I know it.' She spoke coldly now. 'You think we people are stupid, don't you? I've watched you. You give yourself away. You don't look at these rooms for their size, their proportions, their outlook. Your eye is for detail; you've a policeman's eye, and I've seen enough of those to know. You're pathetic, you lot. You searched my house last week; do you expect to find anything more by snooping about pretending you want to buy the place? Now go. You've wasted enough of my time.'

Finn had nothing left to lose. 'Who searched the house?' he demanded.

'Oh, come off it. Or is it all so secret and top-level that they don't tell their hired hacks what's going on at all? You look like a hack, a broken-down one too. Which particular set of thugs do you work for? The accent's wrong for the RUC. It must be Military Intelligence. Or Scotland Yard.'

'Who searched your house? What did they want?'

She mashed out her cigarette. Her face was white, her lips thin with anger. 'Just get out of this!'

'Not before you tell me.'

'Get out!'

She was standing by the dressing table. Suddenly she seized a bottle from it and flung it at his head. He flinched. It missed, shattering with a cascade of turquoise-coloured skin freshener against the wall behind him. She ran at him in a fury, fists clenched, and he seized both wrists and pushed her back against the wall, pinning her there.

'Let me go, you bastard!'

'When you stop struggling, yes. Now you'll listen, you hellcat.

I'm not from the RUC or anywhere else you might think. And I'll prove it. I've found out something they've never known, something you'd rather nobody knew. I know that Kilshaw was your lover.'

'You're hurting me. Fuck you, you're hurting!'

'Nice language for a good Catholic girl. That's what Mrs Downey called you. I know about Mrs Downey's upstairs flat, you see, and squash nights on Mondays and Thursdays. You'll remember the time he stayed the whole night by accident. I can guess what happened: you'd been screwing so hard that you slept through and in the morning he found his car had been towed away. He had to use his influence to suppress the summons. A close shave, that. There must have been some explaining to do when he got home. Is that what frightened him into giving you the boot?'

'You vulgar bastard,' she said. But she had stopped trying to fight back. He held her a few seconds more, looking into the angry sea-green eyes. They were both aware, in spite of their words, of a special undertone to the physical contact. He let go of her wrists; she stood where she was, her face close to his, and took a deep breath.

'All right, so you know. I'm not ashamed. What's it to do with you?'

'I have an interest in making life difficult for Kilshaw. So have you, am I right? Hell hath no fury and all that.'

'Perhaps you're wrong. Who sent you?'

'I wish I knew. Someone who writes anonymous letters to government departments offering to sell information. I thought perhaps you could tell me.'

She was rubbing her wrists. 'The British Government? Information about him and me?'

'Possibly, but I doubt if that's the whole story. The Loyalist firebrand once had an adulterous affair with a rebel, and an IRA man's sister to boot. A fine bit of scandal, but scandal won't stop him. That's what I'm here to do, you see, stop him. It's the rest of the story I want.'

She moved away from him, to the dressing table, to light another cigarette. Finn watched, noticing the slight shake in her hands and the self-consciousness of her movements. She looked up abruptly.

'You look sick,' she said.

'I was sick,' he said testily. 'I'm cured now.'

'You don't look cured. You look like a bloody sick man.'

Uncannily, she had found the only bait that would make him rise. Somewhere beneath the callous tone, behind the steady eyes, he sensed the demon pity. He said harshly, 'That's got nothing to do with anything.'

'I was just curious. I'm always curious about people.'

'I don't need any condescending bloody sympathy!'

She stared at him. Abashed at the violence of the outburst, he felt the blood rising to his face. Then she gave a bright, mocking laugh, snapping the mood.

'Aren't you the sensitive one then!' She was bantering now. 'All right. I don't want to know. I couldn't care less. What makes you think I should help you at all?'

'You're a Catholic. Kilshaw is Kilshaw, whatever he once was to you. Who searched the house?'

'The RUC Special Branch.'

'Looking for what?'

'Explosives, so they said. They took me for a fool, too.'

'Did they find anything?'

'There was nothing to find.'

'Did they tell you Kilshaw's office safe had been robbed?'

The surprise in her eyes could have been genuine. 'When?'

'Sometime in the last two months. Officially, the police were never notified.'

'He's got friends,' Caragh said. 'Sympathizers in the RUC. They'll cover up for him, do anything he asks.'

She walked to the window, which looked across the neighbours' well-kept lawns, and stood silhouetted in the fading afternoon light. 'Did you think I'd be more surprised, at your coming?'

'Slightly.'

'I've been sort of expecting something...' Suddenly choosing not to elaborate, she changed the subject. 'There's not a lot I can tell you. I had an affair with him – so what? He was a different man then. Religion, politics: they become a joke to share when you're attracted to each other. In those days he could still afford to have a Catholic working for him. I was twenty-two when I started there, a neurotic virgin with my head still stuffed full of nonsense put there by a crowd of nuns. What would they know about men and women's feelings for each other, I'd be thanking you to tell me? He was the first man to treat me like a woman, to make me feel like a woman – it's corny but it's that simple. We had to stay late at the office, the two of us, working every night for a week on a big case at the City Commission. He used to get dinner sent up, and a bottle of wine. That was how it started. It went on for two years. We were careful. There were just those two evenings a week, and sometimes he'd go away on business or a political trip and I'd travel separately and take a room at the same hotel. Sordid it sounds, perhaps, but for a while there we were pretty close to being in love with each other, and that was all that mattered.'

Finn went across to join her at the window. He was still surprised, even slightly alarmed, at the reaction she had provoked in him. It had seemed suddenly important that she should not place herself outside the wall he had built against other people's feelings. Why? That in turn had something to do with the sharp yearning he had felt as he held her wrists. He asked gently, 'What went wrong?'

'It started when the Vigilantes were formed. No, I suppose the seeds were there long before. I started to see a side that I'd not realized was there. The power went to his head. Suddenly things mattered again; I was a Catholic, he was a Prod. We fought. He told me he couldn't keep me in the office any longer. After that it just crumbled. I moved out of the flat without telling him. These days we just look through each other.'

'So you've seen him since?'

'Not to speak to.'

'When was the last time?'

'You're a terror for the questions, aren't you?'

'When?'

'You speak as if you've some right to interrogate me. I don't know – a month ago, perhaps.'

'Why did you hesitate?'

'I didn't. Look, I've to drive to Dublin.'

'When did you last see your brother?'

She gave him a sharp look. 'I'm not after seeing him. He's on the run, isn't he?'

'And you're telling me you haven't been in touch in the whole year that he's been on the wanted list? Come on. You were always very close, weren't you?'

'In a way you wouldn't understand,' she said defiantly.

'What was special about the last time you saw Kilshaw?'

The technique was to exasperate, then confuse. Caragh responded well, but again with the hesitancy that told him he was on to something, that somewhere here lay a fact of central importance. She said, 'Nothing was special.'

'Are you afraid of him?'

'Of the things he represents, yes. I don't hate him.'

'Does your brother know you saw him?'

She flared. 'You stupid git, you've got it all wrong! I didn't see him, not that way. We didn't meet.'

'Then what happened?'

'Let this be on your own head,' she said, taking a breath. 'I'll tell you what I know. I expected to be telling it to someone sooner or later. After, I expect to be left in peace. There's a quiet wee car park up behind Queen's University where he and I used to meet sometimes. We'd chat, and maybe go for a stroll in the Botanic Gardens. There'd be very few people; we were pretty safe from being seen. Around the middle of last month – it was a fine day – I went back there for a walk by myself. When I got back to the car park Kilshaw's car was there. He'd remembered how useful the place was.'

'Who was he meeting?'

'Walter Barnett was with him, his little sidekick. And then another car arrived and a man got out and climbed into the back seat of the Rover and they sat talking. I happened to recognize him from three years ago. His name is Gustave Brouhin. He's a Frenchman.'

'Should I know the name?'

'Not unless you're in the same line of business. Arms smuggling.'

She took a final draw on her cigarette, went back to the dressing table to stub it out, and returned to the window. Finn waited for her to continue.

'Just after the Vigilantes started up, Brouhin paid a visit to Kilshaw's office. He'd written from France offering to sell some small ships to Marine Services; he's got some interest in the same kind of business over there. Later, when we met, Kilshaw told me what he'd really been interested in selling: guns.'

'And Kilshaw didn't buy?'

'The Vigilantes weren't that kind of organization – not then. Besides, they couldn't have found the sort of money Brouhin was asking. He's one of the biggest dealers in Europe. He sells only in bulk.'

Finn considered. 'So they've finally found a way of doing business, it seems.'

'It's the only thing that could have brought Brouhin back to Belfast. It was too important, that knowledge, too dangerous, for me to keep to myself. Knowing what you do about my background, you'll appreciate that. From there on you start guessing, Finn, because I'm not going to say any more.'

'Did they see you, up at the car park?'

'I kept out of sight till they left.'

'And then you told...'

'I've said. No more.'

'You could have gone to the police,' he said, half joking.

She snorted. She still stood looking out of the window. Now she turned sharply, uncertainty in her eyes. 'You told me you'd nothing to do with them.'

'Nothing.'

'I know that car. What's it doing here?'

He looked. The car was parked fifty yards behind his waiting taxi. It was still identifiable in the gathering autumn dusk as a green Vauxhall Cresta. There were three men in it.

'That there is an RUC Special Branch car,' she said. 'They came in it to search the house. Kilshaw's friends. Why is it back here?'

'Have they come again since they searched?'

'No.'

'Then they can only have followed me.'

He spoke calmly, concealing annoyance with himself. It had perhaps been inevitable sooner or later, but why now? He should have taken more precautions on the way here, especially after his encounter with Howarth the night before.

'I'd better go,' he said.

'Yes.'

'Maybe I'll see you again.'

'Maybe.' She gave him an ambivalent look. 'Don't bring those back with you,' she said, gesturing out of the window.

They went downstairs. Finn left the house with an odd reluctance. He had rejected, yet in some way been affected by, her empathy, pity, interest, whatever it was. He had also enjoyed the ambience of her sexuality; in the past weeks he had wondered seriously whether desire had been burned out of him as well.

Riding back in the taxi he had a lot to think about, including the fact that Miss Caragh Hughes knew more than she was telling. But certainly the central fact he had been seeking had emerged. Kilshaw was buying arms for the Loyalist Vigilantes, arms that could be used for only one purpose, war against the IRA. And, by implication, against any Catholic who got in the way. He had committed himself to the probability of civil war.

So? Prove it and remove him. To remove him seemed now a more urgent priority than even Partington had realized. But assuming the proof existed, it must have been in the safe that was burgled, and whoever now had it intended making his own conditions of sale in his own good time. This was a very cool customer. The motive for the burglary had at least become clearer; so had the likely identity of the burglars.

It was time he had a long talk with Partington. But meanwhile there was an important gap he could fill tonight. The typewriter.

Down the Falls and the Grosvenor Road, the few street lamps that still worked were coming on as the taxi drove through the gloom of early evening. The charred hulk of the lorry that had been burned the night before still stood on one corner. On the Boyne Bridge a group of Vigilantes, helplessly watched by a small army patrol, were stopping and searching cars.

The men in the green Vauxhall did not seem to care whether Finn knew they were following him.

9

Partington closed the file he had been reading and drew a small bunch of grapes with his pencil on one corner of the cover. He sat back and thought, not about the subject of the dossier – dull, on the whole – but about Finn.

Partington's view of people generally was an uncharitable one. He was not ashamed of it; indeed, he enjoyed his reputation for urbane malice. He detected weaknesses, not virtues, and got a certain amount of pleasure out of exposing them. He had an insufferable talent for annoying others while remaining invulnerable to their spite – a talent which, it had been rumoured among his colleagues, had driven his wife into an early grave ten years before.

Finn was different, though. Somehow Partington had not got the measure of Finn. There was a core of something – indifference, self-confidence, a weary wisdom? – which did not respond to the usual provocation. Perhaps, Partington thought with a twinge of discomfort, there was also something of his own kind of strength.

It was natural that Partington should admire writers like Hobbes, Machiavelli, Swift, who had all rubbed people's noses in the mire of their own natures. Unfashionable oracles, of course, but then it was also part of his armoury to hold unfashionable views. It gave him the latitude that his ego needed to dogmatize, argue, and turn polemical somersaults – in a phrase, to impress people with his intellect. But at bottom he considered himself a realist. He was a civil servant who had to practise politics, and politics was what Lord Butler had called it, the art of the possible. Its true fascination lay in stretching the limits of possibility. Take someone like Niccolo Machiavelli: the maligned Florentine, he considered, was the true father of *realpolitik,* condemned less for the cynicism of his views than for their honesty. By implication his view of human nature was dismal; a few squeamish critics had said the same of Partington in reviewing his pseudonymous Irish history.

Perhaps, he conceded grandly, he did lack sympathy. Perhaps he also became childishly querulous when things did not go well. In the matter of the Kilshaw letter, things had not gone well for some time, but he did not believe in rushing them. When in doubt, do nothing. In time decisions will make themselves. For several days now he had felt the decision approaching.

At first he'd wondered whether they were trying to trick him, compromise him. Or even kill him? One had to go cautiously. In retrospect it seemed improbable. More than three weeks had gone by since the first letter and he no longer expected a second one. Not, as he had thought at first, because they had taken fright, but because they knew by now that the bait had been firmly seized. Finn was plodding away over there, getting himself noticed as he'd been meant to. And yet, and yet... Three weeks. He could no longer afford to work to their time scale. The committee was anxious for a positive plan of action. At least the connection he had been seeking was finally established, confirmed by Finn's telephone call that morning. Ultimately that was all Partington had needed from Finn, though there was really no point in telling *him* that.

Partington stared across the room, through the window into the deepening gloom of Gosfield Street. Finn would have no reason to complain, he thought. Nothing had been kept from him but a single fact that would only have served to prejudice his inquiries. One couldn't be too careful. They, on the other hand, hadn't been careful enough. They had not reckoned with

Partington's memory, with his powers of observation honed over thirty years, and certainly not with the comprehensiveness of his files. It was typical enough.

Idly he opened the dossier again and looked at the photograph clipped inside the back cover. A face from long ago, still distinctive in its own lugubrious way, still familiar. The face he had picked out among the crowd at Victoria station on the evening of the seventh and had been brooding over ever since. Stand and be recognized – and recognize in turn! From a certain point of view it was comical, like so many things Irish.

Finn might as well keep plodding. Partington suddenly knew that it was time to make his own move. It was time to renew another old acquaintance.

10

Finn paid off the taxi outside his hotel. The Vauxhall had drawn up twenty yards behind. He let himself be searched, walked down the L-shaped path of steel hurdles to the front door, then changed his mind and went back again. At the security guard's hut a confusion of whispers among the three from the car suddenly ceased. Two of them stepped aside to let him pass; the third, a great slab of a man with a face as grey and craggy as a Hebridean cliff, stood his ground and made Finn squeeze by. Without looking back he crossed the street and entered the Crown Saloon.

Apart from a television set in one corner, now showing a children's programme, the Crown was much as it had been for a hundred years. The windows were stained glass, the top of the long bar counter was marble, and porter was still drawn from the wood. A row of solitary drinkers in workmen's clothes lined the bar, solemnly watching *Magic Roundabout*. Opposite was a row of head-high booths made of massive carved oak and glass. Finn entered one of them, sat down, pressed a button that activated a clapper in a small opening on a beam traversing the ceiling, and from the waiter who appeared ordered a gin and tonic.

'Major Finn.'

The craggy man's head and shoulders towered above the partition. He opened the door of the booth, slid into the seat opposite Finn, and said to the returning waiter, 'A double McKinnon's.'

To Finn, he pushed across the table a plastic-covered warrant card, palming it back again in almost the same movement of one enormous hand. He was announcing himself anyway.

'Crombie. Detective Superintendent, RUC. A word, if you please.'

Finn poured tonic into his gin and stirred it with a finger. 'I thought you might want to talk. I didn't want you calling on me in the hotel.'

'Indeed.'

Crombie's voice was a nasal Presbyterian boom. His face was massive and Scottish and immobile, with a drinker's complexion, deep blue eyes edged with red, a brow tortured into a hundred corrugations beneath a receding crescent of wild grey curls. His name was familiar from somewhere.

'Is this official?' Finn asked.

'No.'

'Then I'm under no obligation to listen. Do you usually put a tail on journalists?'

'Only when I'm interested in their friends.'

'A man of your rank? I'd have thought you'd have more important jobs. I could put a complaint through my union.'

'But you won't, Major, and we both know it. We both know better than to fence.'

Crombie's rum had arrived. He paid for it, enveloped the glass in one paw, and emptied it in a swallow, smacking his lips around the fumes. He grinned at Finn.

'I would just like to be reassured, Major, that you and I are on the same side.'

'Meaning what?'

'It disturbs me to find you having dealings with rebels.'

'Rebel equals Catholic equals IRA, is that it?'

'It worries me to find you knocking about with Seamus Fortune.'

'Did Howarth tell you that?'

'Who?'

'Major Howarth of the paras. He happened to see us together last night. Did he tip you off?'

Crombie gave an enigmatic smile, but Finn knew from the flicker of sudden caution that crossed the policeman's eyes that he was right. Howarth – he might have known.

'Fortune is a wee troublemaker, known to us from way back. Private detective, so-called. Associates with criminals, ex-internees, all the worst rubbish from the Falls. Caragh Hughes is the sister of a prominent IRA man. You can't expect me not to be a little disturbed, Major.'

'A journalist has to make contacts.'

'Of course. You've spent a fair wee while making contacts. Isn't it time you wrote your first article?'

He grinned again and signalled to the waiter to repeat the order. The rum had already brought a flush to his cheeks, showing up the bouquets of broken red veins just beneath the skin.

'There's that scrambler you use on the hotel telephones, too. Why don't you and I think about a useful exchange of information? Just think about it, that's all.'

'Why not just take me in under the Special Powers Act?' Finn said.

'Och, why should I want to do that? We're in the same trade, you and I. We've learned to survive through compromise.'

'I've told you I'm a journalist. I was warded out two months ago.'

Crombie sighed. 'You'll have gathered I'm after making a few inquiries, Major. You've an interesting history. Malaya, Cyprus, Berlin, the Rhine Army. A talent for working in sensitive situations, evidently. Yes, I know you were warded out. I also know that that can be used as a device to give deeper cover. I've spent time at Scotland Yard catching up on their gadgetry; I know about those wee MOD units tucked away round the back streets of London. And I don't want them freelancing in my parish. We've got to know what's happening if we hope to survive as a community.'

'As a Protestant community?' Finn asked.

'Don't you believe in majority rule, Major?'

'Not at the expense of the minority.'

'The Loyalists aren't shooting soldiers, bombing –'

'Not yet.'

'Not ever, as long as we're not provoked. We've the right to run our own country.'

'Depends what you call a country,' Finn said. 'One fifth of the population of London scattered about one small corner of Ireland? No control over defence, foreign policy, finance? Yet there you went for fifty years flaunting all the trappings of a state: a parliament, a cabinet, a prime minister. Do you know what that kind of self-delusion breeds? Mediocrity. Some of your so-called political leaders wouldn't do credit to a good borough council. As for the ones who depend on violence and confrontation – Kilshaw, for instance – they've come to have a vested interest in it. If peace should magically break out tomorrow he'd fade back into the obscurity where he rightfully belongs.'

Crombie flushed a little more and the furrows in his brow deepened. Finn had found the sensitive spot he'd been searching for. 'You've no right to talk like that, Major.'

'The same applies to the IRA. But you're a Kilshaw man, aren't you?'

'He's the only one with the guts – the integrity – to save us. Only for him we'd be ruled from Dublin by now. Or Rome – some would say it comes to the same thing. The British Government is waiting for the chance to sell us out.'

Finn understood Crombie's position more clearly. He was out to protect Kilshaw by every possible means. And although he had no clear idea what Finn and Fortune were doing, he suspected enough to see them as a threat. For all the rough edges, he was anything but a hick provincial policeman.

The second round of drinks arrived. Again the Ulsterman enfolded the rum in his huge hand and took it at a swallow.

'You're not very co-operative, Major Finn. That's your privilege. But if it should ever emerge that you'd withheld information from us, don't expect sympathy. You'd find it embarrassing to be prosecuted, I imagine.'

'What information are you thinking of?'

'Whereabouts of wanted terrorists, shall we say? Location of their bases.'

'If you're talking about Sullivan's Volunteers, I can tell you now that I know nothing. I met Con Michael Hughes's sister for the first time today, that's all.'

The policeman cocked a shaggy grey eyebrow at him. 'I think there's more to that lady than meets the eye.'

'You can't want her brother badly. He's a theorist, a kid.'

'True enough, but he's also a weak link. He's a spoilt middle-class boy among a hard-headed bunch. If he could be got at, he might lead us to their Belfast HQ, to his pal Billy McGarry. Maybe even to Number One himself, Colin Sullivan. Ó Súilleabháin, as he calls himself in Irish. We've an idea he comes North from time to time. It would be interesting to know when, where, how.'

Finn doubted that Crombie's interest had much to do with legitimate police work, but he said nothing. The big man stood up, looming over him. The blue eyes suddenly seemed very hard.

'I don't know why you're here, Major Finn, but I intend finding out. In the meantime, if you put one foot wrong I'll find an excuse to lift you. Your operation will be split open. There are subtleties to this situation that outsiders don't understand.'

He pushed open the door of the booth and then glanced back.

'Another thing. For your own good, don't trust those bloody Fenians.'

Crombie snapped the door shut and strode off, his great head and shoulders thrusting a path through the crowd at the bar.

Finn sat there for another twenty minutes, breathing the stout-laden air of the Crown more freely but feeling a new and deeper anxiety. The pressure was growing – pressure to trace the origin of the note to Partington and to get out, before Crombie or the Vigilantes made it unhealthy for him. There was one thing he still had to do tonight; probably he would have no better opportunity.

He left the pub. In front of the hotel opposite, the Vauxhall was still parked, although Crombie had gone. The other two men sat in the front, bundled up in their overcoats, watching him. All right. Rule one: Make them wait. Get them bored and tired.

He went up to his room. He had just remembered where he had seen Crombie's name before: scrawled across the notice of intended prosecution that had never been sent to Kilshaw.

11

By ten thirty he was getting worried. The two detectives had tailed him all evening and showed no sign of giving up. In spite of putting them through four hours of mesmerizing boredom he had not yet succeeded in the simple strategy of separating them both from their car, even for a few minutes.

At the hotel he had bathed, changed his clothes, and had two drinks in the cocktail bar before strolling to the nearest cinema, followed at a professional distance by the Vauxhall. For two hours he had sat grimly through a low-budget musical with one of the RUC men three rows behind while the other, keeping to the book, remained outside. Then he had wandered around main streets that were already practically deserted, window-shopping and giving the appearance of a man trying idly to fill his evening. Finally, an hour ago, he had settled into the upstairs lounge of McGlade's bar and ordered a medium steak and a half bottle of burgundy.

The detectives had probably been on duty since morning; they'd be cold, tired, hungry. The one who had come in behind Finn looked grateful enough just to be indoors. He stood at the other end of the bar with a half of stout and a cheese roll – nothing elaborate, in case he had to leave suddenly. You had to be phlegmatic to stick at this kind of thing for long without weakening, and that was what Finn counted on. But time was running out. He was on his second after-dinner brandy. He had studiously been reading every item in that evening's *Belfast Telegraph,* and by now he was on the sports pages.

McGlade's had two entrances – a fact the detectives would know but would not necessarily count on Finn knowing. One door, out of sight from up here, opened off Donegall Street into the public bar; the other was down a flight of stairs that gave onto a narrow entry off Little Donegall Street, directly behind. On the wall by the head of the stairs was a public telephone; Finn had chosen to sit at the table closest to this to discourage the other man from using it.

He finished his brandy. He was reading an account of a split in the Gaelic Athletic Association when a shadow crossed the page.

The RUC man who had been with the car for an hour had succumbed. He looked blue with cold. He did not acknowledge his colleague but stood close to him as he ordered a drink and a sandwich. He'd come in from behind, through the public bar entrance, which meant that the car must be parked in Donegall Street. Better and better.

Finn forced himself to finish reading the report before going to the bar and ordering another drink. Then he turned casually to the telephone, shielding it with his body so that Crombie's men would not see the number he dialled.

Paddy Keefe's mother answered; it was a number through which he could always be found. Tonight he was out at his club, she said, and gave Finn the number. When he dialled it he had to wait, churning with impatience, hearing Paddy's name bellowed against a background of thunderous revelry. He sounded a little drunk when he came on but he was willing to help. Finn gave him instructions softly and concisely and he rang off, promising to be outside McGlade's in no more than eight minutes.

Along the bar the policemen had been watching with uncertain curiosity, but they could not have overheard him. He put down the receiver, waited exactly six minutes, dialled another number and gave his message in the same soft voice. When he was asked a question he hung up without answering. With a thumping heart he returned to the table to finish his final brandy.

He barely made it. The RUC man who had come in first was about to return to the car. He halted halfway across the room as a siren wailed outside, suddenly and alarmingly close. Then a police sergeant in a flak jacket was lumbering up the stairs shouting, 'Everyone out! No panic, mind, just get a move on!'

Finn, nearest the stairs, was first down them. Behind him a glass broke and a girl gave a single hysterical shriek. The two detectives were caught up somewhere in the rush of twenty or thirty people, but Finn dared not take advantage of this by running; he would probably be shot at.

After three years of practice the drill for bomb warnings was extremely efficient. It was the same whether the presence of a bomb could be immediately confirmed or not. A platoon of Guardsmen were trotting down the entry to cordon Donegall Street, and other soldiers and policemen were shepherding civilians to the safety of side streets. They stood huddled round the corners, their breath frosty in the lamplight, neither terrified by a danger they lived with every day nor excited by a novelty that had long since worn off, simply waiting for it to be over.

Finn walked on, across Little Donegall Street, hearing running footsteps behind him as one of the detectives broke free of the crowd. The other must have gone for the car. He turned into Union Street, walked twenty yards to where Paddy Keefe's small van stood waiting, and opened the passenger door. The footsteps behind him stopped, turned, ran in a panic.

He got into the seat. Paddy gunned the engine and made a tight circuit of the block to head south-west. They were waved on across the intersection with Donegall Street, which now was sealed off for a hundred yards on either side of the Vauxhall. The car stood isolated by the accusatory beams of searchlights, waiting for the ATO specialists to arrive. Finn caught a glimpse of the two RUC men flashing warrant cards and indignation as they argued with the Guards officer in charge.

They reckon there's a bomb in that car there,' Paddy Keefe said.

'So I believe,' said Finn.

They drove up the Falls Road and through the dark and brittle streets of Andersonstown. Outside the Glen Road police station a boy of eight or nine stood throwing stones at the sandbagged army observation post – idly, the way he might throw them at a stray cat.

Paddy turned into Coolnasilla Park and drove past the darkened house a couple of times before parking in a street two hundred yards to the rear. Finn thought it unlikely that the police were watching the place. They might have liked to; but the only way of doing so in these suburban surroundings was with the co-operation of a neighbour, and affluent and law-abiding though the neighbours might be, they were still Catholics.

Finn and Paddy Keefe walked quickly along the pavement, through the gate, up the garden path, and into the shadow beside the house. Caragh's absence was providential. Finn had made careful mental notes during his conducted tour of the house: there was no alarm system, but the modern steel-framed windows were impossible to get through without breaking the glass. There must be no trace of the entry. The front door had an Ingersoll deadlock, the kind for which keys were supplied only to individual registered owners; it required two turns of the key and could take a considerable while to open. Relocking it afterwards would take just as long. However, there was a standard Yale lock on the back door, which opened into a small yard adjoining the garage where Caragh's Mini was normally parked.

Paddy had been looking at the house strangely. But he said nothing as they entered the yard and he unslung an old army rucksack he had brought from the back of his van. First he produced a new pair of surgical rubber gloves and pulled them on. Then, after using a pencil torch to examine the face of the lock briefly, he took out a slender probe, inserted it a little way into the keyhole, twisted it this way and that, and grunted. He took a selection of six Yale keys cut to different patterns, rubbed charcoal from a drawing crayon onto the serrated edge of each, and inserted them one after the other, slowly, feeling for slight changes of resistance as the tumblers were forced back and pressure was brought against the cylinder to turn, drawing back the bolt. He examined each key carefully after withdrawing it, comparing the points at which charcoal had been rubbed off by pressure from the tumblers. Now the profile of the key that fitted this lock was lodged in his mind; he rooted about in his rucksack among a hundred or more keys till he found the one that came closest to matching. It needed filing down at two points. Paddy was still slightly merry on Republican club whiskey, and hummed as he worked.

'It's nonsense to say no two keys are alike,' he said. 'They're all alike, if only you've the sensitive eye to see it. Sure, it's a dying art, of course. Nowadays they'll use nothing only gelly and gas cutters, like your lads who did the office safe there. There's no finesse at all.'

He slid his key into the lock and twisted it. The door swung open. The whole thing had taken seven minutes.

'Nothing more you're wanting, boss?' said Paddy, slipping into his pocket the wad of five-pound notes Finn had handed him.

'You can lend me your torch. Otherwise nothing but discretion. I'll find my own way back to town.'

'Good night now. Any other time.'

Paddy Keefe hiccupped, took his bag of tools, and vanished. Finn entered the house, closing the door behind him.

He kept the beam of the torch pointed down, using it to guide himself slowly from the scullery through the kitchen, where he almost tripped over a cardboard box full of groceries that stood in the middle of the floor. He crept down the hallway to the study door, which faced the foot of the staircase, entered, and let the torchlight linger over the bookshelves and the bureau. Finally, with relief, he picked out the typewriter; he had half expected her to remove it. He looked around for a sheet of paper, eventually tearing the flyleaf out of a paperback and rolling it into the machine. He held the torch in his left hand and with his right index finger tapped out in capitals at the top of the sheet: IN CONNECTION WITH JAMES KILSHAW.

The typewriter made an unearthly clattering. And in the vacuum of silence that followed there was a sound outside the study door.

It was a distinct but rather random sound, a noise incidental to movement, a soft brushing of metal against wood. Finn's mind made the connection instantly: the wood of the staircase banister, touched lightly by a ring, a button, a wristwatch. Or a gun.

He listened, his mind ice-sharp with concentration. In a moment he heard the familiar giveaway, the light swish of clothing, a sound so much part of the wearer's existence that he was not even aware of it. Someone was easing his way down the stairs, someone who knew enough about the house to avoid the creaky spots but who had never been trained in silence. Finn remembered the newly bought groceries in the kitchen and was appalled by his own stupidity. Without attempting to be quiet himself he stood the pencil torch on top of the bureau, so that its light narrowed into one corner, and flattened himself against the wall beside the door. He had no weapon; his movements would have to be swift and certain.

The door sprang open; light exploded into the room. The man

came in at a crouch, revolver in one hand and torch in the other, a textbook entry but much too slow. Finn lunged, using both hands to seize and twist back his right arm, hearing a quick yelp of pain as the knuckles were smashed against the edge of the door and the fingers opened reflexively. The gun thudded onto the carpet.

There was still the torch. Its heavy metal case crashed twice against the base of Finn's skull before he could block the young man's left arm. Circles of light dashed giddily about the room. For a moment they stood straining in a. wrestler's embrace, trying to throw each other off balance, but Finn no longer had the stamina for this kind of thing. He brought his heel down hard on the other man's right instep and followed through with a knee to the groin as he felt him convulsively release his grip. He fell to the floor and lay doubled over, whimpering and gasping, hands clutched to his genitals.

Finn groped for the light switch and turned it on. A wave of nausea washed through him, the penalty for sudden exertion. He felt dizzy and leaned, panting, against the bureau for a minute, hearing the sounds of pain become slowly less strident. Then he walked to the doorway and picked up the revolver, a superannuated British officer's Webley, checked the chambers – all loaded – snapped the cylinder back into position, and let the gun hang by his side.

He looked down at Con Michael Hughes, who stared back with brown eyes full of mingled uncertainty, anger, and fear. There was an odd familiarity about his face, which at the moment was streaked by a tear. He still clutched his groin. The boy was as soft as putty.

12

Billy McGarry had the gift of relaxing, like a cat, whenever he chose. He could alternate periods of intense concentration with long intervals of static idleness, his muscles limp, his head empty. He had learned how to prepare for a night's wait, with four hours' sleep in the afternoon and a light supper. Like a cat, again, he took care to make himself comfortable, stretching out on a bed or sofa with as many cushions as he could find. If there was any halfway-decent music in the house he would get them to put it on, softly – in this case two Ray Charles albums had been played again and again on the tinny record player. The boy, finding excuses to enter the darkened room where he lay, had already been in half a dozen times to turn the records over.

The boy was a typical Falls kid, twelve or thirteen, cheeky, trying hard to seem unimpressed by the great man's presence in the cramped council flat. Billy basked contentedly in the warmth of hero worship, rarely thinking about its transience; his was not a strong imagination anyway.

He pressed the smooth, warm butt of the rifle to his cheek again and squinted through the enormous night scope. The battery-powered image intensifier gave a ghostly, arc-light illumination to his field of fire, a twenty-yard stretch of Broadbent Street visible between two wings of Unity Court, the council complex in which the flat had been set up for him. The range was a hundred yards. This was a sensitive area, its fringes constantly toured by foot patrols. Logic suggested that at least one of them would pass by that gap before dawn. He laid the butt of the rifle on the divan again. Only an inch of its muzzle, resting on a cushion, protruded through the half-open window.

Billy had grown up rather like a cat too, more as part of a litter of strays than as one of a family. Not that they had fought for scraps, exactly, in these days of social security, but there had been the same rootlessness, the same savage, tenuous hold on life, and the same readiness to rend. He had never known his father. He was one of six illegitimate children – by at least four men – of a stupid, soft-hearted Lower Falls woman with neither the will to resist men's attentions nor the wit to practise contraception. Billy could not recall a time when they were not living on the State, when they were not moving or about to be evicted from one set of squalid rooms to another. In the urban sense he had 'run wild,' his schooling effectively over by twelve because no school could hold him. Nor could the council welfare home in which he periodically found himself. The family, such as it was, was in permanent mutation, constantly moving, constantly losing and reacquiring members. And always there seemed to be some new complacent face at the tea-table, some new set of grey underwear drying in front of the fire. Billy's hatred for these men, jealous and puritanical at first, widened to encompass more and more of the people he encountered: teachers, truancy officers, priests, shopkeepers, welfare workers, policemen. Even before his voice had cracked there was a taut steel spring of hatred inside him, waiting for release.

Ray Charles was singing 'In the Heat of the Night.' A shaft of light was reflected in the window as the boy opened the door quietly.

'What is it?' he said, not turning.

'There's some of 'em up Tyrone Street. Soldiers.'

'How d'ye know?'

'The weemin's bangin' bin lids. You can't hear it in here.'

'Okay.'

'They'll come down to the Old Lodge Road, won't they? You'll get 'em in that gap there, won't you?'

'You keep out of here now.'

The boy left. Billy raised the rifle butt again, checked the setting of his sights, and moved the weapon back and forth through its narrow field of fire. He felt his heart begin to beat a tiny fraction faster.

There were only two men in the world for whom he had any respect. Sullivan was one, because he was the first person he had known whose authority was starkly unquestionable, and Billy since childhood had unconsciously craved the security of discipline. Con Michael he respected for obscurer reasons. He in turn was the only 'intellectual' Billy knew, but he never looked down. You had to like him for being earnest.

In his early teens he had drifted through a few meaningless jobs and long periods on the dole. He did the usual amount of rutting and fighting, though never as one of a group. Apart from a primal response aroused by the rhythms of black American music, he had no real interests. Finally he drifted into Borstal for a year, for stealing a car and deliberately crashing it into the Lough. Inside, he was taught a bit about welding. When he came out his probation officer managed to get him into the shipyards as an apprentice. Surprisingly, he found himself enjoying the work. He did it well and got on with the men around him, even if they were mostly the Protestants he had grown up to dislike and distrust. He seemed to be settling down. Then, with only a few months of his time still to serve, had come the incident when a foreman had called him, half in jest, 'a wee papish bastard.' In a blind rage Billy had gone for him with a sledgehammer.

Other men pulled them apart before any damage was done and they ended up apologizing to each other. But the story reached the Loyalist Association of Workers, by this time militant supporters of James Kilshaw, and they managed to get Billy sacked as a 'disruptive element.' He was back on the streets and twice as bitter.

A chance meeting with Con Michael at a Republican club jazz evening had drawn him into the movement; a weapons training course in the South had discovered his unsuspected talent, that remarkable combination of nervelessness, a steady hand and a superb eye, fast reflexes and – the most important, most elusive quality – the willingness to kill. Even the first time had not been difficult: some sweat, a slight tremor, that was all. Since then he'd got better and better; the conviction grew that in a round-about way he had found his true vocation.

He started. He had been looking over the scope, not through it, and had caught a tiny twitch of movement in the gap below. He raised the sight to his eye and the scene became clear: a patrol moving line ahead along the far pavement. The scope was perfectly focused; in the artificial daylight it produced he could see the black tam o'shanters of a Scottish regiment, the leader who had darted into a patch of shadow halfway across the gap beckoning his men to follow. They moved warily, their eyes flicking from window to window of the buildings opposite. They looked straight at Billy without seeing him.

Slowly he slid his left hand forward to take a firm grip on the plastic stock. The thumb of his right hand went up from the pistol grip to release the safety catch. He chose the third man in the line, settling the junction of the blurred cross-hairs on a point where the tam o'shanter touched the top of the left ear, following him with the rifle.

He took a deep breath, expelled half of it, held the rest. A warm feeling flowed down from his stomach to his loins. His finger was round the trigger. When he gently squeezed it he was filled not with hate but with the nearest thing he had known to love.

13

'So you're Finn,' said Con Michael, still lying on the floor.

'She told you about me, of course.'

'She told me nothing, we hardly ever meet. It's not safe.'

'Then she left you a note with the groceries. Has she been keeping you fed ever since you went on the run?'

'You wouldn't know anything about it,' the young man said.

'I can guess. The hideouts down the Falls must be pretty ropey. No bathrooms, outside lavatories, four to a room, and the grub can't be up to much. Every so often Caragh fixes you up with a hamper and you sneak home to clean up, am I right? Risky, I'd have thought.'

Con Michael began to sit up but thought better of it and lay back on the carpet, still nursing in both hands his bruised and vulnerable testicles. He looked much as he had in the family photograph upstairs, with that terrible innocence about the dark eyes, a sensitive mouth, and a brooding expression. Only the hair had changed, from a length which might just have passed inspection on a parade-ground four or five years ago to a profusion of black curls that grew richly behind and over his ears. He was dressed for moving about at night, in a shapeless navy sweater, denim jacket, and black corduroys. There was still that haunting familiarity, something to do with his general cast of features, that Finn couldn't place.

'Don't you think it's dangerous, coming back here?' he said.

'What is it you want?'

'You know damned well.'

'That doesn't mean I can talk about it. I don't know who and what I'm dealing with.'

'Why not tell me who and what *I'm* dealing with?'

Con Michael stood up slowly, wincing. He leaned on the desk and looked at the single line of typing on the paper in the Smith-Corona. 'Is that all you came for at all?'

'To establish whether the note about Kilshaw was typed on that machine, yes.'

'I'll tell you for free. It was.'

'Good. We can talk business then.'

'You're jumping the gun, Finn.'

'I've been in this town three weeks and spent most of it waiting for one thing or another. I'm tired of waiting. I know that you found out from your sister that Brouhin was in Belfast and that he was apparently doing some deal with Kilshaw. For some reason that was a hot enough tip to make it worthwhile breaking into Kilshaw's office and burning a hole in his safe. Details about the type of safe supplied by his former employee, your sister. And it would be your friend Billy McGarry, some-time welder, who did the cutting. You found something in there that would incriminate Kilshaw. Right so far? What's the merchandise and what's your price?'

'Not mine,' said Con Michael.

'Whose, then?'

'The movement.'

'Sullivan's Volunteers? You think the British Government will do business with the IRA?'

'Sullivan seems to think so.'

'So he's in charge of the whole prank himself, is he?' Finn stared hard at the young man. 'Tell me something. How did he know there was anything worth stealing in that safe?'

'You'd better ask himself that.'

'Is he willing to meet me?'

'That's the idea. He'll negotiate with you personally.'

'When?'

'Whenever there's the chance.'

Finn took a threatening step forward. 'There've been plenty of chances, sonny, ever since you did the safe. He's kept us waiting to get us impatient, to give us time to convince ourselves that what he's holding is valuable. Why does he need to try so hard? *What was in the safe?*'

'Och, to Jasus!' Con Michael made an irritable gesture. 'All right, there were documents. Company records. They don't make much sense to me, but Sullivan is after studying them. He says they prove that Kilshaw has been swindling his own people to find the money for guns. The books tell the whole story. They'd earn him ten years and discredit him in the eyes of the Loyalists – exactly what the British want.'

'And Sullivan thinks we'd buy the stuff from him?'

'Why not? For once you've more to gain out of knocking the Vigilantes than the Republicans.'

'What proof is there that the documents are genuine? Why should we trust him?'

'He's a man of his word. A patriot. Socialist. Sure, he'll offer you some proof, all the same.'

Finn said nothing for a moment. In some weird way you had to admire Con Michael's innocence. You also had to respect the sheer nerve of Sullivan in offering to do business with his natural enemies; if the documents were as Con Michael described them, they were all Partington wanted and more. They were also one of the hottest political potatoes in years – another reason for Sullivan's devious approach. Somewhere, he felt, there must be a catch.

'What's the price?' he asked finally.

'That I can't tell you either. Would you ever have a cigarette for me?'

'No.'

'D'you mind if...?' He glanced at the revolver, still hanging by

Finn's side. A man who threatens another with a gun needs the will to use it, and both of them knew the will was not there.

'Go on,' Finn said. He slipped on the safety, put the revolver down, and watched Con Michael go gingerly to the kitchen to search in the box of provisions. He came back unsealing twenty Gallaher's. Suddenly Finn realized whose face the Irishman's reminded him of – his own, perhaps twenty years ago. It was an odd sensation. It took only a moment to see that the resemblance was superficial, and the last traces of it must have vanished with the disease anyway, but there it was – a similar physiognomy, the same colouring, and the same dark Celtic look with its deceptive hint of fragility.

'There's something else,' Con Michael said. 'The money Kilshaw collected all went on a single big shipment of arms. The cash is already handed over. The shipment hasn't come yet.'

'So?'

'I gather it's due pretty soon now. For myself I wouldn't know how or when, but I guess you'll be wanting to know the details. Only one man can tell you.'

'Sullivan?'

'He's got it all figured out from the books there.'

Finn nodded slowly. Sullivan seemed to consider himself pretty indispensable – and with good reason, by the sound of it. There was no point in trying to learn more from Con Michael, because he'd obviously been told very little.

'Did you know about your sister's affair with Kilshaw?'

Con Michael nodded curtly. Finn had guessed he would find the subject uncomfortable. 'I tried to stop her,' he said. 'She told me all about it. Wasn't ashamed.' He lit a cigarette and sat carefully in an armchair. 'We were always that close, you see, always confided. As kids we spent a long time side by side in hospital beds, kind of clinging to each other because we were afraid of everything else. Diphtheria – we both caught it; touch and go it was for us both. She was at that mothering age, more concerned for me than for herself. She has been ever since.

'But that's by the way. I couldn't stomach this idea. I mean – him! Even before the Vigilante days he was typical of everything our people despised, a Unionist, a bigoted Orangeman. It was like a French girl carrying on with a Nazi during the war; feelings run just as deep in this community. But she wouldn't listen. She had that self-satisfied air, you know, impervious to criticism, of a woman who's – well –'

'In love?' suggested Finn callously.

'She was fooling herself,' growled Con Michael. 'It went on through my last two years at UCD, and then when I came home she'd broken it off and was living back here. We never spoke about it again till last month, when she told me about Brouhin. She *had* to tell me, the implications were that serious.'

'And you reported it to Sullivan, who assigned you and Billy McGarry to finding out more.'

'He said to take anything we could in the way of company books, accounts, all that there. I hardly even looked at what we took. We were damned lucky to get the right stuff. I knew Sullivan wouldn't miss anything that was there to be found.'

'You admire him, I take it.'

'I joined the movement on account of him alone. He came round to College to address our Socialist Society, and he impressed me more than anyone I'd met before. He still does. He's a man of little education, yet his grasp of political thought is astonishing. He thinks clearly, simply; he's just never learned the bourgeois art of self-justification. Everything important that's ever been achieved in Ireland was achieved by workers and peasants. We're basically a *nation* of workers and peasants, there's the truth. It's not the middle classes that are in the thick of the troubles down the Falls and the Shankill at the minute, and that's the whole point. Sullivan taught me to find my origins. After I'd graduated I went over to London among the navvies for a few months. I lived with them, worked my hands raw, drank with them. It was the greatest time of my life, so it was. Only the troubles brought me back. Of course I stayed with Sullivan when the movement split into factions.'

'And you're going to lead the revolution between you?'

'It's got to come. People are waking up to one fact, that their real enemies aren't those of the opposite religion. There were sound reasons of bourgeois economics for partitioning Ireland in the first place. Ever since then it's been in the interests of capitalist governments on both sides of the border to keep them divided.'

Finn could not be bothered to argue. 'When do I see Sullivan?' he asked.

'Soon. You'll be contacted and brought to a safe meeting place.'

'Here? In the North?'

Con Michael looked at him indulgently. 'He's across the border at least once a week. We've a route that's so wide open we've given it a nickname: Boyle's Bypass. It's safer than crossing the street.'

'I'd better warn you that the police have been tailing me. Kilshaw's friends among the police, rather. I guess they'd like those documents too.'

'We're used to being careful. You'd better go now.'

Con Michael let him out. He walked to the top of the Falls Road and phoned for a taxi to return him to the hotel. He was tired but his mind was active. A good night's rest was called for, and then a talk with Partington. Events had moved swiftly; there were decisions he could not make alone.

He was back in time to hear the one o'clock news on the BBC. Kilshaw had made a speech saying he could not hold back the Vigilantes much longer from finding and destroying the IRA for themselves. And Billy McGarry had killed another soldier.

14

Seamus Fortune left Tooley's club in the Ardoyne at two in the morning, in as much of a hurry as he politely could. Tooley's was only a club in one sense, that it did not have a pub licence and was therefore not restricted to inconvenient closing hours. Anyone indiscreet enough to inquire more closely might have learned that it did not have a club licence either, or a committee, or a fee-paying membership. What it did have was a large stock of liquor, sold at such sacrificial prices that even the most curious patron never dared ask where it came from. But Fortune found Tooley's useful for other reasons; it was a marketplace for gossip and rumour. Very little happened in Republican circles that didn't sooner or later filter through there, and Fortune's hours of drinking and listening tonight had been well spent.

He drove his Austin out into the Crumlin Road and headed for the city. He was pleased to be able to do Finn a favour. Fortune was a conscientious man and still had lingering guilt feelings over walking out on the Englishman. He'd promised to keep his eyes and ears open, and the news he had to bring tonight should go a long way towards making up for his backing out.

He turned down Tennent Street towards the Shankill Road. Vigilante country, this, but there was no way of avoiding it without a major detour. NO POPE HERE, said the wall scribblings. JAMES KILSHAW FOR GOD AND ULSTER.

He'd phone from the call box behind the bus depot, he thought, and just hope that Finn was back at the hotel by now. If not he'd have to wait. The news was too important to keep till tomorrow.

Too late, he saw the roadblock.

Too late, that is, to stop and reverse and get out, which would have been the safest thing to do, taking a chance that they wouldn't shoot at him. But several men had stepped out of a side street behind him now, closing off his rear, and from the roadblock itself – a row of oil drums supporting a length of fence railing laid flat – four others advanced. One carried a hurling stick, the others heavy clubs. The Vigilante armbands stood out against the drabness of their combat jackets. Fortune brought the car to a halt, licked his lips, turned down the window. A torch shone insolently into his face.

'Where yez goin'?'

'Into town.'

'Where d'yez live then?'

'Antrim Road,' he said, careful not to specify which end of it.

'Got any identification? Driver's licence?'

He nodded and took out his wallet. Inwardly seething at their nerve, he said nothing. It was easy to laugh at these comedians until you found them surrounding you in a lonely street. A corner of his mind prayed for the approach of an army patrol, another car, anything. He handed over his licence and the man with the torch deflected its beam onto the pages of the booklet.

'Fortune,' he read out loud. Then, 'Seamus?'

It took a second or two for the significance of the Catholic forename to penetrate. Suddenly the torchlight was full in his eyes again.

'Get out,' said the Vigilante quietly.

'What for?'

'Just get out. Ye're in a Loyalist area. Ye'll have to explain what ye're doin'.'

'Nothing, only passing through. You've no right –'

'It's Kilshaw's writ that runs here. We've every right.'

Panic seized him. The car's engine was still running. He

slammed the gear lever into first, but before he could get his foot off the clutch someone had reached in and twisted the ignition key out of its lock. He scrambled across the seats to the near-side door, opened it, tumbled out. He'd had some notion of crashing through the barricade, but now all he could think Of was running. Anywhere.

The Vigilantes had raced around the car. As he got to his feet the broad flat blade of the hurling stick caught him across the cheek and jawbone and sent him reeling.

'Taig bastard!'

'Fuckin' Fenian bastard! What yez tryin' to hide?'

This time he managed to duck as the stick was swung again, and it grazed the side of his head. The Vigilantes, seven or eight of them, were all around him with their clubs but he dived across the bonnet of the car and slid feet first to the ground, and miraculously there was an opening, through which he ran.

They chased. There was a gap between the barrels wide enough for him to scrape through. Someone swung a club which missed his head by a foot. Then he was pounding down the deserted street, followed by a confusion of running footsteps and obscenities. His fear was that he would run into more of them.

The brassy crash of a shotgun filled the street, and birdshot whistled past him. He slewed into a dark opening on his left, staking his life on its not being a cul-de-sac. It wasn't. There was a turning to the right twenty yards on and he ran down it, his heart and brain hammering in terrified unison, hearing a couple of determined runners now at the front of the pursuit.

Ahead were the lights of the Shankill Road, beyond that the Catholic Falls. Until he got there he could hope for no sanctuary among the mean Presbyterian houses. His breath came in choking sobs.

He ran into the last crossing before the Shankill, suddenly aware of bulky shapes in the street a second before he crashed into someone stepping round the corner. Something scalding spilt on his hand and the man was swearing. Fortune, his balance gone, went down to the pavement thinking, This is it. He rolled on his hip and finished up in the gutter, unable to find the strength to get up again.

Another torch shone in his face. Someone with a quick intake of breath had snapped back the cocking handle of a sub-machine gun. Belatedly he registered the fact that the swearing had been in public-school English. He glanced up the street: the Vigilantes had been stopped thirty yards behind, fretting and stamping like hounds denied their kill. They were being shoved back by paratroopers from the patrol into which Fortune had stumbled.

From the back of one of the armoured vehicles Major Howarth had fetched himself more tea to replace what Fortune had spilt. He came up holding the mug between two gloved hands.

'Now here's a coincidence,' he said. 'Seamus Fortune, private investigator. I've an idea we want to talk to you.'

15

Partington felt more than usually in sympathy with Machiavelli this morning. It was little wonder, he thought, that the man had never been popular. His analysis of power came too near the truth; he knew it was something people aspired to quite naturally, not an aberration of some kind. It was worth having for its own sake, and he had set out to explain how, once acquired, it might be retained. A certain amount of ruthlessness was necessary – the fact was neither here nor there; what mattered was that Machiavelli had not moralized about it but, with the true instinct of a Renaissance scholar, had spelt out how and when it ought to be employed. Bear in mind that his hypothetical ruler governed with the consent of the people. Dictators who professed to admire Machiavelli – and it was said that Stalin had kept his major work, *The Prince*, at his bedside – did his memory a disservice.

Besides, the man had been true to his own teaching. He had survived several turns of the rack and still he could write in support of the Medici. There was detachment for you! Such a facility for separating the intellect and the emotions was rare – rarer still among the Irish, where that tricky factor of temperament tended to get in the way.

But it was a different sort of mind he was dealing with, Partington thought. Cranky, perhaps, but with a grasp of immediate realities. Not afraid of the truth, not squeamish; you could tell that just at one remove. It seemed a mind rather like his own, given to grand designs. Without even meeting they had made great progress.

At last Partington had a project to lay before his committee.

He had no doubt they would agree to it, even if at first sight it was almost unthinkably bold. At a second viewing it would seem much less so. In his own eyes it was simply Machiavellian. *Realpolitik.*

Partington stood, jacket and waistcoat unbuttoned to ease the constriction of his paunch, staring down into Gosfield Street. He yawned hugely. He'd had a busy night – phone calls, coded telegrams, couriers back and forth like airborne commuters. It reminded him of Dublin in wartime. Finn's morning call, irritatingly, distracted him from some pleasant reminiscences.

He turned the two code knobs on the scrambler to the preselected code for the day, placed the conventional receiver in the transistor unit, and sat listening on the scrambler handset for five minutes, drawing on his blotter the outlines of a row of comestibles, one by one – a French loaf, a bottle of hock, a dressed duckling. Finn spoke concisely. Finally Partington said, '*Well.* An embarrassment of riches, hm?'

'The first question,' said Finn, 'is whether we're in the market for goods sold by the IRA.'

'If Kilshaw is due for a big arms shipment, we must do everything in our power to stop it. Agreed?'

'Reluctantly, yes.'

'That information is vital. The rest is very promising too. IRA or not, we've no choice but to talk to them. Discreetly.'

'I can be discreet. The problem is, can they?'

'Sullivan runs a tight ship. Or so I believe.'

'What bothers me,' Finn said, 'is that he's coming North to meet me. Apparently they've got a route across from the South –'

'Yes, yes.' Partington waved carelessly at the ceiling. 'Boyle's Bypass, I hear it's called. It's a safe crossing. There's very little chance of his being lifted on the way. *I* keep up with things too, you see. Good, then. Sullivan knows by now that we're interested. You'll wait to hear from him, listen to his terms, establish exactly the *value* of what he's offering, and we'll take it from there. Are you with me, Finn?'

'Yes. I'm a little surprised, that's all, at how eager you seem to do business with him.'

Partington had drawn a Jarlsberg cheese. 'My dear fellow, you must get your priorities right. Take a high moral tone and the state totters. Kilshaw becomes more dangerous every day. If the only way to get rid of him is by co-operating with an equally revolting but weaker set of people, then so be it.'

'All right. But be warned. The RUC are onto me. They're keen to find out what I'm doing here. If I lead Sullivan into a trap we've lost everything.'

'You'll have to keep your head down,' Partington said. 'Toodle-oo.'

He put the receiver back with a sigh. Perhaps he'd been too flippant. Damn; he still couldn't strike the right note with Finn. He found himself trying to impress, saying things he didn't mean to. The man must not be underestimated, fancy ties notwithstanding. He had a way of looking at you as if through you. He also had a dangerous tendency to display his scruples.

It was a problem to know what to do with Finn, not so much now as later. A point was always reached where the intermediary became an inconvenience. Meanwhile he would still be useful, though not in any way he understood. The best possible form of security lay in what he did not know.

Of one thing Partington was quite certain. It wouldn't do to tell Finn about the project. He was not enough of a Machiavellian to appreciate it.

Partington stood up, took a deep breath, and began to button his waistcoat from the top down. The first thing to do was to get onto somebody about this Brouhin fellow. Then he could think with a clear conscience about lunch.

16

Fortune was led into a room strangely without windows. The light from a low-hanging bulb was so bright that he blinked for a couple of seconds before recognizing the man who sat next to Major Howarth behind a trestle table with a single hard chair placed defencelessly in front of it. The man was Detective Superintendent Crombie. To the right a military policeman stood with arms folded. Fortune heard the key turn in the door behind him.

He was very apprehensive, for no reason he could define. As far as he could make out he was somewhere in the Hastings Street RUC station. For six hours he had sat alone in a cell with nothing to think about but the pain on the left side of his face, grotesquely swollen from the blow with the hurling stick. Yet that bothered him less than the knowledge that he had not reached Finn, that he had not been able to repeat to him what Paddy Keefe, locksmith and forger, in a rare moment of indiscretion, had told Fortune at Tooley's club shortly before passing out across the table and having to be carried home to his mother.

'Good morning,' said Crombie, mock affable.

'I want to see a lawyer,' Fortune said.

'More complaints?' said Howarth. 'I think you've got a complaining nature.'

Fortune looked at Crombie. 'Maybe I'll get some sense out of *you*. I was trying to get away from the Vigilantes. I ran into his people and they lifted me. He won't give me a reason. I was lifted for no reason at all.'

The policeman cleared his throat. 'I can't agree there. That's to say, we've since found a reason. A gun. A Colt forty-five auto-matic. Familiar to you?'

Fortune stared. 'You've searched my house?'

'Your wife raised no objection.'

'Then she must have shown you the certificate. It was in the same drawer. That there's a legal gun. I've had it five years.'

'I dare say,' Crombie said. 'Trouble is, a lot of firearms certifi-cates are being forged these days. We can't take chances. It'll take a couple of days to check that it's genuine.'

'I want to see a lawyer,' Fortune repeated.

'Meanwhile,' Howarth said, 'you'll be held under Regulation Ten.'

'The Special Powers Act?' Fortune heard the disbelief in his own voice. 'You must be mad! You'll need a better excuse than that.'

'There are certain things we need to know from you,' Howarth said. 'Under Regulation Ten we can hold you for forty-eight hours for interrogation. *Without* access to a solicitor. It doesn't specify what we have to question you about.' He smiled. 'Does it, sergeant?'

'No, sir,' said the military policeman, moving forward.

17

Finn sat on his bed, thinking about what Partington had just said. The man had his own sources, of course, and Finn knew better than to ask silly questions, but there lingered like the half-remembered taste of last night's dinner the memory of a phrase he had heard twelve hours before, and which Partington had just repeated. Coincidences like that bothered him. If the coincidence was intended there might be even more to worry about.

Finn had his sources too. For all practical purposes the cover he had been using was already blown. He picked up the phone and dialled another number.

In ten minutes' time he was in a taxi being driven south along the Malone Road. Where the suburbs thinned out among rich green meadows and the road twisted across the Lagan, between low stone walls and farmhouses and copses of oak, he had no difficulty picking out the car that was following him, a black Humber, this time with four men in it. At least with Crombie's people he knew more or less where he stood.

The taxi drove him through the small town of Lisburn and dropped him outside the main gate of GHQ Northern Ireland at Thiepval Barracks. The sentries had been notified of his arrival. He was searched and admitted, and a couple of minutes later was drinking a pre-lunch sherry with a lieutenant-colonel named Barney Wilson in the bar of the Victorian-Gothic folly that did as an officers' mess.

Barney Wilson was an old friend. They had been in the Rhine Army together, had spent fishing weekends at Finn's cottage in the Höhe Eifel, and were much the same in age and temperament. About the time Finn was having his tumour diagnosed,

Barney had been shunted out of the SIB into Int Records and given two years' penance at Lisburn. He was something of a loner, and it had always worked to his disadvantage. The two of them stood at one end of the bar, away from the noisy crowd of young Ops and Public Relations men.

'Will you stay for lunch?' Barney asked.

'I want a favour from you,' Finn said.

'Go on, Harry. I thought you'd come for my company.'

'I want to look at one of your MPO files.'

'Members of Proscribed Organizations? Any particular one?'

'Sullivan.'

Barney Wilson smiled and shook his head. 'I'd need to clear that with the old man.'

'I can't afford that. It might get back to the RUC.'

'What is this lot you're with, anyway?'

'Sort of Home Office. PVP. It's all above-board, I promise.'

'Are you telling me the Home Office want a PVP on Sullivan?'

'Not exactly. Look, we both know the way armies work. Nobody questions anyone with enough brass on his shoulder who looks as if he knows his way to the lavatory. You can do it, Barney. I'll finish with the file in twenty minutes and your old man need never know.'

'Don't you want lunch?'

'No, thanks.'

'There's hotpot on the menu.'

'I'll bet there is.'

Barney gave his slow, resigned smile and drained his glass. 'Come on,' he said. He led the way from the mess to the Main Hall, where a guard admitted them both on the strength of his pass. Upstairs the records office, closed for lunch, was locked behind a barred gate and Barney had to fetch the key from the adjoining Ops Room. Finn waited there a minute for him. It was a quiet day for the field units, to judge by the number of incidents chalked on the panel of illuminated glass covering the 'tribal' maps of Belfast and Derry, segmented into Protestant and Catholic areas. Photographs of wanted IRA men lined the walls. The only Ops officer on duty was a young lieutenant who showed no interest in Finn's presence. He was on the phone to someone asking for the winner of the one-fifteen at Chepstow.

Barney returned, carrying a black loose-leaf binder.

'Bloody marvellous,' muttered the lieutenant, putting down the receiver.

'Did you back it?' Finn asked conversationally.

'I own it.'

They walked next door to Barney's office. Finn sat down and opened the file, noting with quick professional appraisal its thickness and the CONFIDENTIAL marking. That meant that however comprehensive it might be, the information had all come from official or secondary sources. With an informer to protect, an upgrading to SECRET would have been automatic.

Barney had locked the door. Finn went through the binder quickly, skipping what was obvious, skimming over the biographical section, hardly even pausing to note those odd inconsequential facts that often give the best insight into character. It was still that coincidence of phraseology that interested him.

Colm Ó Súilleabháin, as he now was, had been plain Colin Sullivan for the first thirty years of his life and had an average-enough background for one of the middle generation of IRA men. Even the fact that he had not set foot in Ireland until he was seventeen, and then only as an occasional conveyor of illegal Irish Sweepstake receipts from England, was not specially remarkable. He had been born in north London, one of many children of a Wexford farm labourer turned bus conductor, and had grown up with that romantic vision of Ireland that is held only by long-term expatriates and those who have never been there. But his entry into radical politics seemed to have happened entirely by chance.

The traffic in Irish Sweep tickets was brought to a halt by World War II, in which Sullivan proceeded to serve honourably, if without distinction, in the Royal Navy. His mustering at the time of his discharge was wardroom steward. It was 1946, and he was twenty-five, before he returned to Dublin on a sentimental pilgrimage. His dream seemed to have survived the reality of postwar Ireland, whose neutrality during the hostilities had not prevented the opening of old internal wounds. Several hundred members of the IRA had been detained without trial because their pro-Nazi (or at least anti-British) sympathies were held to have jeopardized the country's neutral position.

It was these men, newly released, who were busy reorganizing the movement in the spring of 1946. Sullivan, on holiday in Dublin, wandered into a Republican bar and got talking to a group of them. Imprudently, but characteristically, they invited him along to a clandestine meeting in a church hall. He went out of curiosity – or so he was to claim at his subsequent trial. The Garda Siochána raided the meeting, arresting everyone present. The court did not believe Sullivan's story, and he was jailed for twelve months.

That was the turning point in a career which, up to then, seemed to have lacked any clear purpose. His spell in Mountjoy prison tapped some hidden reserve of dynamism, and with it an almost fanatical stubbornness. He surrendered his British citizenship for Irish nationality. In jail he met hard-core IRA men and studied the Irish language and history. The aimless young Londoner who entered the prison emerged from it a bitter and dedicated Irish patriot.

It was not his last spell behind bars. During the disastrous border campaign of the fifties and early sixties, in which the IRA fought to assert Republican control over the British North, he too was interned. Meanwhile he had moved up into the highest echelon of the movement. He had also married an Irish girl and established himself as a self-employed bookkeeper, with a sideline of dubious legality as a tax adviser.

In the mid-sixties the fortunes of the IRA were at their lowest ebb. Its leader at the time, however, Cathal Goulding, was having some success in turning it away from narrow republican-nationalist principles towards an actively socialist policy. Many of the old guard distrusted this shift, but Sullivan was an enthusiastic disciple. He dug deeply into the right literature, and with the zeal of the convert he ended up far to the left of Goulding. When the movement finally split up over the crisis in the North in 1969, the traditionalists formed themselves into the Provisional IRA, Goulding retained control of the 'Officials,' and Sullivan, almost unnoticed, broke off to the left with a hard core of revolutionary followers committed to establishing a united and socialist Ireland. Among these followers was Con Michael Hughes.

Finn chewed his lips, contemplating. A thinker, Con Michael had called the man. Sincere. But in his background there was a whiff of opportunism, just a suggestion of the eye on the main chance. Those Irish Sweep tickets, for instance, and then in the navy the talent to find himself a soft number. Still, it wasn't that relevant. What mattered to Finn was the last report in the file, an attempt to analyse Sullivan's personal influence on the fighting in the North. Most of the active guerrillas stayed north of the border, with occasional visits to the South to collect supplies or simply to rest; they were being pushed hard. Sullivan and a small tactical-logistical command directed their operations from any of a number of more-or-less secret addresses in Dublin, keeping them supplied with whatever arms and explosives they could lay their hands on.

It was assumed that Sullivan occasionally paid a clandestine visit to the North, but no evidence was offered that he had ever actually done so. There was no mention of that nickname for the route, Boyle's Bypass, which had been used last night by Con Michael and this morning by Partington.

Finn looked up at Barney Wilson. 'How do you rate this file?'

'It's the best there is. It's a pool of our own data and raw stuff from the RUC, Scotland Yard, MI5 operatives in Dublin, and of course the Garda, who don't like these lads any more than we do. You'll have noticed it's right up to date, too.'

'There couldn't be reports from other sources, independently, reaching, say, the Home Office or one of the MOD agencies?'

'There'd be hell to pay if there were. Everything must be pooled.'

Barney was fidgeting for his lunch. 'One more thing,' said Finn. 'Do you know anything about a British intelligence unit that worked in Dublin during the war with official sanction from the Irish Government? Based at Mountjoy prison?'

'I've heard a bit about them. They stayed on till forty-seven or eight, tying up loose ends.'

'What were they up to?'

'Basically, helping the police round up IRA men, particularly German sympathizers. All under the counter, of course, in view of the country's neutrality. The IRA were a pain in the neck to the Irish Government, then as now. Quite simply, Dublin asked our people for help. Our methods were more sophisticated – better interrogation, better staff work, better techniques for collecting tactical intelligence. The lads were brought into Mountjoy by the lorry-load and then shipped off to the Curragh camp for internment. What we got out of it was an almost total suppression of Nazi activity and propaganda in Ireland, plus a few German agents in the bag and a lot of information about the IRA.'

Finn nodded, satisfied. 'You've been a great help, Barney.'

'Just don't let it come back at me.'

'No. Enjoy the hotpot.'

The taxi that took him back to Belfast was picked up again by the police car. They were pretty persistent; soon they could become a positive embarrassment. Sullivan would soon be making contact with him, Sullivan on a visit to the North by a secret route which the army and police didn't know about but that Partington, by some strange divination, did. The conclusion was inescapable: Partington had a source deep inside Sullivan's Volunteers, a source so delicate that its information could simply not be given currency in the files. Was there any connection between that and the years Partington had spent on a clandestine anti-IRA operation during and after the war? Impossible to guess.

There was a further point, very likely insignificant but tantalizing all the same. Sullivan had served his time in Mountjoy during the period Partington was stationed there.

He let himself be frisked outside the hotel and went up to his room. He was tired, with the day not yet half over. Without quite knowing why, beyond some vague feeling of apprehension, he removed his pistol from its place beneath the mattress, cocked it, slipped the safety catch back on, and placed the gun beneath his pillow before lying down.

For the rest of the afternoon he dozed, and read, and waited. By six o'clock he had enough appetite to go downstairs to the snack bar and eat a hamburger. When he came back to his room he found Caragh sitting on the bed, weighing the pistol in her hand.

'British Army issue,' she said. 'I should have known, shouldn't I?'

18

Partington had been reading a file too. The French Sûreté had been able in less than a day to supply a report from their own archives on the activities of Gustave Brouhin, and the Special Branch at Scotland Yard had managed to trace his recent movements closely.

Brouhin was to outward appearances a middle-aged Norman from an artisan's family who had done increasingly well for himself in a variety of businesses. A streak of hardness was evident from the start. In his early twenties he had been sent to Indochina as the representative of a machine-tool manufacturer. Within a month he had quit his post, set up his own import agency, and secured franchises for the distribution of a rival range of products. Today, with the help of a good deal of palm-greasing, the several branches of this company still managed to operate profitably in both North and South Vietnam as well as Cambodia and Laos.

He had fled from the Japanese invasion of Indochina, returning to occupied France where he joined the Resistance, was wounded, and, after the liberation, decorated. It was a time when war heroes could do no wrong. Somehow the authorities never got round to prosecuting him for his extensive involvement in the black-marketing of petrol and scrap-metal during the hostilities. Once he had been back to the Far East to rehabilitate his business, he turned his attention to the sea – or rather to the enormous profits to be made from salvaging war wrecks. Timeliness was always his great talent. He bought a majority shareholding in a salvage firm at Le Havre called Compagnie Havraise de Radoub et de Sauvetage, later investing some of the profits in property development in Rouen and an export-import agency in Paris mainly concerned with finding markets for light machinery from Communist-bloc countries. He was a great believer in diversifying.

This was the legitimate side of his business activities, although – in France, at any rate – the other side could not quite be called illegitimate. Brouhin had never allowed a scrap of proof to exist that he had knowingly brought a consignment of illegal arms into France.

The new enterprise had begun six years ago while he was on a trip to Prague. An official of Omnipol, the Czech state arms corporation, had approached him with a business proposition. Omnipol was perhaps the world's largest supplier of modern military weapons to insurgents. Their Kalashnikov automatic rifles and sub-machine guns and Katyushin rockets, made under licence from the Soviet Union, had become practically standard equipment for guerrilla organizations on every continent. Their catalogue was freely available. Anyone with hard currency and political credentials that were in the vaguest way revolutionary would probably be allowed to buy whatever he could afford.

But times had become difficult for Omnipol. Czechoslovakia's neighbours had tightened up their transit regulations, refusing the passage of weapons that were not accompanied by the international Final User Certificate proving that they were destined for an established and acceptable government. The corporation's proposal to Brouhin was that he should act as their unofficial agent in Western Europe. He accepted. The work involved doing nothing more than he always had in his capacity as an exporter of Czech machinery – arranging and accepting delivery of the goods at various ports, notably Le Havre and Marseilles, obtaining customs clearance, and organizing their onward shipment to Africa, Latin America, the Middle East, the Far East. The difference was that about one in five of the packing cases whose contents were described on customs declarations as tractor parts, machine tools, or cutting equipment actually contained arms from Omnipol.

It might appear that the Sûreté, having established all this, would be in a position to prosecute Brouhin. But it was not that simple. First, he was protected by a system of double-invoicing which offered no proof that he had any knowledge of what was in the packing cases. Then, legitimate as well as illegal consignments reached their ports of loading by an infinity of different routes, making interception almost impossible. The police, in any case, were less interested in preventing revolution in some distant part of the world than in catching Brouhin at it.

His commission from Omnipol must have been high, but he could not be expected to work for long on someone else's behalf. Once he had learned the international arms business, he moved in himself. Again, his timing was right. It happened that the largest pool of black-market weapons in the world was to be found in a country where he was already well established – Vietnam.

Partington thoughtfully drew a string of onions down the margin of the last page of the report. Then he turned back to the account of Brouhin's movements that had been prepared by Scotland Yard. Business in Belfast must be booming. The Frenchman had been there three times in the past month, staying each time at a different small hotel. He was there now. Good. He was expected to leave tonight. Better still. There was also, of course, the trip to Dublin in September, which would have looked odd were it not for what Partington now knew.

He stared out at the deepening gloom of Gosfield Street and lit a cigarette. Self-satisfaction came to him easily. He felt that he could talk sense to Brouhin, that this – like that other one – was surely a mind that worked on the same line as his own.

19

The helicopter engine drove a high-pitched whine through the cabin. You had to shout to be heard and so nobody was saying much, which suited Seamus Fortune. For once there were no voices; for once the noise was uniform and bearable.

His brain, saturated with fatigue and confusion, seemed suspended like a waterlogged hulk below the surface of reality. It had softened, fibrillated round the edges. He knew that at the centre it was still healthy and resilient, but something that might have been common sense told him that time would change that as well. Time and the military police sergeant.

Physical sensations came to him with a certain numbness. He felt the length of parachute cord that bit into his wrists. He felt the constriction of his blindfold, tightly tied and thickly folded to prevent his knowing day from night. He felt also the continual cold blast of air which meant that the rear door on his side of the Scout helicopter must have been removed.

The helicopter puzzled him. For fifteen minutes they seemed to have been flying aimlessly. From the pilot's remarks and from what was said occasionally over the R/T set, he gathered that they'd headed north-west over the city and then gone back in a wide arc over the Lough. He'd worked out where the other passengers were: Major Howarth in front next to the pilot, Crombie and himself at the rear with the sergeant between them, keeping Fortune's upper arm in a tight grip. Twice when he'd been in danger of falling asleep he had had the triceps painfully squeezed.

The sergeant smelt of cheap after-shave and spoke with a Geordie accent. He was a professional, who had worked on

Fortune with the same systematic detachment that he must have applied to the blancoing of his perfectly white web-belt. He also had the professional's knack of doing things his own way while appearing to defer to his superiors. Now he yelled to Howarth, 'Would this be a good time to talk to him, sir?'

'Go ahead, sergeant.'

'Very good, sir.'

Fortune smelt the after-shave as the sergeant's face was thrust close. He enunciated carefully, half shouting each word above the engine noise. 'So? Do you know why we brought you up here?'

Fortune shook his head.

'Because you're a stubborn fool. Because you want it squeezing out of you. All right, we're going to squeeze. This is your last chance.'

There was an ominous pause. The rotor blades cut through the air; the cabin was full of noise and vibration.

'It's a grand view of the Lough,' Crombie shouted eventually.

'What's our altitude?' Howarth asked the pilot.

'Twenty-two hundred, sir.'

'Do you know what would happen if you fell out, Fortune? Do you know what water does to you, hitting it from that height? You might as well land on concrete. You split open like a sack of potatoes.'

'You wouldn't do it,' Fortune said hoarsely. Probably no one heard him.

'An accident can happen so easily,' Howarth shouted. 'A sudden lurch, a frantic grab – but it's all over in an instant.'

'Bullshit,' said Fortune, but to his shame he had felt a loosening in his bowels.

'Nobody would question it. We've no reason to ill-treat you.'

It was true. There was no need for rough stuff. The enforced standing, the blindfolding, the non-stop questioning were all part of a disorientation technique that had made physical brutality obsolete. Worst of all, the thing that pushed the sense of isolation to its terrible limit, was the noise. An air compressor in one corner of the interrogation room had been fitted with a special nozzle producing a high-pitched shriek. A few minutes in the same room and you were crawling up the wall.

Fortune no longer knew what to believe, but a vestigial stubbornness made him repeat, 'Bullshit!'

'Look,' the sergeant yelled, 'all you've got to do is promise to answer the questions.'

'No.'

'We're obviously wasting our time,' Howarth snapped. 'Get on with it.'

The order seemed to shake the sergeant for a moment. Fortune sat confused, hearing the tone of the engine change and the rush of cold air diminish. The helicopter had gone into hover. Then he was pushed.

His reflexes sprung him back from the doorway. He flung his body to the right, across the sergeant's lap, before his feet were kicked off the floor and the bottom half of him slid out of the door. He could hear himself screaming.

He found a footing on the helicopter skid. But with his hands tied, his torso writhed on the cabin floor, trying uselessly to find some grip of its own. The sergeant's boot shoved against his chest. His heart lurched. His bowels opened. He fell.

He fell three feet onto the damp grass of a rugby pitch at Holywood Barracks. Grit and water vapour sprayed over him in the backwash of the rotor blades as the Scout settled a few yards away. When the sergeant reached him he lay crying uncontrollably.

'I think that should do it, sir, don't you?' The sergeant's voice was gentle now.

'Yes. Get him inside, give him tea, cigarettes, food if he wants it. We need him calm.'

'Good idea, sir.'

'And get him cleaned up before we see him. He smells of his own shit.'

'I've known that happen before, sir.'

20

Finn shut the door of his room behind him.

'Who let you in?' he asked.

'A chambermaid. Girl from Andersonstown. Sure, you need your friends in these times.'

She laid his pistol down on the bedside table and gave him a half-scornful look. 'British Army after all, is it? After what you told me yesterday?'

'I told you the truth.'

'How do I know you're not just a spy?'

'Whoever sent you here knows it, that's all that counts.'

She snorted. 'You're a rude one. I'm doing a job, true enough. I'm to bring you somewhere.'

'Where?'

'You'll find that out in time.'

'To meet somebody?'

'You're not meant to ask that sort of question, Finn.'

He went to the window, parted the curtains, and glanced down into Great Victoria Street. Beneath a lamp standard the dark Humber was still visible, parked across the street in front of the Crown.

'The RUC have been tailing me,' he said.

'We can evade them.'

'If we're going where I think we're going, you'd better be sure about that.'

'Trust me,' said Caragh. 'I drive well. I've driven more important people than you.'

Something clicked into place in his mind. He turned to her. 'You! The trips you make to Dublin. Boyle's Bypass.'

'What do you know about that?' she said sharply.

'Not much. Only that your brother mentioned the name to me last night. Only that by some queer coincidence the man who runs me in London knows the name too. And that I should have realized earlier that you're involved up to your neck with Sullivan's Volunteers.'

'I've done nothing only for my brother's sake.'

'Ferrying Sullivan back and forth over the border – what good does that do Con Michael?'

'Don't you see, you fool? Con Michael lives for the man. I started doing it because my brother asked me to, because they needed someone clean.' She paused. 'I wasn't all that unwilling, true enough. No Catholic can afford to sit on the sidelines these days.'

'You'd also started to worry about Con Michael, hadn't you? Go on, admit it. You think he's gullible, vulnerable, a boy in a man's world, and as it happens you're right. You wanted to be near him and keep your eye on him, and the only place to do that was inside the movement. I'm not fooled; I've seen the mother come out in you.'

For a second she looked as if she would like to throw something at him again. Then, in that way she had, she leaped to another subject. 'There's only half a dozen of us know about Boyle's Bypass.'

'So it's not my trustworthiness you should be worrying about,' Finn said. 'It's your friends'. What time is the rendezvous?'

'We can't leave here before seven.'

'Then you've come too early.'

'I thought we might talk. I'm after thinking how we don't really know each other.'

He stared at her and then, nonplussed, sat down on the other bed, facing her. She wore slacks and a T-shirt, a black leather car coat, and a tight, defensive smile. Her red hair was pinned up to emphasize the fine, porcelaneous structure of her face. She sat forward with her chin in her hands, elbows on knees, returning the gaze he had fixed on her with unconscious intensity. He remembered the curious undercurrent that had passed between them yesterday as he had held her, struggling, against the wall.

'What do you want to talk about?' he said at length.

'Anything. Cars, if you like, or guns. I never have trouble talking to men because I can talk about cars and guns. By the way, you can't take that with you,' she indicated the Browning.

'No.' He paused. 'I'm not that interested in guns.'

'What are you interested in?'

'Trout-fishing. Jazz instrumentalists.'

She spluttered. 'You're weird, Finn. You don't care what anyone thinks of you. What matters to you in life at all?'

'I have a small cottage in a secret place in Germany. That matters. Very few people know about it. I spend a lot of time on my own there, with no one around to ask inane questions about what matters to me in life.'

'You're not a real cynic, you only pretend to be. Do you care about women?'

'I haven't met one for a long time worth caring about.'

'The same with me and men. Kilshaw was the only serious one. I won't get involved with people who are no good for me.'

'Strong-willed, are you?'

'Where men are concerned.'

'All men?'

'Most.'

Involuntarily, it seemed, their faces had drawn closer together. There was an unreal quality to the conversation, as if the words were being uttered just for the sake of their sound.

'You still look sick,' Caragh said. 'Why do you do this job at all?'

'I suppose because I enjoy it.'

'It's dangerous. They should give you something easier, a sick man.'

'I've told you I'm not sick!'

The mood was punctured. He stood up and stalked across the room. Why did she have this ability to get at him as no one else could?

'I don't want your bloody pity,' he said. 'I've told you before.'

She sat watching him equably. 'You're wrong. Pity is one thing, compassion is another.'

'Whatever you call it. It's dangerous. I could have succumbed to it and let it kill me.'

'You got close to death, didn't you?'

'What if I did?'

'You put a lot of work into preparing yourself for death,' she said. 'Then when it doesn't come you find you don't really know how to live any more, like as if you'd sold off everything that was worth staying alive for. Life had become an empty house; you have to start refurnishing it sometime.'

'You would know all about it, of course,' he said sarcastically.

'I nearly died of diphtheria once. I was a kid, but old enough to understand what was happening.'

'Ah. Hence the morbid interest. You Irish are all the same. Superstitious. Limp with reverence for death, and wet with sentimentality on top of it.'

His spite was real, not the calculated provocation it had been yesterday. He couldn't help himself; he felt obscurely threatened, perhaps because he sensed that she was somewhere near the truth. This time she hit back.

'I'd rather be like that,' she said with a fierce toss of her head, 'than like you. You're empty, Finn. You might as well be dead because you're dead and cold inside. You're an empty house.'

He couldn't help what happened next either. He was in a rage to prove her wrong. He walked over and kissed her.

She showed no surprise. Her mouth yielded gently, moistly, and he tasted the sweetness of her breath and smelt the milky scent of her skin. She stood up and let his arms go round her, then pulled away.

'You shouldn't be doing that, Finn.'

'I had to do it.'

'Mother of God, I'm all goose-flesh!'

He kissed her again. Their bodies arched together. Finn's blood raced with the sudden, chaotic, unfamiliar access of desire and tenderness.

'Caragh?'

'Yes.'

'God damn you.'

'What do you do to me, Finn? You're a funny, lovely man. You'll get us both in trouble.'

'No.'

'Your hands are hot. This wasn't supposed to happen.'

Her coat had slipped off. He took the heavy warmth of her full, firm breasts in his hands. Somehow her hair had come un-pinned, and she shook its rich red curls down over her shoulders. They looked with amazement at each other. A shudder of anticipation went through them.

The telephone rang.

The sound filled the room with alarm. They clung together, both wanting to ignore it but knowing they could not.

'Christ,' muttered Finn. He detached himself from Caragh and picked the damned thing up.

'Finn?' It was Partington's voice. 'Scramble. I was rather ex-pecting to hear from you,' he went on, once Finn had gone through the ritual. 'I'd got just a little *concerned*.'

Finn silently cursed. Caragh hugged herself.

'I'm all right,' Finn said. 'I'm fine.'

'That wasn't exactly what I meant. Can you talk? Are you alone?'

'I can talk.'

'We've obviously got to find a way of speeding things up now. Can you think of –'

'You're running ahead of me. Why obviously?'

There was a short, irritated pause. 'Do you mean you haven't heard about Kilshaw's ultimatum? It's all over the evening papers.'

'I've been stuck in my hotel room.'

'He's given the British Government exactly seven days to end all violence by the IRA – either by negotiating a truce or by smashing them. *Effectively* that means Sullivan's Volunteers because they're the only fools still fighting. If not, he says his own armed men will go into the Catholic areas and hunt them down. We all know what that means.'

'Right. Civil war. Open season for every maniac who can raise a gun to his shoulder. Has the man finally gone round the twist?'

'Anything but,' Partington said. 'He can only thrive in an atmosphere of crisis. But he's putting the ball straight into the other court, don't you see? He challenges Sullivan to declare a truce. He doesn't *want* a truce, but when the fight begins he wants Sullivan to take the blame for starting it.'

'Bloody Irish,' Finn said, and then was struck by another thought. 'If you were planning something like this and expecting a big arms shipment at the same time, wouldn't you hold off until the hardware arrived? You'd have that much more to back up your threat.'

'Quite so.' Partington never admitted to being beaten to an idea. 'The Vigilantes aren't generally well equipped with firearms. If this shipment, whatever it is, hasn't arrived already, then he expects it during the next seven days. Priority one: stop it. Priority two: get hold of the documents. They'll give us the excuse we need to lift him. *And* on a straightforward criminal charge, not a politically loaded one like incitement. You've got exactly a week, Finn.'

'I've a meeting arranged for tonight.'

'Good. I'll want an immediate report. I'll be on this number all night.'

He put down the phone. Caragh had drawn her coat protectively back around her. They looked at each other uncertainly.

'That sounded like powerful stuff there,' she said.

'Too powerful for my liking.'

They could not disguise one dismal, embarrassing fact: their passion had evaporated. Partington could hardly have timed the interruption better.

'Do you want a drink?' Finn asked lamely.

'We ought to go now.'

'Kilshaw is threatening to attack the Catholic areas. Suddenly we seem to be depending on Sullivan's help to stop him.' He did not add the thought that Sullivan's timing had been almost providentially accurate. 'The idea in London seems to be to nip Kilshaw in the bud. But how do they do that without precipitating the very thing they want to avoid?' He glanced out of the window again; the Humber was still parked opposite. 'Maybe Partington has something else up his sleeve. Half the trouble is not knowing what anyone's motives really are.'

'I'd be in no doubt about the RUC,' said Caragh, pinning her hair up. 'The extremists among them, anyway. They're behind Kilshaw.'

'And they want to smash Sullivan. Are you really sure you can get us to him safely?'

'I don't promise you a smooth ride.'

They were both composed. The memory of their lust for each other, the startling power of the attraction, seemed an illusion – but one which still had changed the nature of their relationship. She joined him at the window.

'I'm sorry,' he said.

'We'll make up for it, Finn. Another time.'

'Do you mean that?'

'I promise it.'

'You were right about me,' he said. 'I've got to learn to do what you talked about – furnish the house.'

'Let me help,' she said, brushing her lips against his. 'I've wanted to do that since yesterday.'

21

Gustave Brouhin, arriving from Belfast at Terminal One of Heathrow airport, was apprehensive, and not only at the prospect of eating dinner in a British Rail dining car. It was a choice of that or waiting till eleven o'clock when the ferry sailed from Southampton and the restaurant would open. By then he hoped to be settled in his cabin and asleep under the kindly influence of two Librium tablets.

No, it was not the problem of dinner that bothered him, though an indifferent meal could throw its shadow across his day. Nor was it fear of the British authorities. If they had discovered something they would surely not have allowed him to leave Northern Ireland, where the laws permitting detention and interrogation were much wider than those in England. There was nothing to fear here. What worried Brouhin was what awaited him in France.

He was a small, dapper man. His black beard was flecked with grey and trimmed very close, his suit was hand-stitched black-cock tweed with wide lapels, and his cufflinks had been fashioned from gold Napoleon coins. He walked briskly down the long passenger pier towards the arrivals hall, thinking what relief he would feel when the shipment finally left Le Havre. Perhaps he could stop taking the Librium. Perhaps he could concentrate on his other, neglected interests, those which did not require him to take such appalling risks. For the first time in a long and careful career, Brouhin had allowed himself to be talked into an arrangement that could possibly compromise him. Looking back, he wondered if he had gone soft in the head, *faible de cerveau*. But there had been no alternative unless, unthinkably, he was to turn away half a million francs' worth of business.

He reached the baggage claim area and waited restlessly, pacing back and forth, for his single suitcase to be disgorged onto the revolving drum. He slit the end of a cigar and lit it, anticipating the usual queue for a taxi, the usual traffic jams on the way to Waterloo station, the usual wait before he'd be allowed to board his train. Wealth did not easily cushion one from inconvenience in the British Isles; yet tonight he found himself almost welcoming delay.

The Irishmen had been largely to blame. They'd been fickle, dilatory, constantly changing their minds about things already agreed. They had been somewhat distrustful of him as well, which was foolish. That little upstart Walter Barnett, in particular, who had raised the same stupid objections time after time. They seemed to appreciate only dimly that in this business, given the kind of customer it attracted, a man like Brouhin could not afford to cheat. He had an established method of working; they had managed to change it to his disadvantage. Yes, he must have gone soft.

The baggage from his flight had begun to tumble out onto the drum. His Chinese pigskin suitcase was among the first to appear. He seized it and turned to find two men blocking his way. One in a plastic raincoat, holding out a plastic-sealed card illegibly reflecting the overhead lights, the other in a mulberry-coloured suit.

'Mr Brouhin?' said the man in plastic. 'British Airports Authority Police. We must ask you to come across to our office.'

Brouhin drew slowly on his cigar. 'What is the problem?'

'We're acting on behalf of the Home Office. They'd like to speak to you about an alleged offence under the Explosive Substances Act. That's all I can tell you, sir.'

'Do you mean you are arresting me?'

'I'm only entitled to ask you to accompany us, sir. I might add that you'll probably find it in your best interests to do so.'

Brouhin half smiled. The more lethal the British were, the politer they became. There was something he wanted to establish. He said, 'You realize I am a citizen of France? The consul must be notified.'

'Perhaps you'd rather not rush that, sir.'

'Why on earth not?'

'Only thinking of your best interests. There's a gentleman from the Home Office who'll explain.'

Brouhin nodded. He felt tired. He said only one more thing.

'I have bookings on a train to Southampton and a ship to Havre. Would you be good enough to cancel them?'

22

Finn and Caragh left the hotel openly and went to her car, which she had parked in the forecourt after allowing it to be searched. They drove left into Glengall Street and saw what they had expected to see, the police Humber moving round the corner behind them.

'We drive quite normally,' Caragh said. 'Get them off their guard. We can't afford to lead them towards Sullivan.'

'But he can't afford to wait for us,' Finn said. 'You'd better lose them damned quickly.'

She drove on, taking two sharp turns into the Grosvenor Road before swinging right again, in among the confusing little streets where the shooting had been two nights ago. There was little traffic and few street lights were in operation, factors which also worked to the advantage of the men in the Humber. They stayed fifty yards behind.

'Never worry about Sullivan,' Caragh said. 'He can't go anywhere unless I bring him.'

'You brought him across the frontier today? Boyle's Bypass?'

'At dawn. It's safest at dawn. It's a farm that belongs to a man of the name of Boyle, right up against the border.'

The front windows of the little back-to-back houses were identically lit by flickering television tubes. The Mini went across the Falls Road and on to what was now jokingly called the Peace Line between Catholic and Protestant streets, a row of wooden barricades, barbed wire, and army observation posts, where a wall sign subliminally caught in the headlight beams, UP THE IRA, had been amended to FUCK THE IRA. But there was no fighting tonight and few people were out on the streets;

a big football match on television was as much to thank as any-thing.

The Humber stayed just behind. Finn's hands were sweating and he felt faintly nauseous at the thought of the RUC men staying with them all night, preventing the rendezvous. But Caragh seemed confident. She braked as they approached a sandbagged army observation post. As usual, two ramps a foot high had been set across the road twenty yards apart, one on either side of the OP, to deter gunmen from firing from cars and speeding away. Trying to cross a ramp at anything more than a crawl would cause, at the very least, the front suspension to col-lapse.

Time us,' said Caragh, shifting into first gear, and Finn checked his watch. The Mini crawled; the Humber crawled behind it.

'Twenty-eight seconds,' he said, once they had negotiated the second ramp and were accelerating towards the next corner.

'We can cover a quarter-mile in twenty-eight seconds,' she said. 'We can lose them. Let's find another one.'

They turned right again, from the painted union jacks to the painted tricolours and back again, and approached a second ob-servation post. Finn's glance went to the pavement opposite: narrow, overlooked by the usual row of terraced houses, but perhaps with the kerb just low enough to jump, and enough of a gap between the wall and a lamppost for the Mini to squeeze through. Perhaps.

Twenty yards short of the first ramp Caragh was already in second gear. 'Ready?' she asked.

He gripped his seat. 'Now!'

She swung right, thumped the car onto the pavement, aimed for the gap, and accelerated. The Humber's headlights blazed in the mirror; it turned after them; there was a warning shout from behind the sandbags. Then the lamppost and the wall rushed at them, an impossibly tiny gap seeming to narrow as they hurtled into it. A jarring bump, a shriek of metal: the offside door scraped the wall and the wing mirror snapped off and then they were through, racing along the sidewalk at forty miles an hour. Behind, one of the Humber's headlights was suddenly extinguished and there came a flat metallic crash. It had hit the lamppost.

Another shout came from a soldier in the OP, and just as Caragh punched the car into a turn that flung it off the pavement and round the corner, a single SLR shot bit a chunk of brick out of the wall four feet away.

Safety. From the gloom of the empty streets they had turned in less than a minute into the Shankill Road, where they could move rapidly and anonymously as long as they didn't run into a Vigilante patrol. But the anonymity wouldn't last. Once they'd sorted out the muddle back at the OP, every soldier and police-man in Belfast would be watching for the Mini.

Caragh and Finn were both trembling, and his nausea was more acute. 'Great driving,' he said, 'but bang goes your clean record. They'll be knocking on your door in half an hour.'

'I'll be bringing Sullivan back to Dublin later tonight. There are hidey-holes I can use till then. Maybe I'll stay down South for a week or two, give them time to forget.'

In a couple of minutes they were on the Ligoniel Road, climb-ing away from the city with the lights of linen mills picked out in the deep blackness of the valley on the left. There was little danger from Vigilantes up here, but they had to make a detour to avoid another OP before continuing up the winding road. Here, on the flanks of Wolf Hill, the city dissolved into the country in a series of steep meadows divided by hedges, and away from the street lamps rural darkness suddenly closed in on the car. It had begun to rain. Finn and Caragh sat silent until they approached a huddle of low buildings on the left, where she pulled up.

The buildings were cottages. Between two of them was the entry to a narrow lane that ran off along the hillside.

'Walk down there now,' Caragh said. 'After a quarter of a mile there's an old chalk quarry. Wait there, in the open. You'll be met.'

'And you?'

'I've to meet Sullivan at another rendezvous.'

'Go carefully.'

'Och, I did nothing illegal, only drive on the pavement.'

He climbed out of the car. A narrow fluted dent ran half its length from contact with the wall. He leaned in to kiss Caragh. There was tenderness and a strange dread between them.

'We'll be in touch,' she said lightly.

He shut the door, watched her turn the Mini round, and waited till its tail lights vanished round the hairpin bend below. Then he entered the lane. The house on his right had a name-plate on its wicket gate, Rose Cottage, and from its parlour and those of its neighbours came the same electronic flicker and the roar of a crowd. Glasgow Rangers were playing, traditionally a side supported by Protestants and therefore both deeply loved and heartily disliked in Belfast. Where did you begin, when even soccer was feeding their prejudices?

He walked on. The lane twisted between a few more cottages and then broke up into a potholed track running between two hedges. Rain still fell, lightly but steadily, though enough moonlight filtered through the clouds to allow him to see his way without stumbling. He had walked for five minutes when the track turned down a steep slope and crossed a stream. Here, guarded by the shells of two abandoned cars upended in the mud, was the entrance to the quarry. Disused, by the look of it, the floor turned into a quagmire, with rain glistening in the hollows of old cattle hoofprints, and car tyres and rusted oil drums lying about in the puddles. He went tentatively into the mouth of the pit, shoes squelching, and peered round the floor and up the sides, perhaps thirty feet high. There was no sign of anyone.

He turned to face outwards again, down the hill. He hadn't brought a raincoat, and now he could feel his clothes beginning to cling to him unpleasantly.

Ten minutes went by. From here all the lights of Belfast were visible, from the gleaming Lough to the floodlit shipyards to the pinpoint symmetry of housing estates crawling up the flanks of the hills. The lights of occasional cars vanished and reappeared as they twisted slowly through the hairpin bends of the Ligoniel Road. It was a good vantage point, this, especially if you needed to guard against being taken by surprise.

From behind him came a sound, instantly recognizable, a snap and a sliding of metal as the cocking handle of an automatic rifle was released.

He did not turn. To move was still dangerous. But his mind mechanically sought the location of the sound: behind and above, on the rim of the quarry, perhaps fifty yards away. A twitch of tension was overtaken by relief. They'd let him stand about to be sure he had not led anyone else here. For ten minutes he had been framed in what could only have been – in this darkness – the night sight of One-shot Billy McGarry's rifle.

At the extremity of his vision he caught a movement against the side of the quarry to his right. Then came sounds: a squelch and a voice.

'Fuck this mud!'

Con Michael. If he'd intended surprising Finn he had lost the initiative by sliding down the quarry face. Finn risked turning his head to look; the Irishman's dark figure was groping about at the foot of the slope.

'Finn! Come over here, for Jasus' sake. I've lost my shoe.'

Finn suppressed a laugh and moved over to him. Above the

quarry another figure stood up, faintly silhouetted in the moonlight, and began to walk round towards the opening.

'It came off in the mud. D'you have a torch?'

'No.'

'Oh, to blazes, I've no time to look.' He straightened up and stared intently into Finn's face. 'Nobody followed you?'

'The RUC tried. We shook them off.'

'You'd better be sure about that.' Con Michael reached out and patted up and down Finn's torso and damp trouser legs. 'Is my sister safe?'

'She was all right when she dropped me.'

From the darkness beside them Billy McGarry materialized silently, a lean figure who stood in an easy, alert slouch, saying nothing. Finn could see only the faintest outline of a wide-cheeked face framed by curly shoulder-length hair, but he recognized the rifle that Billy held at the trail, with its big, clumsy-looking image intensifier, a thousand pounds' worth of weapon that had already killed seven soldiers.

'Let's go now,' said Con Michael.

The rain had softened. They walked a short way farther along the track, the revolutionary in one stockinged foot limping beside Finn, Billy McGarry ambling behind. At a gap in the roadside hedge an old long wheelbase Land Rover was parked.

'Into the front,' Con Michael commanded. 'I'm going to cover your head. It's for your own protection as well as ours.'

Billy went behind the wheel. Finn climbed into the front passenger seat and Con Michael got in behind him, producing something that might have been a black pillowslip which he slid over Finn's head and fastened firmly but comfortably with a length of cord around his neck. He could breathe easily enough. He could see nothing in outline, and when he turned to face the lights of the city below, only a faint blur was visible.

'Let's drive,' said Con Michael. Billy, unnervingly silent,

started up, engaged low gear, and eased the Land Rover out along the track. Barely audibly, he began humming a tune which Finn recognized as 'Back Water Blues.'

The journey, to Finn's surprise, was short. It was less than five minutes before they stopped again. There had been a couple of sharp turns but the road had remained fairly level and unmade, and they could not have been moving at more than ten or fifteen miles an hour. Finn was convinced that they were still somewhere on Wolf Hill.

He was ordered out and guided through a metal gate which was shut and padlocked behind him. It was muddy underfoot. To judge from the smell he was in a farmyard, but a very busy farmyard for this time of night. There were movements and whispers from perhaps half a dozen places all around him as he was led to a door which swung open with a squeak of badly fitted hinges. Behind it, lights shone.

Con Michael untied the cord and jerked away the pillowslip. For several seconds Finn blinked against the sudden harsh light of gas pressure lamps. Then, taking a deep breath of air still faintly redolent of pigs and hay, he stepped inside the Belfast headquarters of Sullivan's Volunteers.

23

The first thing he noticed was the television, a small portable set standing at one end of a trestle table and, inevitably, switched to the channel that was showing the Rangers match. Half a dozen young men stood or squatted in front of it, taking up one corner of the room. They turned casually to look Finn over as he entered behind Con Michael.

The opposite corner had been partitioned off by benches to form a kind of makeshift ops rooms, with maps of Belfast cello-taped to the stone wall. There was no telephone or radio transmitter, which made the whole thing slightly pointless. A man wearing earphones sat at a table fiddling with the controls of a small VHF receiver, perhaps trying to monitor army or police calls.

The room in fact was – or had been – a barn, about eighty feet long by forty wide, with a concrete floor, a high corrugated-iron roof, a broad sliding door at one end. Black cloth had been draped over the few high windows, and sacking was stuffed into every other opening that might emit light. The barn had been cleared of straw and muck, but there were still signs of its former function – a few rusted tools scattered about, and against one wall a pile of hessian bags that had once contained feed. Most of the furniture consisted of backless benches and trestle tables at which the men would mess and plan their operations. Many who were on the run probably bunked down here as well; by day those who were not known to the security forces would either be working or – if they had no jobs – spending their dole money in the pubs along the Falls Road.

Finn glanced back. A man with an M-1 carbine had taken up

a position just inside the door, and there'd be more guards outside. Leaning against the wall next to the men watching television was a variety of weapons – two more M-1s, a couple of Thompson guns, a .303, and a Springfield. The place was easily guarded and had the impermanence about it that a guerrilla base needs, but there were far too many people hanging about doing nothing.

Everyone wore warm clothing. The only heat came from a pot-bellied coal stove whose chimney-pipe vanished through a hole knocked in the wall and wadded with sacking. Next to the stove, alone on a bench, sat Colin Sullivan. He rose to greet Finn.

He was of medium height, narrow-chested, dressed in the ubiquitous dark sweater and jeans with a quilted anorak. His face was interesting in a way the few photographs that existed of him had never shown, a face that had aged without softening at the edges. There was something of the lean, haunted look Finn had seen on the faces of middle-aged Communists, men who had held to their faith in spite of Stalin, Hungary, Czechoslovakia, the look of men consumed from within by their own convictions. But Sullivan's eyes, honey-coloured and still contriving to be cold, piercing and yet remotely cynical, struck a note of contrast; so did the slightly dandified way his yellow-brown hair, going on grey, had been trained backwards to cover a bald spot. Looking at the revolutionary, it was easy enough to see also the wardroom steward and the ticket tout. His skin was scaly and a little translucent, like a snake's. He smiled and reached out his hand.

'Mr Finn. Or do you prefer to use your rank?'

'No.'

'Good. We have no ranks here. Was it Chairman Mao who said that an army needs democracy as much as a people does? What do you think of our setup?'

'I'd think better if you hadn't laid on so much for my benefit.

Didn't the Chairman also teach you not to concentrate your forces until you're assured of victory?'

Sullivan smiled again – an engaging smile, it had to be admitted – and shrugged. 'It's a wee bit like a social club at times, right enough. But we're still an effective fighting force.' He turned to Billy McGarry, who had followed them from the door. 'Would you ever fetch in the wee bottle I brought with me, Billy? Then maybe you'd relieve one of the lads out in the yard. Why not sit down, Mr Finn?'

The marksman left the barn. Sullivan returned to his bench beside the stove, and Finn and Con Michael sat down to face him across the table. Sullivan had scarcely acknowledged the presence of his Belfast commander; it was clear who was in charge.

'I think we both like speaking plainly,' Sullivan said. 'We also both know why you're here. If the British Government were not interested in what I have to offer, you would not have come. I take it you speak as their agent.'

'But without power to negotiate,' Finn said. 'I can report what you say, that's all.'

'Tonight?'

'I promise no reply before tomorrow at the earliest.'

'Time is short for you. I would have thought –'

'It's short for you as well,' Finn said with a flash of anger. 'You've stretched everyone's patience too far. You've done more than anyone to drive the Protestants into Kilshaw's arms. If civil war comes it'll be as much your fault as anyone's. There's a premium on irresponsibility in this country.'

Con Michael, flushing, rose to the defence. 'We've no interest in your theories –'

'Be quiet a minute now,' said Sullivan.

His tone was slightly parental. The glint of the dogmatist was in his eyes, but so was the cynicism Finn had noticed a minute earlier. He spoke rather mechanically.

'You misinterpret our aims, Mr Finn. We've never fought a sectarian war. The British disguise its real nature from themselves because they're afraid to admit what it really is, the start of a revolution. Whatever Kilshaw does will be irrelevant in the long run. He's only fighting a rearguard action on behalf of the old feudal ascendancy –'

'Which also happens to be Protestant,' Finn interrupted. 'This war is tribal, you can't get away from it. In the twentieth century, in an industrial society. Marx would have been hard put to explain it. But it's your side that's on the defensive now. Effective fighting force, you call yourselves. Effective at killing a soldier here or there, effective at setting off bombs in busy streets. In a week's time, unless you follow the other IRA factions and declare a truce, Kilshaw's hooligans will be invading Catholic areas, burning houses, killing the very people you set out to protect. Maybe it shouldn't bother me. It's not my war.'

Billy McGarry, the rifle still slung from his shoulder, silently brought a bottle of Paddy and three plastic cups to the table. His eyes were grey, blank, expressionless. He left the barn again. Con Michael brooded. Finn held the gaze of the yellow-brown eyes that searched his face and noticed, when Sullivan finally spoke, the patches of cockney beneath the carefully tailored brogue.

'Can we talk business now?' he said.

'Yes.'

'I'll explain the background briefly and go straight to the point. I heard, by means you know about, that Gustave Brouhin had been meeting Kilshaw secretly. It was obvious that some kind of arms deal was in the offing, and if we could find evidence we knew it would be valuable. I told Con Michael and young Billy there to take out his office.'

'One question,' Finn said. 'What made you so confident of finding something?'

'Only the fact that I had met Gustave Brouhin too. I knew what to look for. He had offered the same deal to me two months previously.'

Finn's surprise must have been obvious. 'You refused?' he said.

'Not exactly. We couldn't raise the money. Your man drives a hard bargain.'

Enjoying himself now, Sullivan reached for a kettle that stood on the stove. He half-filled each of the three plastic cups from the bottle of Paddy, topped them up with water from the kettle, and passed the hot whiskey round.

'Brouhin will sell to anyone, anywhere, who's got the cash to pay for a large order. And I mean large. His supplies come in bulk, mainly from south-east Asia.'

'What was he offering?'

Sullivan jerked his head at Con Michael. 'Show him.'

The young man stood up and went to the pile of sacking against the wall. From behind it he pulled out something tubular wrapped in polythene sheeting. Finn recognized it even before it was unwrapped, a forty-inch length of black steel and plastic with a shape that was very familiar, from the slightly coned muzzle to the perforated stock, the carrying handle, the pistol grip, and the twenty-round magazine.

'This was a sample he sent us – a token of faith, though oddly enough without working parts. M-16 rifle, United States Army issue. You've seen our other stuff?'

'Thompsons and M-1s,' said Finn. 'World War Two and earlier. That SLR of Billy's must be the best weapon you've got.'

'Indeed,' said Sullivan. 'But this is something else again.'

He took the rifle. Grease glinted on the barrel and in the empty breech, though to judge by the scratches it wasn't new. Finn knew the M-16. It was extremely light and fully automatic, but what made it unique as a military weapon was its small calibre. A magnum cartridge behind a tiny .223 bullet gave it a devastating muzzle velocity, so that at a range of up to three hundred yards it struck its target with up to three times the force of larger high-velocity ammunition. With that kind of impact you didn't need anything bigger. Furthermore, the newer pattern of nickel bullets for the M-16 were coated in plastic; when they entered a human body they did not leave the metal trace that had always been vital in X-raying gunshot wounds. Altogether, it was not the kind of weapon that anyone in his right mind would want either Sullivan's men or Kilshaw's to have.

'So you couldn't afford them,' Finn said.

'Not two hundred of them.'

'Two hundred!'

'I told you Brouhin sells in bulk. He was offering a package deal, all or nothing. Two hundred M-16s at two hundred and fifty pounds apiece. He'd throw in twenty thousand rounds of ammunition free, plus unlimited options on further rifles and ammo.'

'That's fifty thousand pounds,' said Finn.

'He mistook the extent of our resources. We're a working-class movement. We spend money as we get it. Two hundred and fifty is the price the market dictates. These are all from Vietnam, Cambodia, thereabouts. Villagers steal them off dead soldiers; others are lost, even sold. There's a thriving black market with Brouhin's Far East company at the head of it, and nobody in authority gives a damn. There's plenty more where they came from. Uncle Sam wants out, and he'll pay them all the M-16s they ask for in conscience money just as long as American boys don't have to use them. Brouhin isn't short of customers. We can't afford fifty thousand; others can.'

'Like Kilshaw?'

'Indeed.'

'Where do the Vigilantes get that kind of money?'

Sullivan reached into his anorak. Unzipping the detachable lining he drew from beneath it a large manila envelope that bulged an inch thick. The flap was open. Several dozen sheets of photocopying paper were folded inside. 'It's all there,' he said, 'only for the trouble of looking.'

Finn took the papers from the envelope and' riffled through them. Page after page of ledger accounts had been copied, together with a series of invoices, deeds of sale, and contract notes. There could be almost no doubting the authenticity of Kilshaw's small, tortured handwriting. But at first glance the documents meant nothing, and he said so.

'A good auditor in London will soon sort them out for you – yes, you can take them. The originals are in safekeeping in Dublin, and you'll need those if you want to prove anything in court. These are accounts of the Shankill Distress Relief, together with two companies that Kilshaw has an interest in.'

'Sydenham Holdings and Marine Services,' Finn said. 'I've already checked them out.'

'Superficially, perhaps. You never saw the books because a private company needn't disclose details of its finances to anyone, only an auditor. Even if you had seen them you'd not have caught on, because Kilshaw and his people were up to one of the oldest tricks – keeping two sets of books, one for the auditor and the taxman, another for themselves. Both sets happened to be in the safe that night. Your people in London can examine them side by side. Even then, they'll have to check every entry for both companies together, and compare them with the public receipt and expenditure accounts of the Shankill Distress Relief, before they can find the purpose of the discrepancy.'

'Which is?'

'I'd never have noticed only for having some training at this sort of thing. For nearly three years Kilshaw and Walter Barnett have been milking the Shankill Distress Relief of five hundred pounds a week. The accumulated capital was paid last month in the guise of a bank loan to Sydenham Holdings. They in turn passed it on to Marine Services to finance the purchase and re-fitting of several small ships. All bought from Gustave Brouhin's company in Le Havre.

'The funny thing is, when you go into it, they're getting very little for their money. The contract is for the sale of one small harbour tug, coal-burning, and two dredgers that used to belong to the port authorities of Le Havre. These two would be worth twenty to twenty-five thousand each. They're a nuisance to Brouhin, taking up valuable dock space, so he's persuaded Marine Services to agree to a penalty clause. They must remove these dredgers from Le Havre under their own power within a month of signing the contract, or the ships revert to Brouhin's ownership.

'Well and good – until you check with Lloyds and find that the dredgers had their engines and boilers removed two years ago. And they've got to be removed under their own power within a month! Do you get the drift? Marine Services sign an agreement that looks all right on paper but that they know is impossible to fulfil. All the same, the Bank of England gives them exchange-control permission to pay the money. If there are ever any questions they can claim delivery delays, union problems – anything. Generally they're a badly managed company, but as long as they're only throwing away their own money, who cares? They end up paying fifty-four thousand pounds for one small tug that any Lloyds underwriter will tell you isn't worth more than four. The penalty clause takes effect in two days' time. Brouhin makes fifty grand without getting out of bed.'

'The price of two hundred M-16s,' Finn said.

'Funny coincidence, now, isn't it? But there's another thing even odder. Marine Services haven't collected the tug yet either, although she's quite seaworthy and on the face of it they were free to take her weeks ago. I can only find one explanation for that, Finn. The merchandise must be on board the tug. Brouhin is holding onto it until the full month is up and the money is securely his, legally irrecoverable. The boat is called the *Astrid*. I'd bet you good money that she'll be steaming out of Le Havre and heading full speed for Belfast exactly two days from now.'

'Arriving just in time to arm two hundred Vigilantes with lethal weapons before Kilshaw's ultimatum runs out,' Finn said thoughtfully. He took a sip of whiskey. It all made sense, but for one glaring discrepancy. 'Why have you told me this?' he asked.

'Is it not what you wanted to hear, then?'

'You can't expect us not to act on the information,' Finn said. 'Whether we agree to buy the documents or not, we can seize this shipment when it arrives. We can get the French police to seize it before it leaves. I find it hard to believe you're giving away one of your hands for nothing.'

'Ah, you're not slow, Finn.'

There was a subdued roar from the group round the television set as someone scored a goal. Sullivan said, 'This brings us to the delicate question of price, you see. My price for the documents is that shipment.'

Finn thought he had misheard. 'The rifles?'

'The rifles. I give you the rope to hang Kilshaw with; you find a way of delivering the shipment to me in Dublin.'

Slowly Finn replaced his plastic cup on the table. 'You're mad,' he said.

'No. Realistic. The British need to crush Kilshaw more badly than they do me. It makes sense for us to co-operate. In the greatest secrecy, naturally. Of course you can seize the rifles, but how far does that take you now? Kilshaw will be marching into

Andersonstown in a week's time with or without the extra weapons. The only way you can nail him is with hard, legitimate proof linking him with the theft of charity money and the purchase of illegal arms. All the existing proof is in my possession – you'll see from the photocopies. You'll also appreciate that legally the copies are useless without the originals to back them up. You must pay my price, Finn.'

'We've been fighting you for three years. Do you seriously expect us to equip you for more fighting, no matter what you offer in exchange?'

'I accept that the idea may be unpleasant,' Sullivan said. 'Why do you think I approached it so obliquely? But it's a quaint notion of political morality you have, Finn.'

'Maybe yours is even quainter.'

'If you paid us money, what do you think we would spend it on? The difference is that this way you will guarantee that the shipment reaches Dublin. There's no risk for us. If you still have scruples, we could undertake not to use them against British troops in the North.'

'Keep trying,' Finn said. 'In a minute you'll make me laugh.'

Sullivan brought his plastic cup down with a snap – the first sign of a temper reputed to be short. 'You refuse to understand, Finn. We are Irish socialists, not nationalists.'

'A distinction which often escapes me.'

'We're fighting class oppression in all of Ireland. Revolution is inevitable, whoever supplies the weapons. That's why we won't and can't declare a truce, because history is on our side. In the end we can't lose. Maybe you don't understand that, but Partington will.' He drained his cup and smiled humourlessly, highlighting a pattern of shallow creases in the shiny matt of his facial skin.

Finn said casually, 'You know Partington, then?'

'In forty-six I was in Mountjoy prison. He came to see me, introduced as a welfare visitor; there was a laugh! The pretence was soon dropped, though. He was trying to recruit me as an informer. I played along, pretending to be interested. What struck me under all the bluster was his coldbloodedness. He knew the movement would remain a powerful factor in Irish politics, and he wanted a bright young man who'd slowly work his way up through the ranks. The retainer he offered was handsome.' Sullivan looked mock-wistful. 'We've all had that kind of approach, one time or another. I'd practically forgotten Partington till last year, when his name cropped up again. It turned out he was running a man named O'Meara who'd tried to infiltrate the movement here in Belfast. O'Meara told us all about the queer fellow.'

'You mean, don't you, that you tortured the information out of him before he was strangled and thrown into the Lagan.'

'This is a war, Finn. That's the way with informers.'

Finn was uneasily aware of the conclusion he had reached earlier that day, that Partington still had an informer among Sullivan's Volunteers, that somebody, sometime, had succumbed to the inevitable approach. He said, 'All right. I'll report your proposals. I still can't see them being accepted. Have you any idea of the political consequences if there was a leak? The British Government supplying arms to the IRA – that makes the Profumo scandal sound like a stroll in the park.'

'There are ways of doing these things quietly, smoothly. We've many influential friends. The exchange must take place in Dublin; then I can guarantee secrecy. Getting the shipment there will be your problem.'

Finn shook his head. 'I'm telling you, the price is too high.'

'I'd prefer to hear Partington's judgement on that, once his boffins have had a go at the photocopies. They'll confirm that the incriminating entries are in Kilshaw's own handwriting; what better proof could you ask for?'

Sullivan's calculating eyes watched him.

'I expect an answer tomorrow evening. At exactly six o'clock I'll be at this phone number in Dublin.' He produced a small card with the six-figure number scribbled on it. 'To save you the trouble of checking, it's a public callbox behind the General Post Office. Too many private numbers are being tapped by the Garda these days. Just yes or no, that's all I want to hear. If it's yes, I'll be there every subsequent evening for a week, but I want no more calls until you can tell me that the stuff has arrived in Dublin. We'll then arrange the handover. Clear?'

'Perfectly.' Finn sighed. For plain overacting you couldn't beat them.

Sullivan snapped his fingers at the group who still watched television in the corner.

'Switch that thing off now,' he called. He turned to Con Michael. 'Tell Billy to take him back down.'

24

The Land Rover bumped along the track, still running south-wards, and then turned left onto a paved surface that went steeply downhill. Finn was hooded in the black pillowslip again, but he had learned enough of Belfast's geography to guess that they were on the Glencairn Road heading back towards the city. With the help of an ordnance map he would probably be able to pinpoint the Belfast headquarters of Sullivan's Volunteers – a handy thought, but a disturbing one too. There were certain things it was better not to know. Their arrangements for getting him there and back had been typical of everything he knew of them – partly clever, partly amateurish bungling, a combination that the English found hard to understand. Indeed, in sceptical moments it was easy to think that the whole Northern Ireland thing was some grotesque joke being played on the English. There had been a kind of mocking laughter on Sullivan's face, an expression that dared him to find the truth in a wilderness of irrelevance.

Con Michael, returning to the quarry to search for his lost shoe, had left Billy McGarry to take Finn back on his own. It was a queer feeling, no matter how level-headed you were, to be alone with a man who had taken deliberate aim at seven complete strangers and shot them dead. His driving seemed smooth and competent. Finn wished he would speak. All he had done was hum another jazz tune, scatting quietly to himself.

'"Vine Street Breakdown",' Finn said suddenly. 'Have you heard Buddy Tate doing it?'

The humming stopped. There was a moment's hesitation. 'Yeah,' Billy conceded. 'Yeah. Great.'

'Do you go for West Coast stuff?'

'I like it all. Blues, mostly, I s'pose.' Another pause, and then the question that even he could not avoid. 'You? You know somethin' about jazz?'

'I've a bit of a collection. Original seventy-eights. Pre-twenties New Orleans stuff, King Oliver, cakewalks, stomps. Trouble is they're getting too valuable to be played. Still, for a real buff I might make an exception. If you're ever in Germany with nothing better to do...'

He sensed a smile. The ice had been broken. A minute later they turned left, made a U-turn, and stopped. Billy tugged off the black hood. Finn found they were parked roughly where he'd expected, facing the way they had come on an unlighted stretch of the Ballygomartin Road at the western fringe of the city.

'I miss the music,' Billy said. Suddenly, disconcertingly, he was talkative. 'Me and Con Michael started a bit of a jazz club before I went on the run, like. Just an old house across the town there that we tarted up. I suppose it's back to bein' a ruin now. It was more my idea than his, him likin' the classical music mainly. Did you know now that he brought all his classical records to London when he went over there to work and he'd be spendin' every night tryin' to get the navvies interested in Brahms? Always tryin' to convert someone to something, so he is. Never mind, he's a powerful brainy wee lad. I've to drop you here. The buses don't run at night no more, but you can phone for a taxi up at the Wood vale Road there.'

Finn got back to his hotel room to find Crombie sitting on the end of the bed. He'd been watching television too! Highlights of the football match were being repeated on the ten o'clock news.

'Who won?' said Finn.

'Rangers.'

The policeman switched off the set and turned to look at him resignedly. 'I'm not pleased with you this night, Major.'

'No?'

'I hoped you would take to heart what I said yesterday.'

'You think I haven't?'

'I know you haven't, Major.' Crombie stood up, towering over Finn, his massive face heavy with suppressed anger. 'Why did you shake off my men?'

'Maybe I don't like being crowded.'

'You were in Caragh Hughes's car. Why?'

'Not for immoral purposes. It's difficult in a Mini.'

'Don't fool with me, Major. I warned you about mixing with these rebels. I could make things embarrassing for your people. For Partington.'

'You've been steaming open my mail, Superintendent.'

'No. I've been talking to your friend Fortune.'

'Talking? Or leaning on?'

'He was lifted early this morning. He's being held under Regulation Ten for interrogation.'

Finn tried not to let his apprehension show. 'Fortune has no idea,' he said.

'He'd enough idea to send me to your left-luggage locker at the station there.'

'I suppose he fell down the steps just before he talked.'

'It's an interesting collection you've made there, Major. There's any number of charges I could bring against you – bribing the police, fraudulently obtaining confidential government documents. On the other hand –'

'Oh, for Christ's sake!' In sudden exasperation Finn stepped round Crombie and went to the bedside table. A pain had sprung into his ear; he found his pills. 'Listen,' he said. 'Yesterday you were saying let's come clean with each other. All right. Let's. Stop talking police jargon about charges and fraud. You're not speaking to me as a policeman. You're here to protect Kilshaw because you admire him. I'm here to screw Kilshaw because I'm being paid to do it. It's a game we both understand. There are no rules. We use whatever resources we have, and you have more than I do because you're a policeman. You've seen what Fortune and I collected. You know it's not worth a row of beans.'

'And the stuff the IRA have got?' Crombie said quietly. 'The stuff you've been trying to buy – what's that worth?'

'I don't know,' Finn said. 'I just don't know.' He walked round the policeman again, to the bathroom, and ran water into a glass. 'They're being cagey.'

He swallowed his pills, chasing them down with water. Crombie's frame filled the bathroom doorway and he brought his face close to Finn's. His brow was knit into a hundred furrows; there was rum on his breath. 'Let me tell you something,' he said. 'This isn't a healthy town for your kind of work. For an outsider, specially. There are two or three unsolved murders every day – men with their hands tied, shot in the head, dumped. No witnesses ever come forward. I wouldn't linger here, in your position.'

'Is that a threat?' Finn said.

'It's advice. Well-meant advice, believe me.'

'I might just take it. I have a regard for survival.'

'Good.'

Crombie turned, ducked under the lintel, and left the room. Finn latched the door behind him and released a breath. The policeman was catching up fast. The danger increased with every minute he stayed in Belfast.

His call to Partington first. He went to the cupboard to get out his scrambler. It had gone.

He began to search the room. He found it within a minute in the wastepaper bin, its transistors smashed, the handset lead cut off.

That settled it, then. He would not be sorry to leave.

25

The sun had been up about an hour when Caragh Hughes and Sullivan came into the northern outskirts of Dublin. For the third time on this journey she was aware that the hand he had rested carelessly on the edge of her seat had made its way across her left thigh and was crawling up the inside.

She had made her own rule for this game, balancing the risk of encouraging him further against the possibility of appearing prim. Automatically she let go of the wheel with her left hand, took his right one, and replaced it in his lap.

'I've told you it doesn't mix with driving,' she said. 'Like drink.'

'You mean it affects your control?'

'No. After a while it affects my temper.'

'Come on now. And us old friends.'

'I'd not say that. Three months ago I'd never set eyes on you.'

'You're an attractive woman, Caragh.'

'Thank you.'

'After hearing that too often, are you?'

'How's your wife?' she asked pointedly.

'Away to Galway for the week.' He paused for a decent interval. 'I could do with some coffee. Could you?'

'So let's stop at your place, is that what comes next?' She grinned at him sarcastically. 'When will you learn, Colm? The reason I offered to drive you isn't that I'm dying to get to bed with you.'

'Is there something wrong with me?'

'No,' she said, but shuddered inwardly. It takes a certain kind of woman to tell a man that he repels her physically. There were the backs of his hands, scaly and reptilian, and the yellowish-grey hair, and the eyes that had always seemed yellow to her as well. All his colouring was unnatural. She said lightly, 'Perhaps my heart is another's.'

'Who's my rival?'

'Now I think I should make you guess that. What about Billy McGarry? I could fancy him.'

'No time for girls these days. A man's man.'

'Finn, then.'

'Finn!' Sullivan snorted with laughter. 'A funny wee man. I almost felt sorry for him. He looks sick. Wait'll I make a phone call, will you? From home I've the whole of the Garda listening in.'

They were in a redbrick suburban road just past Dublin airport, and a callbox stood on the next corner. Caragh pulled in and waited, watching him go to the cubicle, dial the operator, and then insert seven fivepences separately into the coin slot. Perhaps three minutes went by before he returned, looking pleased with himself. She wondered idly whom he might have been phoning in England at eight in the morning.

'Why *do* you do it?' he asked suddenly, as they continued down the Drumcondra Road. 'Driving me, I mean. Why did you offer?'

'It was for Con Michael's sake,' she said. 'I wanted to stay near him. I'm not playing the big sister, I just happen to know him better than anyone else does. He was a spoilt boy. His judgement is bad. He needs watching over.'

'Never worry about him,' Sullivan said, rather dreamily. 'He'll be all right, never worry.'

Once again the hand had begun its ritualistic advance across her thigh.

26

'He's frightened,' said Partington cheerfully. 'Very frightened. One phone call to Paris could put him inside for ten years. Still, there's no panic. You don't get rich by losing your head in a crisis. He's a canny Norman. Don't they have a *saying* about them in France? *A Normand Normand et demi*, I believe. Roughly equivalent to "Set a thief to catch a thief." He'll co-operate.'

Finn nodded mechanically. He realized that the green tea-stained paper on the desk blotter hadn't been changed since the first day he had entered the Gosfield Street office. Spilt ash was trapped in the corners and the edges were now decorated with innumerable small drawings of hams, cheeses, fish, and fruit.

Partington drew complacently on a cigarette. His interview with Brouhin last night had gone well, quite well enough to redeem even the subsequent vigil by the telephone, awaiting, largely for appearance's sake, news of the meeting in Belfast.

'Normally,' he said, 'his cargoes are shipped as regular freight, documented as machinery. But every port in Ireland is watched very stringently for just that sort of thing. Kilshaw and friends weren't prepared to lay out that much money against a high risk of seizure. They persuaded Brouhin to accept their *own* plan, to send the stuff in on board a ship that he would sell them – on paper – for conversion from a coal-burner to diesel. Officially there'd be no cargo, hence no customs declarations and checks. But the really bright idea was to conceal the weapons *within* the hull of the vessel itself, to weld them into a compartment inside the fuel bunkers, which would be altered as the first stage in the conversion process. The only place where that could be done safely was in the workshops of the company in Le Havre in which Brouhin has an interest. So he agreed. A lot of money is involved. For once, avarice got the better of his judgement.'

'And now?' said Finn.

'Today is Thursday. As Sullivan said, the delay that was built into the contract ends tomorrow. The two dredgers revert to Brouhin's ownership and he releases the tug, which steams for Belfast with a freelance crew. That's the *idea*, anyway.' Partington gave a sly grin and flicked more ash onto the blotter. 'What if Brouhin discovered at the last minute that the tug could carry only enough coal to take her to – oh, *Dublin,* say? Too late to notify Kilshaw. He'd have to change the crew's orders, tell them to put in at Dublin and return to France on the understanding that an Irish crew would be found for the last leg of a hundred miles or so.'

'Then what?'

'Quite simple. The exchange takes place. The rifles for the documents.'

Finn stared. 'You mean you'd fulfill Sullivan's demand?'

'Good Lord, no!'

Never again, Finn told himself, would he rise to Partington's rhetorical bait. He said nothing.

'We have to play for time, don't you see that? He's kept us waiting this long because he wants to rush us into an agreement. For the moment we've no choice but to go along with him. You'll phone him at six this evening and say yes. We'll do what he wants: we'll get Brouhin to send the tug to Dublin. And the exchange *must* take place because it's the only way we'll get the documents. We can't hope to hoodwink him before then.'

'You reckon you can do it afterwards?' Finn said sceptically.

'If I tell you I can arrange things so that Sullivan doesn't *keep* the weapons, will that satisfy your conscience?'

'I don't know whether you realize how shrewd he is; he won't be easy to fool.'

'I realize it very well,' Partington said with a touch of huffiness. 'I also know he's on his home ground in Dublin. But I have friends there too – people in the Garda, for instance, who are looking for an excuse to put Sullivan away. It's too early to go into fine details, but we'll work something out.'

It wasn't like Partington to be this vague. Finn raised another objection. 'What about leaks? How do you guard against the risk of exposure?'

'The risk isn't actually that great. Where's the visible involvement of HM Government? There is none. The only contact with the IRA has been through you. Say the worst happens: interception, exposure of your part in it. What *are* you, when all's said and done? The record shows you were warded out some time ago. Skilful public relations can present you as a type everyone's familiar with from a hundred bad plays and films. Army officer, retired early, time on his hands, bit short of money, gets caught up in a shady venture – arms smuggling. You realize, of course, that the usual rules would apply: HMG would deny any responsibility for you.' Partington leaned forward and crushed his half-smoked cigarette in the Cinzano ashtray, watching it bend and split with the absorption of an infant vivisectionist. 'Understand how important those documents are. My committee will agree to almost anything that offers the chance of removing Kilshaw. *Almost* anything. Sullivan was right. The papers show that half the money paid every week to the Shankill Distress Relief group was being siphoned off into the subsidiary account run by Walter Barnett, *allegedly* to pay for the rebuilding of houses and so on. The best part of all is that we've got Kilshaw's handwriting to prove his part in the fraud. Everything seems quite authentic, to judge by the photostats.'

'And yet it was indiscreet of Kilshaw. Out of character. I've always thought that.'

'He's grown very conscious of his own power. It creates a feeling of immunity. Well. While you're away I shall devote some thought to the handling of Sullivan.'

'Away?'

'*Ah.* Yes.' Partington made a mock-apologetic face. 'I thought it would be rather helpful if you were to cut across to France and sail to Dublin on that tug.'

'What the hell for?'

'To keep an eye on Brouhin. To keep an eye on things generally. You could be introduced as a representative of the buyers. There'll be only a freelance delivery crew, you see, two or three Frenchmen who'll have no idea what the tug is really carrying. And then in Dublin you could be very useful. I shall be over there, but I can't go showing myself.'

'Why me, for God's sake? I'm meant to be –'

'Don't you feel well enough?'

'I feel fine,' said Finn, bridling.

'Good.' Partington stood up, rubbing his hands. 'Very good. Oh, I was talking to the DMI about you, by the way. They seem to think you'll be fit enough to return to your unit in a week or two. Once all this is settled.'

'Back to Germany?' said Finn, startled. 'Then they must have cleared me for the active list.'

'Yes. They've had some kind of medical report.'

'That can only mean one thing. I've been given a clean bill of health. Finally. Completely.'

'Yes,' said Partington airily. 'I gather you have. There's a letter on its way to you. Well, I'm off for a spot of lunch. With any luck there'll be a Deputy Minister paying.'

27

Finn and Brouhin shared a cabin on the ferry from Southampton that night. Finn slept well but woke up once or twice to find the air thick with tobacco smoke, and the Frenchman lying staring at the ceiling, the tip of a cigar redly illuminating his features.

They reached Le Havre at seven in the morning. It was still pitch dark when they checked into the Hotel Normandie, where Brouhin was given the fourth-floor suite in which he usually stayed. Finn made do with a room on the second floor. They bathed, breakfasted in their rooms, and met in the lobby at nine o'clock to set off for an inspection of the tug.

The day was sunny, with a high wind off the Atlantic howling across the enormous open squares which Le Havre had acquired at the price of being almost obliterated in World War II. Brouhin led Finn eastwards along the edge of the Bassin du Commerce, in fact a mainly ornamental lake, to where the quays began to look workmanlike. Behind a row of warehouses a small enclosed dock appeared with a three-storeyed building on the other side containing the offices and workshops of the Compagnie Havraise de Radoub et de Sauvetage. There were several small vessels along the quay – a lighter, a couple of tugs undergoing repairs for the harbour authorities, the two dredgers mentioned in the Kilshaw contract, tied up abreast, and the tug that mattered, the *Astrid*.

Finn had somehow expected something bigger, in spite of knowing that she was only seventy feet long with a displacement of fifty-four tons. She was small even in comparison to the other harbour tugs. She had an A-1 classification from Lloyds, meaning that she was intended to work only in sheltered waters, so a special policy had had to be negotiated for the trip of six hundred miles to Belfast. It should take about three days; putting in at Dublin instead would save ten or twelve hours' steaming.

They walked round the eastern side of the dock, across a swing bridge which, when open, connected it with the main harbour. In the adjoining dock, cranes were offloading cargoes of building sand from Seine barges. There were three or four men working on the *Astrid*, and electric leads and gas lines ran out to her from the workshop doors. The last of the welding was still being done.

A man with the sleeves of his *bleu de travail* jacket rolled back from muscular forearms glanced up, saw Brouhin, and scrambled onto the quay.

'*Ça marche bien, Rico?*' Brouhin asked.

'*Pas si mal, monsieur. Elle sera prête à partir cette après-midi, la vieille coque.*' Brouhin introduced Finn as a representative of the buyers who would travel with the *Astrid*. The workman nodded noncommittally; his name was Enrico Poretti, the foreman welder, a Corsican. He was one of only three people in the firm who knew what the true nature of the conversion work on the tug entailed. He had personally loaded the two hundred rifles and the ammunition, wrapped in plastic and asbestos sheeting, into the bunkers.

Finn knew that Poretti would say nothing of any importance in his presence. He moved farther along the quay, leaving the two Frenchmen to talk, to where a pile of coal sacks stood waiting to be loaded aboard. The *Astrid*, although worked under the French flag for more than twenty years, had actually been built in England. She was a tug of the TID class – the letters standing, in the inverted nomenclature of whoever thought up such titles, for Tugs, Inshore Duty. These vessels had been built in the forties to niggardly wartime specifications, and in most of those that were still earning their living, the big compound-expansion steam engines had been replaced by diesel motors. On paper, this was what Kilshaw's firm intended doing with the *Astrid*.

As an inducement to the purchaser, Compagnie Havraise had agreed to carry out some preliminary work for the conversion, fitting two fuel tanks into the compartments formerly used as bunkers on either side of the stokehold. Since the tanks were less than half the size of the old bunkers, a space of about sixty cubic feet was left empty on each side, sealed in by plates that had been welded over the mouths of the coal chutes. It was this empty space that had been filled with Brouhin's consignment. Only by taking the tug to pieces plate by plate could it possibly be located. Kilshaw had planned well.

Poretti stopped talking as Finn returned. Brouhin told him, 'They are practically ready. The crew I have hired will be here at midday. It takes three or four hours to build up the steam pressure, and you can leave before the swing bridge closes at six o'clock.'

'Good,' said Finn.

'The accommodation is – well, not luxurious. There are several bunks in the forward cabin down below. You will have to share them with the crew, I fear. There is a mess aft of the engine room.' He shrugged. 'She was designed to do a day's work in a harbour, no more. In the open sea she will roll. But she will make nine knots and you are in the hands of a good crew.'

'And you can't wait to get rid of us. All right, I'll come back around three o'clock.'

They returned together to the city centre, taking a short cut along the line of big steel hoppers into which sand from the barges was being loaded to await its final distribution in lorries. At the bottom of one vessel a flock of chickens grubbed disconsolately in the remaining sand.

It was ten thirty when the two of them entered the lobby of the Normandie. In an easy chair beside the reception desk, Walter Barnett sat looking at them.

Finn saw him first, his glance drawn to the head of bright ginger hair that glowed in the filtered sunshine from the windows. The airmail edition of the *Daily Express* lay in his lap, and a coffee and cognac stood on the table by his elbow. Finn felt a moment of blinding panic before realizing that Barnett could not have recognized him, that they had never met; confusedly he knew that it was vital to retain his facelessness. He looked through Barnett, walked to the desk, and asked for his key, feeling the other man's gaze flicker uncertainly over him before switching to Brouhin, who walked a couple of yards behind.

The Frenchman twigged. Barnett must be made to assume they had entered together by chance, must not be allowed to realize they were acquainted. At least the alarm in his tone could be disguised by genuine astonishment as he stopped dead and said, 'Barnett!'

'Surprise, surprise,' said Walter Barnett.

Finn took his key and turned towards the lift.

'What on earth are you doing here?' he heard Brouhin ask.

'Just dropped in. Just came to see everything goes smoothly.'

Resisting the temptation to linger, to eavesdrop further, Finn went with a thumping heart up to his room. It had been foolish not to think that Kilshaw might send someone to do the same job for the Vigilantes that Finn was meant to carry out for Partington.

28

They met an hour later, by arrangement over the hotel's internal telephones, on the first floor of the municipal Fine Arts Museum. They had taken precautions to ensure that Barnett did not follow Brouhin. Among the Dufy and Boudin paintings they stood looking out in dismay over the furious grey-green of the Seine estuary.

'So *he* wants to ride on the *Astrid*,' Finn said. 'God Jesus! What did you tell him?'

'As one of the buyers he has every right. I could not object too strongly in case he became suspicious. He has a suspicious nature.'

'Quite. You know why he's here, don't you? To make sure you aren't thinking of doubling on them.'

'*Zut!* Damn the man! He wants also to look over the tug this morning.'

'Better not try to stop him,' Finn said. 'But make a phone call first, to Poretti; you trust him thoroughly, don't you? Get him to send away the crew and find a plausible excuse to delay the sailing until we've thought of something. Could we leave tonight?'

Brouhin shook his head. 'The Pont Vauban, the swing bridge, can only be opened in the daylight hours. It will have to be to-morrow morning.'

Finn stared unseeingly at a canvas of bright, bold Impressionist strokes. 'Poissonerie de Trouville,' it was called. Twelve hours' delay meant they would not reach Dublin before Tuesday, only three days before Kilshaw's ultimatum ran out. And that was assuming a solution could be found between now and tomorrow morning to the problem of Walter Barnett.

162

'He didn't ask who I was?' Finn said. 'He didn't wonder if we'd been together?'

'Not apparently.'

'That's one advantage we have, then. He mustn't realize we're connected. We may be able to use the fact.'

'I beg your pardon,' said Brouhin, suddenly stand-offish. 'My agreement with Partington was to arrange for the diversion of the tug from Belfast to Dublin, no more. There my responsibility ends. I suggest that the question of what is ultimately to be done about Barnett is your own problem.'

It was a bluff, and both of them knew it. Finn said quietly, 'Do you know what kind of man Partington is?'

'Ruthless, *oui*?'

'If Walter Barnett travels on that tug instead of me and it reaches Belfast, Partington will find a way of getting back at you. That's a fact, not a threat. Barnett must not board that tug. Something must be arranged.'

'Something?'

They both understood what was meant. Brouhin's face was the colour of Roquefort cheese, but a desperate, sharp-eyed re-sourcefulness was there as well, the quality of a survivor. He said, 'Must it be here, in France?'

'You know it must.'

The Frenchman stroked his beard glumly. 'I will speak with Ricco Poretti. Between us we will find a way.'

Finn studied a Boudin painting, 'Entrées des Jetées du Havre par Gros Temps.' By moving a few yards to the window it was possible to see the same scene in its modern setting. The weather was much the same, the wind smashing great Channel seas against the harbour mole.

'Maybe it's just as well we're not leaving today,' he said. 'I'm not much of a sailor.'

'The forecast for tomorrow is better,' said Brouhin.

They stayed discreetly in touch during the afternoon. Barnett had been taken to see the *Astrid* and accepted without apparent suspicion the story Poretti had told about a small problem with the boiler preventing the departure of the tug before nightfall. He seemed satisfied with the other arrangements at this end; his main interest was in seeing that the shipment arrived safely in Belfast. He would return, he said, about four in the morning when the crew would be on board building up a head of steam and preparing to leave at six o'clock.

But that would be too late and too public an occasion for Finn and Brouhin to use. By mid-afternoon they had set out their own plan.

Barnett, too, had checked in at the Normandie. He was an unsociable, rather surly young man who kept to his room and did not respond to Brouhin's hint about spending the evening out on the town. However, somewhat to the Frenchman's surprise, he suggested meeting for a couple of drinks in the hotel bar after dinner. Then, he said, he intended having an early night.

The rendezvous was for nine o'clock. By twenty to nine Finn was installed alone at the bar, nursing a brandy and conspicuously reading an English newspaper. When Barnett arrived, punctually, he merely glanced up, nodded as to a stranger in an otherwise empty room, and buried himself back in the newsprint.

The Irishman drank a cup of *café filtre*. He waited twenty minutes without showing any concern at Brouhin's absence beyond glancing at his watch once or twice. Then he left the bar abruptly, doubtless to check the fourth-floor suite and inquire at the porter's desk. The critical question was whether he'd be worried enough to come back.

He was, though he stayed away longer than Finn had anticipated. He must have been to the news agent round the corner, for now he carried a paper of his own. Finn's heart sank; the man would be difficult to budge. But instead of sitting down Barnett was standing suddenly in front of him.

'Excuse. Are you British?'

Finn lowered the newspaper. 'Yes?'

'I was due to meet someone here. I was wondering if you'd seen him before I arrived. Feller with a black beard?'

'No,' said Finn without hesitation. 'Definitely not. I've been the only one in here.'

'Odd.' Barnett's pale, insensitive face gave nothing away, but his naturally suspicious brain was clearly hard at work. 'The hall porter seems to think he went out around seven and hasn't been back.'

'I see.' Polite indifference was called for. The conversation reached an awkward pause. 'You're Irish, aren't you?' Finn asked.

'I'm an Ulsterman,' Barnett said without humour. 'British.'

'Oh. Sorry.' Finn smiled and then made a show of remembering something. 'Just a minute. A black beard, did you say? Is he staying here?'

'Yes. He's a Frenchman I'm doing business with.'

'Then I know the one you mean.' It was important to sound careless about the next bit. 'Yes, he did go out around seven. I happened to see him walking down the Quai Georges Cinq.'

'Which way?'

'Let me see. Left. Towards the docks.'

Barnett's face hid a confusion of furious thoughts. 'Thanks,' he said stiffly. The conversation flagged again, and only the ringing of the phone behind the bar ended further awkwardness.

'The call you booked,' the barman said to Barnett. 'Long distance.'

'I'll take it in my room,' he said, and stalked out.

Finn seethed. Damn that phone. Who could he be calling?

Surely not Kilshaw at this late hour to warn him of the delay in sailing? Finn's own coded telegram to Partington had been sent before midday. But the main worry about the call was that it might distract Barnett from going out to find Brouhin.

He could only sit tight. In five minutes Barnett returned, looking more relaxed, as if a decision had been made for him. He said to Finn, 'Look, can I ask you a hell of a favour? As one Britisher to another?'

'Of course,' said Finn without conviction.

'I've got to go out and find that Frenchman. I told you we've got a business deal lined up. I don't quite trust him; it's too long a story to go into. The point is I've got to go down to the docks and I could use some company.'

Half relieved, half burdened with new anxiety, Finn could not think what to say. 'I don't know...'

'It won't take long, a few minutes' walk. I know exactly where to find him.' His tone became confiding. 'My company is buying a tugboat off him, see. I don't trust him not to be getting up to some trickery down there over the fixtures and fittings that we're paying for. But this Frog's got some hard friends. I wouldn't want to be going down there alone and catch them stripping the boat.'

A warning note sounded in Finn's mind. This was one possibility he and Brouhin hadn't considered; in a way the deception had succeeded too well. But his own decision now could tip the balance between whether Barnett left the hotel or not. It should be safe enough, with Brouhin and Poretti both close at hand.

'All right,' he said. 'I'll come.'

'Good man!'

They left at once, Finn buttoning up his coat against the raw evening air, Barnett still, perhaps absent-mindedly, carrying the folded newspaper. In the doorway of the hotel Finn, glancing casually around, saw in its parking bay on the Place Gambetta to the right, Poretti's car, a Citroën DS 23. Its yellow headlights came on as the two of them turned and began to walk down the Quai Georges V.

Being what it was, a city destroyed by war and re-created, Le Havre suffered the fate of every town planned as a total and model entity. The crowds who were meant to throng its squares, stroll beneath its colonnades, and admire its soberly elegant buildings were somehow far smaller than those envisaged by the planners. At night, even more mysteriously and to a man, they vanished.

It was ten o'clock. They walked for several hundred yards beside the Bassin du Commerce and crossed the Pont Vauban to approach the dock where the *Astrid* was moored. The maze of streets and quays and wharves and builders' yards here was badly lit and, but for an occasional car in search of a short cut out of the city, utterly deserted. Finn was conscious of the Citroën following them, in fits and starts, at a safe distance. He could understand Barnett's reluctance to come here on his own. Finn had a sour taste in his mouth. The thought of what would happen to Barnett was neither horrible nor tantalizing, merely unpalatable.

They rounded a corner into the patch of shadow thrown by a sand hopper, moving into single file where a protruding iron fence narrowed the pavement. Finn felt something seize his coat collar from behind, twist him sideways, fling him against the fence. Incredulously, instinctively raising his right hand to parry a blow to the head, he took instead a kick in the ribs which doubled him over for a second, fighting for breath.

When he straightened up, gasping, his back to the fence, Barnett was backing off, his newspaper falling to the ground to reveal in his right hand a small black automatic.

'You stay right there, Major Finn!'

He still struggled to breathe. He stared into the pale, suddenly savage face that glared at him indistinctly in the darkness.

'D'you answer to the name then?' Barnett demanded.

'Why not? It's my own.'

'I know about you, Finn. You were setting me up, weren't you? What for?'

'Can't you guess?'

'You treacherous bastard!'

Finn understood his anger. Apart from anything else, there was a terrible effrontery in planning to kill someone. He said, 'All right, you've stolen a march on us.'

'I want the details, double quick. I'm not a fool, Finn. I noticed you coming into the hotel at the same time as Brouhin this morning. Then there you were tonight, where he should have been. It was a wee bit too much of a coincidence. While I was asking the porter about Brouhin I also asked for your name. He found your registration card for me. I made a phone call to Belfast. They know all about you there.'

'Who does?'

'My people. The Vigilantes.'

'From a policeman named Crombie, perhaps?'

'Perhaps. You knew the one thing that would lure me to the docks tonight was the idea that Brouhin was tampering with that shipment. So I let myself be lured; it was the only way to find out more. But I wasn't doing it alone. I wasn't born yesterday. Now tell me what you and Brouhin are planning. Quickly.'

Finn sighed. From the right he had seen the thin glaze of yellow headlights approaching. 'I guess I know when I'm blown,' he said. 'The people who don't are the ones who get posthumous VCs.'

'Tell me,' Barnett said.

'Yes.' But there was more than one way of playing for time. 'It's just that I can't win whether I talk or not.'

'I'd like to kill you. I've no need to.'

'Then put your gun away.'

Barnett hesitated, glancing over his shoulder at the twin

yellow beams rounding the corner, about to pick them out against the fence. He had no way of telling where the danger lay. Still gripping the butt and with his finger on the trigger guard he shoved the pistol into his jacket pocket and moved deeper into the shadows. It was not what Finn had hoped for.

'I'm here,' he said, 'to make sure those rifles don't reach the Vigilantes, just as you're here to make sure they do. It would be nice to think I was doing it because there are already too many psychopaths running around Northern Ireland with guns, but that's not it. This is part of a bigger deal, Barnett. One that people like you and me learn very little about.'

'A deal with who?'

'The IRA.'

'It never is!'

His astonishment was real. But now he sensed that the approaching Citroën was slowing down. With a single vicious glance at Finn he turned, ready for them. The car stopped; Poretti and Brouhin sprang out.

'He's got a gun!' Finn yelled.

They were running at Barnett, both carrying monkey wrenches. He stood facing them and fired point-blank from his pocket. He fired just once because the lining of the pocket caught in the breech.

Muffled, the small gun made no more noise than a firecracker. Brouhin gave a sort of hiccup and went down on his knees by the kerb. Barnett was desperately trying to drag the jammed pistol out of his pocket when the first blow from Poretti's wrench smashed his knuckles. The second broke his forearm with a quick crunch as he raised it to protect his head. He gave a brief, awful gasp. Then he turned and ran, one useless arm flapping by his side. The big Corsican threw aside the wrench and chased him round the end of the fence to somewhere beneath the sand hoppers.

Finn did not follow. He went to Brouhin, who now lay on his side in the gutter. He picked up Barnett's newspaper with some idea of stanching the blood flowing from his chest. But then he saw that it had run, also, down the gutter in a thin stream almost as far as the next corner.

From behind the fence came terrible muffled sounds of struggling and retching. Then there was silence for a minute before Poretti reappeared, panting.

'*Mort?*' he asked, jerking his head at Brouhin.

'It was a fluke,' Finn said. 'A small-calibre bullet. It just happened to get his heart.'

'*Aides-moi.*'

A stunned calm still possessed them both. Finn held Brouhin's legs and Poretti took him under the armpits and together they dragged the limp body around the fence and laid it between the high steel legs of the hopper. A few yards beyond, the white superstructure of a sand barge rose above the edge of the quay. No one had heard the shot, no one had witnessed the shambles they had made of their plan to arrange a quiet accident for Barnett. They did not deserve such luck.

The Irishman lay with his face buried in a sand heap next to the hopper. Poretti had suffocated him.

Finn looked with an impotent dread at the Corsican.

'*Attends,*' Poretti said. 'I know what must be done.'

They rolled Barnett's body to the end of the quay. The features were smudged; sand blocked his nose, mouth, and eyes. Poretti eased the body over the side, and it fell with a thump and an alarmed squawking of chickens into the sand in the bottom of the barge. Brouhin followed him down, and so did the wrenches and the pistol. Poretti found a shovel, tossed it in as well, and then scrambled aboard the barge, down the companionway into the open hold.

He worked energetically for twenty minutes, watched with

huddled resentment by the chickens, while Finn, with carefully placed handfuls of sand, covered the trail of blood leading from the pavement as well as the rivulet in the gutter. The Corsican spoke again when he hopped off the barge.

'They are at the bottom, under one metre of sand. Always twenty tons are left for ballast, one metre deep. This will return to Rouen tomorrow for another load. If we have luck they will not be found for months. I will arrange all at the hotel. You will go now to the tug.'

Poretti spoke with the authority of the executioner. Finn did what he was told.

The crew of three professional French tugboatmen began work at midnight, lighting the fires, oiling the engine, and building up a good head of steam. Finn, after writing and encoding a cable describing the night's events and giving it to Poretti for transmission to Partington in the morning, slept on board for several hours. When he awoke at five o'clock the pressure in the boiler was already up to its working level and the *Astrid* was blowing steam. The swing bridge was opened for them at three minutes past six, and by a quarter past they were steaming out past the main breakwater into the Seine estuary. The wind was down, but a heavy swell was still running in the wake of yesterday's storm. By the time they had passed the Cap de La Hève lighthouse and set a course of 290 degrees to take them round the Pointe de Barfleur, Finn had gone below again, feeling queasy.

<h1 style="text-align:center">29</h1>

A train called the Enterprise Express, notable mainly for the cheerful squalor in which its passengers were expected to travel, left for Dublin at eleven each morning from the bombed-out shell of Great Victoria Street station in Belfast. On this occasion it was three quarters empty; Partington had no trouble getting a first-class compartment to himself. He dusted cigarette ash off the seat, mopped up the spilt tea on the table in front of him, and immersed himself in the *Times* crossword. Beyond the unwashed windows, the flat County Down countryside trundled by.

Once across the border the first stop was Dundalk. Here a man boarded the train, entered Partington's compartment, and sat down opposite. He then proceeded to eat with a teaspoon the contents of an open can of creamed rice pudding. When he had finished he opened a window and dropped the can down an embankment, licking the spoon and returning it to the top pocket of his denim jacket. It was typical; it was his way of cocking a snook. Partington watched him with a mixture of curiosity and distaste.

'We haven't got that much time,' he said.

'You're right there,' said the newcomer.

'First things first, then. The thing is on. It's accepted in principle. But I have a few of our own proposals to put to you. Proposals only come in *packages* these days, like everything else. There's one item on which I must have the final say. Security.'

'Understood. What do you have in mind?'

'Certain people present a very distinct threat,' Partington said. 'Shall we say, ah, subsequent *nonavailability*?'

'You've not changed much over the years.'

'Thank you.'

'There's also the question of those company records.'

'Neither of us can afford to leave any evidence of the connection,' said Partington. 'Nothing must remain. *Nothing.*'

At Pearse station in Dublin an hour later they left the train separately. By the time Partington had had a chalk mark put on his suitcase at the customs barrier, his travelling companion had disappeared among the crowds.

Partington found his right foot sticking to the ground. There was bubble gum from the train floor on his shoe.

30

Dublin appeared hazily, clinging to the edge of its calm and misty bay, in the middle of Tuesday morning. The *Astrid* had made good time, helped by a following wind which had allowed her to average ten knots all the way up St George's Channel. Finn had felt vaguely seasick for much of the journey, but although he was not required to share in the work, for the sake of doing something he had relieved the French crew for a couple of shifts at the wheel. His real work would begin ashore.

For a while they had to steam back and forth across the bay, waiting for pilotage into the harbour. When the launch finally came out to meet them two men clambered aboard. The pilot went straight up to the wheelhouse. The other man, in a brass-buttoned serge uniform, stuck out a hand to Finn.

'Muldoon,' he said. 'Dublin Ports and Docks Board. You the owner?'

'No. She's being sold. I've a letter of authority to act for the seller.'

'You've a cargo manifest?'

'There's no cargo. She's on her way to Belfast for a conversion job. We're stopping over just long enough to take on coal.'

'You'll need a customs clearance all the same. Very tight they are on security these days.' He gave Finn a queer look. 'You've no bonded stores, anything like that at all?'

'None.'

Muldoon sucked his teeth, staring towards the city where dockside cranes had emerged from the mist around the mouth of the Liffey. He made Finn uneasy. He was a thin, consumptive-looking man of about fifty with sceptical dark eyes and a cheerless tone. He said, 'We can't fit you into the docks proper just now. We'll find you a berth along one of the river quays.'

'I was told to go into the Alexandra Basin.'

'Sorry. They're after having a strike. There's a build-up of ships waiting and we hadn't the notice of your arrival, now, had we? You'll be told whenever there's a berth at all.'

'How long?'

'Twenty-four hours, maybe thirty-six.'

Finn despaired. They could simply not afford that much delay in unloading the rifles and getting hold of the documents. 'There must be some way of speeding things up. We're a small vessel; we'll be here less than twenty-four hours.'

'It's either this way or anchoring out in the bay,' Muldoon said.

'I'll have to speak to someone higher up.'

'Sure, you're welcome. I doubt it'll do you much good.'

The telegraph rang and the tug's engine went down to quarter speed as they passed the eastern breakwater and nosed up the sluggish brown river. Bloody Irish, Finn thought. He stood on the low afterdeck and watched the pilot edging the *Astrid* in towards a berth on the south bank in front of the gasworks. A lorry loaded with great steel barrels of Guinness rumbled along the quay. A man took a line from their boat and turned it round a bollard; the stubby little boat swung to starboard, straining gently against the rope to bring her rump alongside. Finn, with an odd prescience, realized that from here there was open access to the city. There were no fences, gates, inquisitive policemen, as there would be in the main dockyards across the river. He said to Muldoon, 'We couldn't take on coal here, I suppose?'

'No coaling along the quays at all. No repair work. If you wanted to do a small bit below decks, now, we wouldn't mind that. We'd turn a blind eye, you might say.'

'We don't want to do any repairs.'

'But there's always a little something cropping up, now, isn't there?'

'Like welding work?'

'Why not? As long as you kept it to yourselves.'

Finn turned to stare at him. His face was ambivalent.

'You've arranged it well,' Finn said softly. 'Very well indeed. There's just one thing you'd better tell me. How did you know?'

Muldoon did not respond.

'*How?*'

The *Astrid* was now fully alongside and tied up. Muldoon, still ignoring him, stepped over the rail onto the quay and waited for the pilot, who was coming down from the wheelhouse, to join him. Then he touched the peak of his cap.

'Good day now,' he said. He sounded as if he expected no good of it at all. The two men walked away towards the city, leaving Finn in an impotent, uncertain rage.

Muldoon was on Sullivan's side. He'd arranged this berth to give the IRA men easy access to the tug, which meant that they'd had advance warning of its arrival *and* knew for certain that the rifles were on board – a fact which had been no more than a surmise at the time Finn had met Sullivan. Their intelligence was obviously better than Partington had realized; the plan he'd been working out had better be sound.

Finn knew he must make contact with Partington at the first opportunity. But there were even more urgent things to do; getting the Frenchmen out of the way was the first of them.

Soon an immigration officer and two customs men had arrived. His passport and the seamen's ID cards were checked; he produced the *Astrid's* British registration booklet, the bill of sale, and his letter of authorization from Brouhin. The customs officers carried out a fairly thorough search of the cabin, the mess, the stokehold, and the engine room, peering under bunks, poking behind companionways, but ignoring the bunkers completely.

The idea was paying off; nobody who did not know that something was concealed there could possibly begin to guess. Still, Finn was relieved when he had signed a declaration and the officers left.

He drank a cup of coffee with the crew. Then he left the tug, walking beside the river as far as O'Connell Bridge. A little way along the quay the stacked barrels of Guinness and Harp lager were being loaded onto two brewery ships that would carry them to thirsty expatriates across the Irish Sea. He crossed the bridge, walked up O'Connell Street to the Allied Irish Bank, and claimed the money that Poretti had telegraphed to pay the seamen's wages and their fares home. Then he went to the Aer Lingus office and booked them on a flight to Paris that afternoon, with onward reservations to Le Havre. Back at the tug, where the Frenchmen had already packed their grips, he said goodbye and watched them leave for a couple of hours' sightseeing and buying blackthorn sticks and leprechaun dolls before they caught their plane.

He was alone. Alone with a lot of questions and misgivings nagging at him, with a hulk of a tugboat and two hundred automatic rifles that could cost him a long time in jail. Yet in a strange proprietary way he was now reluctant to leave them alone.

He walked, rather wearily, back up the quay to the nearest pub and made a phone call. The woman who answered at the small hotel in Glasnevin, on the northern outskirts of the city, said that the gentleman wasn't in at the minute but had left word that he could be found at the Stag's Head, off Exchequer Street. It was lunchtime; Finn might have guessed. He took a taxi.

Rain had begun to fall, a relentless Irish downpour that brought traffic to a halt and filled the platforms of buses with a clutter of wet prams and pushchairs. In the Stag's Head, a cheerful Dickensian chophouse, Partington was finishing a plate of roast beef and drinking burgundy.

'I spend a lot of my time in pubs here, they're the only places one can get away from *children*. The little brutes are everywhere. Contraception would do this country more good than all the German light industry you can think of. Sit down, sit down. Spot of nastiness in France, hm? How was the trip?'

He poured himself more wine without offering Finn any.

'The tug is tied up at Sir John Rogerson's Quay,' Finn said. 'That's just below Butt Bridge. Wide open. It couldn't be better for Sullivan. All he needs to do is come down with a gas cutter and a truck.'

Partington forked a formidable quantity of meat into his mouth and nodded. 'So you make your phone call at six and announce that you've arrived. That's the first step.'

'He must know already. I was greeted on arrival by an emissary. A bent Ports and Docks official named Muldoon.'

'I know Muldoon; old IRA lag. Nazi sympathizer during the war. In and out of TB hospitals. Convicted of manslaughter around forty-four. Question of a bomb that went off *early* and killed two of his own people.'

'Serve his time in Mountjoy, by any chance?'

'Certainly.' Partington blinked at him and then noticed his tie – blue and red balloons floating on a cream background. Other people thought his ties inappropriate; Partington was the only one who found them funny.

'I don't like them knowing so much,' Finn said. 'Somewhere there's a leak we've not taken account of.'

'Ah. You must accept that down here they're a lot better organized than in the North. They've got influence at the highest levels – a problem the police are always up against.'

'I'm sure. But that's no help to us.'

'You make everything sound so *difficult*, Finn. Now listen. You phone Sullivan at six. They'll certainly want to take the stuff tonight. You'll wait on board the tug. I rely on you to effect the exchange as you think best. They'll probably want to inspect the consignment before they hand over the documents.'

'And I'll want to see the originals. But it's all a trifle one-sided, isn't it? I'll be alone. They'll come in mobhanded.'

'Now, now,' Partington said soothingly. 'There is actually no reason why Sullivan shouldn't keep his part of the bargain, is there? We won't be keeping ours,' he added thoughtfully, 'but then he's not to know that. It's as much in *his* interests as in ours, remember, to get our friend out of the way.'

'All right. So I've got the documents and I've got the rifles. Then?'

'Yes. There's a little street off the quay where you're tied up, farther east though, called Peterson's Lane. I'll be waiting there in a car, about halfway down.'

'It could be a long wait. Why not let me phone you?'

'Because if Sullivan's got any sense he won't specify a time of arrival. We must be ready to go at a moment's notice. A private plane will await us at Dublin airport. In London we'll have two clear days to use the stuff in the best possible way.'

'But... Sullivan? The rifles?'

'A simple phone call to the Garda Siochána tomorrow morning. *Anonymous,* of course. The stuff will be cached in Dublin for a couple of days before it's distributed to their units. I happen to know that, you see. I also happen to know the exact location of the cache.' Partington finished eating, touched a napkin to his mouth and beamed through it.

Finn had to fight hard to seem unimpressed.

'Very *clean,* you see,' Partington added. 'The whole shipment bagged in one swoop, but no arrests. Nobody to go dragging us into it. Nobody's going to come forward and *claim* the stuff.'

Finn nodded, reluctantly admiring the simplicity of it. 'You know about the cache because you've got someone inside Sullivan's mob. I've known that for a while.'

'Now, now,' Partington said again.

'It's someone near the top. Someone who knew enough to tell you the nickname of their border crossing, Boyle's Bypass. You gave me the first clue when you mentioned the name.'

'Careless of me,' said Partington impenitently. 'All right. True enough. It's very recent, you see, it only dates from then. I could only make an approach once you had established a connection between the IRA and the Kilshaw letter for me. Old acquaintances, you know, a bit of give and take. Invaluable. Where *do* you get your ties, anyway?'

'London. Jermyn Street. Do you really think those documents will do the trick? Eliminate Kilshaw *and* prevent the fighting?'

'We can but try, my dear fellow. Those of his supporters who choose to stick by him may run riot, but that's an acceptable risk.'

'I'd like to get some sleep now,' Finn said.

'Of course. One more thing. We don't want trouble from the Garda. I'd rather you weren't wafting about Dublin with that British Army pistol.'

'I'm not. I left it in London for that very reason.'

'Good. Take care.'

Finn left, feeling about as benevolent towards Partington as it was possible to be.

31

He slept for three hours, wrapped in a sleeping bag on his bunk in the forward cabin. When he awoke he felt fresh, rested, better and more whole than he seemed to have been for a long time. He shaved with his battery razor, washed in cold water drawn from the tank on the afterdeck, changed his clothes – a clean shirt, corduroy trousers, a leather car coat – and packed the small duffel bag he had taken with him to France. He glanced briefly into the cracked mirror that hung beside the bunk: his features still seemed distorted by the radiation treatment, as if they were not quite his own, but the sea voyage had given him a healthy ruddiness.

The first stars were out. Up the river, behind the elegant silhouettes of Georgian houses lining the quays, the sky still held an afterglow of the sun. At ten to six he left the tug, strolling up the quay past the gasworks and coalyards and warehouses. In the pub from which he had tried earlier to phone Partington, one of those desolate Dublin 'lounges' the size of a dance hall, he entered the cubicle again and dialled the number of that other callbox behind the General Post Office.

Sullivan's cockney-Irish voice was unmistakable, even in a monosyllable. 'Yes?'

'Finn,' said Finn.

'Be back at the tug within half an hour. Alone. Don't leave it again.'

'You're bringing...?'

The line had gone dead. Finn shrugged and replaced his receiver. The call had been superfluous anyway, more Irish theatricality, because Sullivan must have known through

Muldoon of the tug's arrival. Their preparedness was worrying and still unexplained. He hoped Partington was not underestimating them.

He killed the half-hour at the bar with two whiskeys, an egg roll, and a newspaper. The paper was full of Kilshaw and rumours of civil war; the tension in the North was close to breaking point. He also turned away a whore, a pretty girl with a desperate edge to her voice and eyes that reminded him of Caragh's. He had not thought much about Caragh in the past few days, but suddenly he found himself missing her. Then he realized she might still be here, in Dublin. The reminder was depressing. He couldn't risk a phone call. He would fly out tonight with no way of knowing when he'd see her again. Would he want to see her again? Yes. The answer came easily. He was still in some awe of her, of that ability to penetrate the strange deadness in his soul.

He took his time strolling back to the tug, in spite of Sullivan's half-hour warning. He didn't expect the IRA men to show up until much later; it wouldn't make sense to come until fewer people were about. However, a natural caution made him pause for a few seconds behind the stacked Guinness barrels higher up the quay, watching the *Astrid* before he approached her. She was in darkness. She strained with a gentle creaking sound against her moorings on an outgoing tide. And a shadow moved across her deck.

Finn's hand groped involuntarily for the butt of the pistol that was not there. His mind quickly dismissed the thought that Sullivan's men had come early after all. This was a figure on its own, a figure that had moved between the wheelhouse and a big ventilation cowl and for a few seconds was hidden in shadow. Now it reappeared, stepping cautiously out into the starlight, crossing the rail, walking quickly up the quay.

He waited till the man had gone five yards past him. There was a tiny red glow, the whiff of a cheap cigar.

'Stop!' he commanded.

The intruder's hands rose automatically, one holding the cheroot, as he halted. He half turned towards Finn.

'Jasus! Harry!'

'Stay where you are. What were you doing?'

Fortune peered at him more closely through the gloom. 'Jasus, that was a turn you gave me! You've a right nerve, Harry, and you not even tooled up.' He lowered his arms and approached Finn.

'What do you want?' he asked, still distrustful.

'You, Harry. I've wanted to talk to you for the past week.'

'How the hell did you find me?'

'You know how I work, Harry. Whispers and rumours and friends of friends. I'm after searching all over Dublin.'

'But why Dublin?'

'That was a hunch, no more. Wait till I tell you.'

Finn studied his face in the filmy light that reached them from distant street lamps. It was indefinably different, the eyes more withdrawn behind their long lashes. A huge bruise was fading from the left side of his face.

'They took you to pieces, did they?'

'That was Kilshaw's lads. The other is called interrogation in depth. *They* never lay a finger on you. They don't need to.'

'Did you talk to them?'

'I told them everything, Harry. Everything I knew about you and me and Kilshaw. I won't apologize. Anyone would have done the same.'

Finn shrugged. 'It can't make much difference now.'

'That man Crombie. The Vigilantes have got him in their pocket. And Howarth – he's so intent on smashing the commie revolutionary IRA that he gets used by the others. They'll make it dangerous for you back there.'

'I've no intention of going back.'

'That's not all I came to tell you, mind.' Fortune raised his cheroot to his lips. It had gone out. He tossed it into the river, which in the sudden silence could be heard discreetly hurrying by.

Finn kept looking carefully back along the quay; there was still no sign of anyone approaching.

'You're doing some sort of deal with Sullivan?'

'What do you know about it?'

'Nothing. Only my own conjecture. Crombie kept on about you striking a deal with the IRA, a deal to get rid of Kilshaw. I realized you must have got very close to what you and I were looking for. That's what brought me to Dublin; I thought where Sullivan was, you would be. I've no idea what your deal is, Harry. I just reckon you'd better be sure Sullivan keeps his part of it.'

The river whispered in the silence again. Finn said, 'What do you mean?'

'Let me tell you just what I know. Remember last Tuesday? That was the evening you borrowed Paddy Keefe there to fiddle a lock for you. The same night I was lifted. In between I was drinking with Paddy up the Ardoyne. Bear one thing in mind: Paddy does a bit in the forgery line as well. He was after making a lot of money just lately, and he was out celebrating. Normally he's discreet; that night he was drunk and talking to an old friend. There were two things bothering him that he wanted to tell me about, two coincidences, and they both involved you and me.

'The first coincidence had to do with that B and E job he did for us. He'd said nothing at the time but it had been a fair surprise, he said, to find out whose office that was, for hadn't he done a very fine facsimile of the same man's handwriting for another client a short while ago?'

'Kilshaw's handwriting? Are you serious?'

'As I live, Harry. Of course I wanted to know who the client was but that he wouldn't say, drunk as he was. He got on to the second coincidence, which is just as interesting. Whoever it was that hired him took him to a particular house to pick up the stuff they wanted forged, and then went on to another place where he did the job under their supervision. The first house was the one where you'd taken him to pick a lock that very evening.'

'The Hughes house,' Finn said blankly.

'I realized right away,' said Fortune. 'And of course I made the connection. Con Michael Hughes. IRA. Sullivan. I would have asked him more but he passed out, beyond reviving. Then I was on my way to see you when I got lifted.'

Finn's brain seethed. Down the quay, the tug moved with the tide, her rubber fenders squeaking gently against the concrete.

'Jesus Christ,' he said numbly. 'He didn't mention what the forgery was about? What it was written on?'

'Nothing.'

'You may as well know this. Sometime in the next few hours Sullivan is handing me a set of company records supposedly proving that Kilshaw has been robbing his own people to pay for illegal guns. The vital parts are the entries in his own handwriting; if they've been forged they're worse than useless. If only I could make absolutely sure...'

'I've repeated every word Paddy Keefe told me,' Fortune said.

Yes, it fitted into a pattern, Finn thought. Suddenly it answered several questions that had worried him – questions about the writing of the Kilshaw letter, about Sullivan's delaying tactics, about the arrangements for the handover. There was some irony in the realization that Partington, intending to cheat Sullivan of the rifles, might instead be cheated of the documents.

'I need your help,' Finn said.

Fortune looked uneasy. 'I can't get involved, Harry, that I can't.'

'You don't need to. I want you to run a message, that's all.'

'I took a risk coming down here, Harry. It was for your sake personally.'

'So is this. Listen.' He explained, in as few words as possible, the terms of the deal with Sullivan. 'I've got to be here to meet him. I've got to confront him with what you've found out. If the stuff really is faked, if he set the whole thing up just to get his hands on those rifles, then he's not going to let me go off and announce it to Partington. We might turn nasty. We might spoil things for him by tipping off the police. On that account I could wind up at the bottom of the Liffey.'

'Then why not get out while you can?'

'Because I've got to *know*. If the stuff is genuine after all, I've got to have it. You can help without showing your face to anyone but Partington.'

'If you're sure...' Fortune said reluctantly.

'Here's what you do. Partington is sitting in a car parked in Peterson's Lane about a quarter mile back that way. Go to him now. Tell him what you know, warn him that Sullivan may be trying to trick us, and tell him to wait for more information. Then come back here and hide among these barrels. You'll be quite safe. Wait for Sullivan and his mob to arrive. Give me twenty minutes to come off the boat and join you. That will mean everything's okay, that I've got the genuine stuff. If I don't appear, get back to Partington. Tell him to get out. Tell him to blow the gaff on Sullivan before he goes – a phone call to the Garda. Then disappear yourself.'

'And leave you as a hostage?'

'They've got to use a gas cutter to burn the rifles out of the bunkers,' Finn said. 'It'll take the best part of an hour and they don't want to jeopardize the thing. No noisy murders – not till the end, anyway. I can't let them just have those rifles. With luck the police should arrive about halfway through.'

'If you say so, Harry.'

'One more thing. Have you got your pistol?'

'Yes.'

'Lend it to me.'

After a moment's hesitation Fortune dipped into his overcoat pocket and took out the heavy, compact Colt .45. 'Here. I've taken to carrying it since the Vigilante business. It made me kind of nervous. Watch yourself, Harry.'

Fortune moved across the quay and vanished down an alley beside the gasworks. Finn returned to the *Astrid*. First he needed a place to hide the pistol. In the mess there was a small steel table fixed to the deck towards one corner of the room. He went to the engine room, found a roll of masking tape on the workbench, brought it back, and taped the gun firmly to the underside of the table top. Remembering what had happened to Barnett, he took care not to cover the trigger or the moving parts and laid it left side up so that an ejected shell would not jam the breech. The safety catch was on the left and would not be accessible. For once, breaking the sacred rule, he left the safety off. The pistol was cocked, ready to fire.

Had Sullivan tricked them? The more he thought about it, the more the likelihood seemed to grow. The arrangement had been weighted in Sullivan's favour from the start; Finn had tried to warn Partington but he'd taken no notice. Why not? The bumptious fool had relied too much on his newfound informer in the movement. If this source had failed, as it obviously had, to alert him to the intended double-cross, then they couldn't rely on the accuracy of its other information, the location of the cache where the arms were to be stored. Finn was determined – with a stubborn vehemence that surprised him – that Sullivan must not keep the rifles. The only time to stop him was now.

He was afraid. The fear was still under control, invigorating rather than flustering him, lending an edge of precision to his thought and movements. Experience could not abolish fear, it could only help keep it in check.

The mess was lit by a gas pressure lamp. He got two more lamps going and hung them on either side of the deckhouse above the manholes that led down into the bunkers. He lit the paraffin stove that heated the mess. Then he sat down beside it, allowed his mind to go blank, and waited.

The heat from the stove made the room stuffier. He dozed off in spells of five and ten minutes, starting awake once at the sound of footsteps and a kind of stifled, coughing noise higher up the quay. But it was not Sullivan's men. There were other ships tied up here, other people occasionally passing – sailors, tramps, drunks. He drifted off to sleep again.

32

They made a good deal of noise arriving. He could hear the vehicle rattling over the cobbles when it was a hundred yards away. It stopped beside the *Astrid* with a long squeak of brakes, and the engine expired asthmatically. It sounded like an old three-tonner. The time was ten to ten.

Several pairs of feet thumped across the steel deck, then came Sullivan's voice.

'Finn!'

'I'm here,' he called. 'Where the light is.'

He stood up, close to the steel table. He wanted to avoid moving from the mess. A pale face appeared at one of the scuttles on the port side, and then the hatch opened and a man in an olive-drab combat jacket and battle-dress trousers, carrying a Luger, came down the companionway. It took a few seconds to recognize Muldoon, the Ports and Docks official, in a different uniform. Sullivan followed, then two more men, one armed with a Thompson gun. Above, there were more footsteps and the sound of a steel gangplank being shoved into place.

The four men crowded together at the foot of the companionway. Muldoon seemed his usual melancholy self; his pistol pointed at Finn absent-mindedly. The others looked flushed, faintly excited. Sullivan gave Finn a penetrating stare. His eyes were bright, his manner seemed different – intense and malevolent.

'You show a touching degree of trust,' Finn said. He was more than ever sure that his guess had been right.

'One needs to be careful,' said Sullivan.

'I want to see the documents.'

189

'Do you now?'

'Yes,' said Finn. 'And I mean this minute.'

There was a hostile pause. From on deck came the sound of the port manhole cover being removed and a man dropping into the bunker. A trolley holding the oxygen and acetylene cylinders was trundled along the quayside.

'Why the great hurry?' Sullivan asked coolly. 'I've yet to see the rifles. I don't even know they're on board.'

'And I don't know that the documents are any good. I've got reason to believe they were partly forged.'

'Oh?' The manner was even more dangerous, but he showed no surprise.

'You probably didn't even bother to bring them along,' Finn said. 'They're useless, aren't they? And you've got what you want within your grasp. What do you owe us? Nothing. I think I've got you all figured out now.'

'Let's hear your theory,' Sullivan said.

'You couldn't afford those weapons when Brouhin offered them to you. But once you found out he was negotiating to sell them to Kilshaw you thought you could see a way of getting them. You'd need outside help, and who better than the British Government to help, through your old acquaintance Partington? They were looking for something to use against Kilshaw. If you could provide it there was still the chance of getting the rifles. Yet it was a high price you were asking – arms that could be used against our own people – so what you offered in return had to be pretty good stuff.'

Sullivan listened neutrally. Muldoon sucked his teeth.

'So you went looking for the proof,' Finn continued. 'You got Con Michael and Billy McGarry to burgle Kilshaw's office. What they found didn't amount to much – perhaps a few dodgy sets of accounts implying but by no means proving Kilshaw's in-volvement in the swindle and the arms deal. What Partington would need was proof, and now you got a really good idea – to manufacture your own proof. With a bit of expert treatment those papers could be made to look pretty incriminating. Provided they stood up for long enough, until the moment when the rifles were handed over in payment, that was all that mattered.

'You studied the documents carefully, worked out exactly what was needed, and got Paddy Keefe to add some notes and names and figures in an imitation of Kilshaw's handwriting. On the photostatic copies it passed for the real thing. You were also careful not to oversell. Approaching Partington direct would have made him suspicious. Instead you sent an anonymous letter, knowing he would be interested, guessing we would investigate it and find evidence, *some* evidence, of what Kilshaw had been doing. You hoped that in the end we would convince ourselves that what you had was valuable. And we did. I've got to hand it to you.'

Now there was a faint smile – of self-satisfaction if nothing else – on Sullivan's haunted face. 'How long are you after reaching this conclusion?' he asked.

'A couple of hours.'

'Yet you waited here to find out for sure? Admirably fair, Finn. Very English. But is that the only reason you stayed?'

There was a thump from the stokehold as one of the gas cylinders was lowered, and then a muffled curse. Someone had got his fingers or toes jammed.

'No,' said Finn. 'There's more.'

He consulted his watch deliberately. 'I took precautions in case my hunch was right. Within five minutes from now a phone call will be made to the Garda. They'll be told what's happening here. Nothing can stop that call being made. They'll be down on you before you get a single rifle out of the stokehold.'

The atmosphere was electric. Muldoon and the two volunteers

glanced uncertainly at each other and then at Sullivan, awaiting a cue. His yellow eyes had narrowed but he still watched Finn with that slight, mocking smile on his face. There was something worrying about that smile.

'You reckon, do you?' he said eventually.

'I don't care whether they find you here or not. If you want to get clear you'd better leave now.'

Muldoon regained some confidence. 'It's a bluff, isn't it?'

'No,' said Sullivan quietly. 'It's not.' The smile was suddenly gone. 'He'd have doubled on us, all right. He did fix that phone call and he thinks it can't be stopped. He needs to be told it already has been. He needs to learn not to interfere.'

'Who's bluffing now?' Finn said, but in the face of Sullivan's confidence he felt a terrible doubt flood through him. Sullivan did not answer. He stepped forward and punched Finn in the face.

The blow snapped his head back against the steel bulkhead. He lurched to one side before regaining his balance. The numbness in his left cheek began yielding to a fierce pain. Sullivan stared at him with neither anger nor fear, only with the calculated indifference of a disciplinarian. Finn was to be punished. For this reason alone he perceived through his shock that what Sullivan had said was true. Something had gone wrong. The phone call would not be made.

'You're not stupid, Finn. You figured out more than I expected you to. But that still only gets you halfway there, you see. A lot is missing. A lot you were never meant to know and never will.'

He hit Finn again, a twisting hook to the left eye before Finn could get his guard up. He felt his eyebrow split and blood begin to crawl stickily through the hairs.

'Your trouble,' said Sullivan, 'is that you still don't know your friends from your enemies.'

His fist moved again. Finn, ready for him this time, blocked the punch and threw back a jab that grazed Sullivan's head. The volunteers rushed forward, seized his arms, bundled him against the bulkhead. He struggled for a few seconds until his head reeled with the exertion. Then he let himself go limp, raising his arms to shield his head and face.

Only half a dozen more blows came from Sullivan, each carefully, dispassionately aimed to cause the maximum hurt in a different place – his ear, his throat, his solar plexus. Blinded by pain, he felt himself sliding down the bulkhead. Agony shot through his back as Sullivan's knee took him under the kidneys.

He was unconscious for possibly a minute. He found he was lying on his side on the cold steel deck without quite understanding how he had got there. Sounds drifted back into his cognizance – the noises of people moving about the tug and, from the stokehold, a sharp hissing as the oxyacetylene cutting torch went to work on the port bunker.

Many parts of his body seemed to throb in unison, though the worst pain was still in the thinly fleshed cheek which had taken the first punch. He opened his eyes experimentally. The left was blocked by congealing blood from his brow; the right focused at once on the steel table, with the Colt pistol taped to its underside, about three feet away. He let his gaze drift to the companionway. Muldoon squatted on the bottom step, watching him, relaxed but alert, the Luger resting in his lap. Sullivan and the other two men had left the mess.

'Here.'

Muldoon tossed him a damp cleaning rag that someone had brought from the engine room. With an effort he raised himself onto an elbow and dabbed away enough of the gore to be able to see Muldoon through both eyes. In the hard light the skin of the Irishman's tuberculous face looked dead and bloodless. He had not helped in the beating. He sat looking at Finn with – well, not sympathy, but perhaps the covert curiosity of a fellow invalid.

'Better get back there,' he said, indicating the bunk where

Finn had sat earlier. Slowly, bruised muscles screaming, Finn worked his way into a sitting position. He rested for a minute. The smell of molten steel reached him from the stokehold, and the sound of voices and the tramp of the lookouts' boots across the deck echoed through the boat. Like the pain, a dismal knowledge of failure sank deeply into him. He had discovered Sullivan's double-cross in time to forestall it and had then been betrayed himself. What else was he to assume? The police would not come. A quarter of a mile away Partington sat waiting for a set of documents which might as well not exist. The message that should have reached him had been taken to Sullivan instead. By whom? Fortune. The idea was hard to escape. But then why in the first place had Fortune bothered to approach Finn with his discovery about the forgery?

Clinging to the small table for support, Finn forced himself to stand. Nausea swelled in him. He discovered that he had a blinding headache. He began working his way round the table to the bunk diagonally behind it. When he sat down he would be no more than two feet from the pistol.

A sudden realization struck him. It was both curious and alarming. When Sullivan and his men had arrived they had not searched him for a weapon. Nor had they searched the boat. He had been grateful for it at the time, but in the light of what he knew now it seemed incredible. If, as he suspected, it had been Fortune who warned Sullivan of Finn's plan to trick him, he would also, surely, have mentioned that Finn had borrowed his pistol. Sullivan would have turned the boat upside down to find it. There was a second implication, more vague, more sinister, as difficult to accept as slander about a friend: even without a warning, would Sullivan in the normal way be careless enough not to search at least his body? It was almost as if he had been confident in the belief that Finn was unarmed. What – or who – could have led him to believe such a thing?

Finn had reached the bunk. He sat down on it, catching his breath in agony. Muldoon, watching with a mournful interest, had followed him with the Luger. He fished with his free hand in the pocket of his combat jacket, brought out a pocket of Majors, and lit one. 'Fag?' he asked, offering to toss one.

'No.'

'I'm sorry you find yourself on the losing end of this deal, Major Finn.'

'It's not a deal,' Finn said. 'Robbery at gunpoint is not a deal.'

'Oh, I don't know now. There's deals and deals. Like Colm Sullivan said there, you don't know the half of it. Nor do I, come to that. Lookit, people like you and me never get the whole picture. It's the natural way of things.'

Finn looked at his watch. It was nearly ten thirty. Late enough to dispel any crazy lingering doubts he might have had that the police would still turn up, that somehow word of the double-cross had reached Partington and he'd been able to do something. He stared round numbly at the uniform dirty cream of the bulkheads and deckhead. From the stokehold there came a hoot of triumph and then an excited babble of voices. They had found the rifles. For a couple of minutes the torch continued biting through the metal until the cut was complete. Then there was a squeal of pain as someone over-eagerly touched the hot metal. Another voice called for wet cloths to cool it down.

'What we want is Billy McGarry through there,' said Muldoon conversationally. 'He's your real expert. He's something special on in Belfast tonight, so I'm told, else we'd have him down here for sure. No idea what that job is either. I don't get told too much at all, and sure it's better not to know, a lot of the time.' He paused. 'You should be after learning that yourself by now, Major. You took on a lot there trying to catch Colm Sullivan out. He's nobody's fool. Nor is your man Partington there.'

'You know Partington too?' Finn asked, without much interest.

'I met him in Mountjoy. Forty-three to forty-seven, it was, they had me in there. Everyone from the movement got the approach from Partington. That's how I was able to recognize him at Victoria station the other week.'

'So you were the one,' Finn said dully. 'We wondered who that might have been.'

'Wondered?' Muldoon snorted. 'Partington didn't wonder.'

'What's that supposed to mean?' said Finn, puzzled in spite of the pain and the apathy it had induced. Muldoon drew deeply on his cigarette, considering whether he should say more. From the stokehold came the sounds of men heaving the oxygen and acetylene cylinders across to the starboard bunkers and the cutting torch being lit again. They were leaving the rifles on the port side until the exposed compartment was cool enough to enter.

Muldoon shrugged. 'No harm in saying it. Somebody had to go to London to check that Partington was interested in our proposition. It had to be someone that knew him by sight and who was free to travel. I'm in the clear here in Ireland and I'm not on any of your British wanted lists, so me it was. What I didn't count on was him recognizing me.'

'What makes you think that?' Finn asked blankly.

'Think it! Sure, I didn't have to think. When the man you're looking for in a crowd walks straight up to you and says, "Muldoon," you're not left in much doubt. That's how it went. Just "Muldoon," with a particular smile that I remembered. Then he waddled away. He just couldn't resist letting me know that he was after spotting me. Smug bastard. After twenty and some years, too. It had never occurred to us that it might happen that way.'

Finn stared at Muldoon, his mind in a turmoil. The man seemed sane enough; his sceptical, slightly bitter expression hadn't changed.

'Do you mean,' said Finn, 'that Partington has known from the start that the IRA were involved in the Kilshaw business? Or guessed, at any rate?'

'Seems like it, Major.'

'But –'

'It seemed like a disaster at first. The way Sullivan had explained, you see, the whole thing depended on keeping us out of it until we had to show our hand. By then Partington would have found out for himself that there was some substance to what we'd said in the letter about Kilshaw. Otherwise, knowing Sullivan for what he is, he'd drop the whole thing for a swindle right away. That's what I thought. But I underestimated your man. It seems he had a different deal in mind altogether.'

'You mean a deal I don't know about?' said Finn.

Muldoon considered again. There was a kind of gloomy cordiality between the two of them. He said, 'There's a lot been kept from you, Major. Why do you think he sent you away to France at all? So you wouldn't be around when he came across to Ireland. You wouldn't be asking the awkward questions, such as why he came to Dublin via Belfast instead of direct, and why he caught a train south instead of flying, and who he might have met on the train. Not that I'd tell you the answers, mind, even if I was sure of them myself. It's no good asking me.'

Finn's head pounded. He felt suffocated by deception. First his plan to have the rifles seized from the boat had been given away to Sullivan. Now this. The two seemed obscurely but emphatically connected. Partington had lied to him – a lie of omission on a vital point. He had known about the IRA's involvement. Why hadn't he said so? Why had he allowed Finn to go through the elaborate charade of investigating Kilshaw's background and reaching the same answer by a different route? Was it only to be doubly sure? To guard himself against compromise? Or had Finn's entanglement been a deliberate part of his strategy?

Uneasily he remembered what Partington had said when they had discussed the danger of exposure: 'The only connection with the IRA has been through you... What *are* you, when all's said and done? ... Army officer, retired early, time on his hands, bit short of money, gets caught up in a shady venture...' Had that been the intention all along, to disown and discard him?

The consciousness of pain was being overtaken by a sick apprehension. It must have been about a quarter to eleven when the men cutting open the starboard bunker broke through to expose the rifles cached on that side of the boat. The work had gone quickly. From the port side the other volunteers had begun passing up the weapons and stowing them in the lorry. There was some excited chatter up on deck, stifled now and then by a sharp word from Sullivan as he supervised their work from the quayside. There could be little time left for Finn now.

'Isn't he coming back down?' he asked.

'I guess not, Major.'

Muldoon took out another cigarette; Finn noticed a slight tremor in his hands.

'I'd like that fag now,' he said.

Muldoon threw him one. He caught it, fumbled, dropped it beneath the small table to his right, and shifted across to retrieve it. Muldoon watched carefully but showed no sign of suspicion. The experiment had worked at the cost of his smoking a cigarette he didn't want. He caught the book of matches that was tossed to him and lit up. The unaccustomed smoke seared his throat. His hands trembled too. He had a sudden compulsive need to talk.

'It looks like you've got what you wanted,' he said. 'Partington and I worked out a scheme to stop Sullivan having those rifles. It looked all right at the time. It was stupid of me, I suppose, to look for morality as well as expedience.'

'I suppose it was, Major.'

'So you've won. You've beaten me, at any rate. But how long do you think you can go on with your madness in the North? Do you think two hundred guns will stop Kilshaw? On Thursday the Vigilantes will take the Catholic areas apart, brick by brick, and you'll be powerless to prevent them.'

'True enough.'

He stopped talking. A dangerous, nervous, patronizing tone had crept into Muldoon's voice. The rest of the rifles were now being moved from the starboard bunker. Men trotted round the deckhouse to throw the weapons one by one into the arms of others waiting on the quay. The old three-tonner coughed into life. Muldoon cleared his throat.

'We'll be going soon, Major.'

'Yes.'

Now the tramping of feet had ceased. The rifles were all on the lorry; the men were ashore, waiting for Muldoon to join them. And Muldoon was standing up slowly, the Luger pointing at Finn's middle. The gun shook visibly; there was a line of sweat along his upper lip.

In a nervous spasm Finn dropped the burning end of his cigarette so that it rolled off to the right. He went to pick it up, changed his mind, and ground it out with his heel. His hand stayed just where it had ended up, on his knee just below the edge of the table.

'You'd better turn round, Major.'

Finn kept his gaze fixed on the fevered eyes. 'To make it easier for you? No.'

'As you like, Major.'

Finn's temples pounded. He had to keep talking, he needed another ten seconds to complete a series of infinitesimal movements with his right hand. He said, 'You've done this before, of course – an accident with a bomb. I wonder if you've got the guts for the real thing.'

'I'm well prepared, Major. This was part of the deal, you see. Nothing personal.'

Muldoon licked his lips. His finger tightened on the trigger. Finn shot him three times from under the table.

The first bullet hit him in his groin, the second in the stomach as he was knocked back into a grotesque, doubled-over sitting position on the companionway steps, both hands clutching his genitals, the Luger tumbling to the deck. He stared at Finn with a tortured, disbelieving frown, mouth agape. The Colt fired once more from its fixed position, smashing Muldoon's front teeth and blowing out the back of his neck in a dark mushroom of blood and tissue that spattered against the bulkhead behind. He sighed and slid down the steps.

Finn wrenched the gun from beneath the table and stripped off the tape that had held it. He listened carefully. Over the hissing of the pressure lamps there came from the quayside only the rumble of the three-tonner's engine idling. They'd expected to hear shots. They were waiting for Muldoon.

The place reeked of cordite. The noise had been shattering in the confined space but would scarcely have been audible beyond the quay. He glanced down once at the dead man, who lay as limp and shapeless as the curiously depersonalized bundle of army-surplus clothing he had suddenly become. Blood gleamed between his legs. The deck was already slippery with it.

Finn turned out the lamp to make his silhouette less distinct. His mind was icily clear, his movements measured and deliberate. He climbed up the companion way and stepped out on deck.

The three-tonner, with a canvas awning over the back, stood about twenty yards down the quay to the left. At least two faces were visible, looking out over the tailgate.

He stepped over the rail, turned right, and began to walk away, not overhastily. You could always rely on a few seconds of confusion, hesitancy. The light was bad. The brewery barrels and the cover they afforded were forty yards away. He had walked ten, and then fifteen, and then came a shout.

'Hey, Muldoon!'

He kept walking, resisting the urge to run.

'Hey! This way, man!'

And then, 'Jasus Christ, it's the other one!'

Only noise would save him, the more of it the better. He turned round, raising the Colt, and emptied the remaining four bullets at the lorry. Then he turned and ran.

Darkness and street lights and reflections from the river swirled about him. He saw nothing clearly but the nearest stack of steel barrels, feeling as he ran a sudden and dreadful need to vomit. A few yards short of the stack he slipped on the wet cobbles, just as three or four high-velocity shots banged into the barrels above and Guinness came spouting down on him. He scrambled on all fours behind the stack, round two more, and then behind another one, where he crouched and tried to fight down the swelling nausea. Sullivan's men had loaded their new M-16s, and the tiny bullets were being pumped into the barrels all around him now with enough noise to wake the dead; foaming black Guinness streamed across the paving to run into the river and the gutters.

He counted carefully to twenty. His breathing became more normal and the nausea receded a little. The shooting had stopped. Behind him there was confusion and shouting as the volunteers realized what a racket they'd been making. Lights had come on aboard one of the brewery ships. And the lorry, which had started to reverse towards him with too much throt-tle, had stalled.

If they'd intended coming to get him it must have been that which finally discouraged them. Escape was now more impor-tant than pursuit. The starter motor rasped slowly for half a minute before Sullivan snapped out some instructions and the volunteers began to push.

A sailor had come out on the deck of the brewery ship, twenty yards away. 'What in the sweet name of Jasus is happening?' he muttered to someone inside the deckhouse. Finn pressed himself back into the shadows as the lorry, with six men shoving at the tailgate, came rattling past his hiding place. The engine gasped into life. Somewhere across the river a police siren began its ululating wail. The volunteers scrambled into the vehicle. Finn watched the tail light recede up the quay until the truck turned to cross over Butt Bridge.

They had got away.

The man on the ship had moved round to the stern, following the progress of the truck. A couple of hundred yards up the quay a small crowd seemed to be forming outside the pub, building up the courage to come down and investigate. Finn moved to cross the road and stumbled. There was a soft recumbent form among the barrels, another shapeless bundle of clothes. He bent down and rolled it onto its back. In the dim light he recognized at once the only two things he needed to know: firstly that the man was Seamus Fortune, and secondly that he was dead.

Finn stood up, slipped across the road, and entered one of the side streets leading south from the river. He turned right up Misery Hill, between two sections of the gasworks, and continued parallel to the Liffey behind the quay until he reached Peterson's Lane.

It was deserted. There were a few parked cars, all empty, no lights in any of the commercial buildings that lowered at each other across the narrow street. He did not even need to walk the full length of a hundred yards before he was certain of what he had begun to expect, that Partington was not there to meet him.

33

Customers were still being poured out of the pubs as Finn moved quickly southwards away from the river, uphill past Pearse station and behind Trinity College. It was a little after eleven; he was amazed at how quickly everything had happened.

He was not yet panicky, just aware of a growing helplessness as he walked the streets of a city where he had no friends. Well, where he might have one friend; it was by no means certain. There was just one place in Dublin where he could conceivably be safe. Stillorgan Road, Donnybrook: it was lucky he had remembered the address. Donnybrook, he knew, was a village that had become part of the suburban sprawl south of the city, and he trusted to luck that he could find it without asking the way. At this time of night and looking as he did – his eyebrow split, his clothes dirtied and bloodied and smelling of Guinness – he could not risk accosting strangers. He must leave absolutely no trace of his whereabouts. Head down, he hurried on through the quiet streets.

By now the police would have found the bodies of Muldoon and Fortune. They would quickly identify Muldoon as an IRA man, and with the other indications on the scene – the secret compartments in the bunkers, the Armalite cartridge cases on the quayside – they'd form a pretty good idea of what had happened. Before daylight they'd be turning Dublin inside out to find the rifles.

They would also be looking for Finn. He was the one who had brought the *Astrid* to Dublin and signed a false customs declaration, who had dismissed the crew and allowed Sullivan's men on board to remove the rifles. Yes, they would want him badly:

whether dead or alive, he was the scapegoat he had been intended to be. The customs and immigration people had his name, description, passport number: there was no hope of his slipping out of the country by a regular channel. There was only one way to go, only one person who might take him.

He stopped in Merrion Square to get his bearings. Then, turning left into Baggot Street, he was confronted by a public callbox. The opportunity seemed too good to miss; at the price of a couple of minutes' delay he could get one fact, at least, clearly established. He entered the callbox and dialled the number of the small hotel in Glasnevin. The woman he had spoken to at lunchtime answered.

'The English gentleman, was it? You've missed him again, so you have, and for good this time.'

'What time did he check out?'

'Sure he'd his luggage packed and waiting since this afternoon. Sharp on ten he was back to collect it. There was a chartered plane waiting on him at the airport, so he said.'

'Thank you.'

He walked on. There it was, then. Partington was almost back in London by now. Partington had not waited for him in Peterson's Lane because he had not expected Finn to leave the boat alive. It had been arranged that he shouldn't, arranged behind his back by the two men for whom he was supposed to be a go-between. Why? Finn felt something of the outrage that Walter Barnett had expressed when he learned he had been set up to be killed, but he could find no proper answer to the question.

There had been collusion, unknown to Finn, between Partington and Sullivan – collusion in effect between the British Government and an organization they were supposed to be fighting. Muldoon had talked about a meeting on a train. It seemed that Partington had guessed at the IRA connection as soon as he had seen Muldoon at Victoria Station, had used Finn to establish the connection more firmly, and then bypassed him to make direct contact with Sullivan. That much was clear. Finn had picked up only a hint of it when he discovered that Partington knew of the existence of Boyle's Bypass. The simple fact was that Partington's man inside Sullivan's Volunteers was Sullivan himself. But what kind of deal had they worked out? Obviously it did not involve the Kilshaw documents, because Partington had discovered they were worthless. They had become an irrelevance, a blind. But the rifles were certainly involved. Partington was giving Sullivan the rifles – in exchange for what? What price had he asked?

In a couple of minutes Finn had reached the Grand Canal. The narrow gash of water and its deserted towpaths could solve one of his problems. For a quarter of a mile he walked beside it, systematically stripping down the Colt pistol, wiping the parts separately with his handkerchief, and tossing them at irregular intervals into the dark water. They might be found eventually; it would not be soon enough to concern him. By the time he had discarded the last part of all, the firing pin, he had reached a hump-backed bridge where Leeson Street crossed the canal. Here he continued southwards, soon entering a broad avenue swathed in orange fluorescent lighting. There was still a fair volume of traffic but almost no pedestrians. He kept to the inside edge of the wide pavement, seeking what protection there was in the shadows of trees and hedges at the front of long gardens. His head throbbed and he ached in many places. He was tiring rapidly; he had not walked this far since his illness.

He also felt emotionally drained. He had been used. He had started out as a front man and finished up a stooge, valuable only for disguising Partington's real intentions from others who were curious – like Superintendent Crombie – because he did not know these intentions himself. Partington had never meant to betray Sullivan to the police. If things had gone wrong, if the shipment had been seized, Finn would have taken the blame. There was nothing to connect him with the British Government. There might have been suspicion; there would never be proof. And yet, again, why kill him? Why go to the lengths Partington had gone to, establishing beforehand that he was not armed so that he could be disposed of on board the tug? Finn was not dangerous simply because he knew of the collusion. There must be something else, some connection of ideas he had not yet made. If only he knew the details of the agreement between Partington and Sullivan, perhaps he might have the answer.

Admittedly, he had come close to upsetting things tonight. Fortune had come even closer. Partington had indeed waited in Peterson's Lane as he had promised – but only till ten o'clock, when he knew that Sullivan's men would have boarded the tug. Abound seven Fortune had brought him news of the discovery about the forged documents and the plan to call in the police. Fortune immediately became a danger. Sullivan had been informed. The noise Finn had heard while half asleep, from higher up the quay where Fortune crouched among the barrels...

There was a sour taste in Finn's mouth. Three men had died – Walter Barnett, Muldoon, Fortune – for what? Partington's original object, to stop Kilshaw, was still not accomplished. How did he now hope to do it? What was the price he had asked?

'Partington's price' – Finn realized he had repeated the phrase aloud. He was getting light-headed. He was suddenly aware of other voices round a corner, twenty yards ahead, and the sound of measured footsteps approaching. He stopped by a garden gate, transfixed. There was only one possible hiding place. He unlatched the gate, stepped into the garden, and stood with his back pressed against the privet hedge. The two policemen took an interminable time to stroll past. They were talking about the fishing in Lough Derg.

He walked on. He was haggard and frightened, his limbs aching, his clothes sticky from their soaking in Guinness. He had no idea how fast the police were working. A couple of times Garda patrol cars had cruised past, but their crews, if they had seen him, had not been interested enough to stop.

He found the house with providential ease.

It found him, really, because with a couple of turns the Morehampton Road, in which he'd been walking, became the Stillorgan Road and the number he wanted appeared almost immediately on his right, fixed to the gate of a rambling old bungalow. And Caragh's car was parked in the driveway, the Mini with the Northern numberplates. She was still here. Relief surged through him; he felt an absurd inclination to cry.

Only one light was on, behind windows with the curtains drawn to the left of the front door, and from the same room came the tail end of the midnight news headlines on the BBC. Finn rang the doorbell, heard the chimes in the hall, the sound of the radio being switched off and feet padding to the door.

'Who is it?' Her voice, down to a whisper and apprehensive.

'Finn. Please let me in.'

There was a sharp intake of breath and a second's hesitation before she unbolted the door. Her face looked pale and dramatic in the jaundiced light of the street lamps. She wore a silk kimono.

'Finn, whatever the hell...?'

'I need help, Caragh.'

'Are you all right? You smell all of –'

'Stout, yes. Spilt, not drunk.'

'Look at you – your eye! What...? Come in now. Just be quiet before you wake my mother.'

She closed the door behind him and led him through the entrance hall. The room with the light on was her own, kept ready for her visits, with warm autumn colours in the carpet, the curtains, the peasant rug on the divan, the tone feminine but slightly muscular. He sat down heavily on the divan.

'I want you to drive me North,' he said. 'Boyle's Bypass.'

'What are you after doing, Finn?'

'I've killed somebody.'

She stood facing him. Her expression did not change; only her eyes seemed to glaze slightly.

'His name is Muldoon. Was Muldoon. He was going to kill me, but I'd never prove that in court. I wouldn't last long enough to get to court. I've got to ask you to believe me. I must get out.'

'You don't have to explain,' she said.

'You've a right to know. You're the only one here I can trust.'

'This Muldoon,' she said. 'He was with Sullivan, wasn't he? So Sullivan's people will be looking for you. They won't look here. You could stay. They don't know that we're' – she searched for a word – 'friends.'

'I can't. The North isn't healthy for me either, but from there I can get to London. Just drop me on the border, anywhere.'

'You'd be safer going right through to Belfast.' She thought for a few seconds. 'I was just making up my mind to go back there anyway. I'm worried about my brother. You've heard about the ceasefire?'

'Good God!' He felt his jaw drop.

Caragh said, 'Sullivan declared a ceasefire in the North at half an hour's notice, starting at midnight. It was just on the news there. They'll stop what they call offensive operations against British troops, they're willing to take part in negotiations for peace with Kilshaw. There was a lot of other waffle about Irishmen uniting.'

'Could that be the price?' he wondered uncertainly.

Caragh didn't know what he was talking about. 'It's three years now we've been hearing this class of thing,' she said bitterly. 'A truce one minute, fighting again the next. I don't believe what any of them say any more – not Sullivan, any of them. What good is a ceasefire without the power to enforce it? Maybe it'll take the steam out of Kilshaw and his hooligans this time. What about the next and the next? Dear God, I begin to think they just enjoy fighting!'

He realized with a faint sense of embarrassment that she was close to tears.

She said abruptly, 'Let's get your face cleaned up,' and left the room.

When she returned, carrying a sponge and a basin of water, she was more composed. She stood over him dabbing at the wound on his eyebrow and washing the congealed blood from his cheek.

'You're probably right,' he said. 'There will be other times. But for the moment the ceasefire is part of the price Sullivan is prepared to pay.'

'What's this price you go on about?'

'Partington's price for supplying two hundred rifles to the IRA. The chance of peace in the North for the chance of making war – one day – in the South. That would be someone else's problem. But I wonder whether there's not more to it.'

'Do you mean,' Caragh said slowly, 'that the British would encourage a civil war here in the South?'

As she cleaned his face he had discovered, absently, that she was wearing nothing beneath the kimono. He said, 'If it brought peace to the North, why not? Revolutionary war is the term Sullivan would use. It wouldn't get far, but of course there'd be casualties. Politicians have to be coldblooded, you know. They'll talk about the sanctity of human life, but they can't help sneaking a look at the statistics. It's unavoidable, like comparing prices on a menu. Five hundred violent deaths in three years, that's the toll in the North. Do a few more in the South matter if it brings peace? In the end, the price always influences your choice. So we give Sullivan weapons to play at staging his workers' revolution some day. In exchange we get a ceasefire and something else. Who knows what?'

'There'll be no peace as long as Kilshaw is around,' she said. 'But it's Con Michael I'm worried about. He and Billy have been preparing for some special assignment. It's on Sullivan's personal orders, and dead secret. They're detached from the rest of the movement as a self-contained active service unit. I'm afraid they may not have heard about the ceasefire.'

'You've no idea what this special job is?'

'None at all. I'm just worried. Ceasefire or not, they won't let Billy get away with killing British soldiers. Con Michael never killed any, but they'll want him too. I want to find him, Finn, before they do.'

'Maybe I can help you look.'

'All right, I'll bring you to Belfast.'

'Is it safe for you yet? That business with the car...'

'They'll have other things on their minds by now.'

While she left the room with the bloodstained water he stood up and felt so giddy he had to slump back onto the divan. The events of the last two hours had caught up with him, flooding him with a terrible weariness. When Caragh returned he was sitting hunched forward with his face buried in his hands.

'What you want is sleep,' she said.

'No. We must get going.'

She shook her head. 'We mustn't cross into the North before daylight. In the dark any car travelling close to the border is liable to be stopped by the British Army.'

'So?'

'We'll be careful leaving Dublin and allow three and a half hours to reach the border. It won't be light till seven so we can't leave till half-three. Meanwhile let's both get some sleep. And let's get those beery clothes off you.'

He nodded gratefully. This was one time he wouldn't object to being mothered. Still sitting, he struggled out of his car coat, and without embarrassment Caragh helped him off with the rest of his clothes. He lay down, pulled the rug over himself, and was asleep even before she had snuggled down beside him and switched off the light.

34

Cars came down the hill at longer and longer intervals.

Traffic was always thin in Belfast at night, and the Ligoniel Road wasn't busy at the best of times. By twenty past twelve there was barely one car every ten minutes winding up or down through the hairpin bends. Con Michael, hunched uncomfortably in the driver's seat of the Land Rover, took out a cigarette, noting from the number left in the packet that it was his eighteenth that evening. He lit it and went on waiting.

He'd never been much good at waiting. His temperament wasn't right for it. Not like Billy, still as a snake, who'd been lying for two hours thirty yards up the hill on a groundsheet and surrounded by cushions and had not made a single sound loud enough to reach Con Michael through the hushed night air. And he'd stay there till dawn if he had to. There were times when Billy didn't seem human at all.

Con Michael drew on his cigarette and fidgeted, wondering whether to start up the engine again and idle it for five minutes to keep it warm. No. It couldn't be more than fifteen minutes since he'd last done that. He wondered if he might get out to stretch his legs. No again, reluctantly. They'd agreed to stay put. All very well for Billy. Con Michael contented himself with flexing the stiffened muscles of each limb in turn. Then he blew a few smoke rings and checked in the mirror, possibly for the twentieth time, that his face was still properly blacked.

From where he sat, facing up Wolf Hill from the entrance to the lane but screened by the hawthorn hedge of the garden at Rose Cottage, he could see the headlights of approaching cars over the brow of the hill half a minute before they began their descent. There was one coming now, the reflection of its lights washed up across the thinly clouded sky. He tensed up, counting the seconds, reaching for the cluster of powerful hand-held photoelectric floodlights that lay wired to their wet-cell unit on the seat beside him. The headlights themselves appeared over the crest, lancing down towards him before veering off to the right and disappearing for a few seconds as the car entered the first hairpin bend. Con Michael relaxed. The car was on its own. What they awaited was a convoy of three.

There were five bends in the road before it reached the sharpest one of all, just above Rose Cottage. It was on a low ridge twenty yards left of this that Billy lay, the night sight of his rifle focused on a point where the curve began to straighten out, the point where a car coming through was down to its lowest speed. Ever since Sullivan had briefed them they'd been measuring, timing, rehearsing. Mentally, they still were. Watching the zigzag approach of the car, imagining it the second vehicle in a convoy, Con Michael recited his drill. First bend, two light taps on the horn to signal Billy. Second bend, start engine; plenty of time left in case she didn't fire right away. Fourth bend, floodlights in position and lined up. Fifth bend, wait. On the sixth there was a marker, a whitewashed stone which they had placed on the inside edge of the road exactly halfway through the curve. The moment the second car obscured this from his view Con Michael would switch on the floodlights for exactly five seconds, full in the driver's face, blinding him and illuminating him. After that, whatever had happened, drop everything. Drive. Above all, don't stall. The leading car full of flunkeys should have overshot the entrance to the lane; the rear one wouldn't get round the sharp corner in one go. Even then, they wouldn't be able to follow the Land Rover far along the broken track. Slow down just long enough to pick up Billy and away. They and the car would be safely hidden down the hill in eight minutes.

The lone car passed by and meandered on down the Ligoniel Road. Con Michael crushed out his cigarette. He'd wondered at times about Sullivan's motive for this, wondered whether they weren't playing into the wrong hands. But Sullivan had offered no explanation and Con Michael knew better than to ask. Sullivan saw things from a loftier height. His perspective was better. It was military common sense for the man on the ground not to know too much about the strategic thinking behind his orders. So Con Michael rationalized; in fact his trust was absolute. All the same, he couldn't help wondering.

He reached out for another cigarette, then noticed light flickering above the horizon again. He waited, watching. The headlights came bouncing over the hilltop and vanished round the first bend to begin the roller-coaster descent. Immediately he saw the second pair, just a few moments behind. Yes; and the third. Here, unmistakably, unbelievably, was their man.

The leading car was through the first bend now and the second was going into it. Faintly he could hear the carillon of changing engine notes as gears were shifted up and down.

Con Michael clenched his fist and bounced it twice on the horn. In answer came the first sound he had heard from Billy all evening, the snick of the rifle being cocked.

35

Sometime around three o'clock Finn awoke. He lay on his side with Caragh's warm shape curled in behind him. He turned towards her. She was awake too.

'Good sleep?' she asked, smiling.

'It helped.'

He still ached, but the sick fatigue of three hours before had receded. He lay for a minute looking at Caragh. In the dimness of the room her face was palely luminescent, like Dresden china, her lips full and dark and inviting. He leaned over and kissed her. Her arms went silkily around him; her body moved against his.

Through the fear and pain and tiredness desire flickered, caught, and burned. The belt of her kimono was undone. He slid his hand beneath it, exploring her body with a kind of sleepy wonder; the full breasts, the firm buttocks, the strong, supple muscles of her back and belly, the coarse warm hair between her legs all had a particular freshness, as if the longings that had been dormant in him so long were not merely awakened but re-created.

'There'll be no phones ringing this time,' she whispered, and wriggled out of the kimono. They caressed each other, languidly at first, then in a mounting feverish rhythm until Caragh's green eyes were fiery and the fragrance of animal lust had penetrated the milk and bath-oil bouquet of her skin. Finn thrust his knee between her thighs and rolled onto her.

With his carnal quickening a strange feeling grew, a lightening of his spirit as if all the sensibilities he had suppressed over the months were being liberated in a rush. There was affection as well as desire, tenderness – even joy – as well as physical release. In the moment that he pushed himself into her and heard her gasp of shock and pleasure he sensed that he was suddenly close to being a whole person again.

Afterwards they dozed for twenty minutes, made love again, and lay for a while looking into each other's eyes.

'I grew to be afraid of emotion,' he said. 'Any emotion. Maybe that's why I hated people pitying me, because I deserved to be pitied.'

'Maybe.'

'It's not like that any more. What I feel for you is... I don't know. Unusual?'

'And me.'

'Maybe, when this business is settled...' He didn't quite know what to say. Did he want her as a mistress, a wife, a friend? He knew only that he needed her. There were so many uncertainties.

'I know what you're thinking,' she said. 'Shall we wait a while and see?'

He kissed her. 'Do you want to be convinced?'

'No!' She laughed and rolled away from him. 'Come on, it's gone half-three.'

Reluctantly they got dressed and left the house.

From Donnybrook in the south-east of Dublin they had to take a long way round the city, moving in a wide irregular arc on deserted rural roads to Clonee, where they picked up the north-westerly T35 to Navan and settled down for the journey to the border. Once clear of the city they did not expect to meet roadblocks. It was more than four hours now since the police must have arrived at the tug, but as long as they had not intercepted Sullivan's men they couldn't yet know the full story. Muldoon's killer would be expected to go to ground in Dublin; for a member of the movement to flee North was to choose the fire against the frying pan. But there was no harm in being careful.

Caragh drove with her usual competence, but not so fast as to attract attention from any patrolling police car. Finn dozed in the passenger seat, wishing there were a radio in the car. Not that it would have helped, since not a single station in the British Isles was on the air at this time of night. He wanted news. Out here on the road, away from the cocoon-like security of Caragh's bed, all his fears and all the misgivings they had both had returned with renewed force.

Beyond Navan, the flat wet farmlands of County Meath rushed by in the darkness. The nearest town to the crossing point was Monaghan; the main road there criss-crossed the border and had customs posts at intervals, so to avoid it as far as possible Caragh turned off among the low hills of Cavan. They picked their way northwards from village to village, moving slowly but unerringly along narrow potholed lanes between the farms. Rich manure smells reached them; the stone cottages were still in darkness, but a streak of grey had appeared on the flat horizon to the right and the first cocks were crowing. In forty minutes they had picked up the road again. Once through Monaghan they stopped in a lay-by, screened by a hedge, and drank the coffee Caragh had brought in a vacuum flask. Between them was the tranquil warmth of spent passion.

'We'll be there in just a few minutes,' Caragh said. 'Boyle's farm is near a wee village called Ballyclareen. He's an old supporter of the movement. His land runs right up to the border, and there's a tractor path leading off to the other side. The police don't even know it exists.'

They sat silent for a minute, finishing the coffee. Then Caragh said, 'Are you really cured of your illness?'

'Really and truly. I've got a clean bill of health.'

'But you hadn't, had you, when you first started this job? Is that why they gave it to you, because they couldn't really believe you would live anyway? You hardly believed it yourself at one time.'

The idea had never struck him before. He was appalled. 'Nobody would do that. But yes – Partington would. That man is capable of anything. *Anything*,' he added, unconsciously falling into Partington's style of speech. He was suddenly irritable. 'Well, I won't give them the satisfaction of dying, not after coming this far. Let's drive on.'

The border between the Republic and Northern Ireland is perhaps the most unrealistic in the world, a ragged and arbitrary line superimposed fifty years before on a pattern of fields and farms and villages that had formed over centuries. The farms and fields were undisturbed by the political abstraction, as were the roads, hundreds of lanes and byways and farm tracks that had been there much longer than the frontier. The authorities had declared all but two dozen of the main crossing points 'un-approved' – a defeatist term if ever there was one. Since the smuggling of arms and explosives from the South had increased, the British had taken to blowing craters in some unapproved roads and patrolling the others frequently. But Boyle's Bypass suffered from none of this attention.

They passed through Ballyclareen, half a mile from the border, and within a couple of hundred yards turned through a pair of gates into the small farm. Across a sloping meadow the sun was rising into a sky that promised to be clear and sparkling. The farmer himself was loading milk churns onto a trailer and he came over at once, touching his cap; then he saw Finn and looked at Caragh questioningly.

'All right now, Mr Boyle,' she said. 'This is a friend.'

'Sure, you'll forgive me staring,' said Boyle. 'If it was any of the wanted ones I'd be advising you not to bring them across this morning. There's a lot of activity across there, what with patrols and convoys.'

'Is something up?' Finn asked. Boyle caught the English inflexion in his voice and studied him suspiciously again until Caragh said, 'You can talk in front of him.'

'Well, I couldn't say what's up at all, only for lorries and armoured cars on the move. Not in this direction, mind, towards Armagh and Belfast. Never seen it like that before, only in a crisis.'

'But there's a ceasefire,' Caragh said. 'There's been a ceasefire since midnight.'

Boyle scratched his unshaven chin. 'There was something else. They know about this route now. There was a group of them hiding in the hedge down the end of my track. Gone now, mind.'

'An ambush!' Finn muttered.

'They gave up waiting whenever it got light.'

'Someone must have told them. What the hell is happening? Have you heard any news this morning?'

'Not this nor any morning,' Boyle said. 'I've no wireless and no papers. What doesn't reach my ears anyway isn't worth hearing, that's my belief.' He grinned and touched his cap. 'You know the way, Miss. It's safe enough now, but you'd be best not to use the route again for a week or two.' He turned and went back to his churns.

The tractor path led off the main farmyard, through two iron gates that Finn had to leave the car to unlatch, and then ran behind a long hedge in which the ambush party had waited. The track suddenly intersected a narrow tarred road where Caragh turned left. They were in Northern Ireland, as easily as that. A few minutes later they were on the main road to Armagh, following a long convoy of Green Howards in troop carriers. The men whistled at Caragh; indifferently, she overtook their vehicles one by one.

Finn said, 'There's two companies of men there. I'd like to

know where they're going. I'd like to know what's going on in this crazy country. Who did they expect to walk into that ambush? Us?'

Soon after that he fell into a doze. He was vaguely aware of entering Armagh and stopping at a filling station. Caragh got out of the car. He sat sleepy and empty-headed, breathing petrol fumes, until she rapped sharply on his window.

She was mouthing at him and holding up a newspaper. It was the *News Letter*. For a second he wondered why she had bought a Unionist paper. Then his gaze was drawn down from the mast-head to the headline that bellowed across eight columns:

KILSHAW ASSASSINATED

Suddenly, sickeningly, he knew what Partington's price had been.

36

It had happened early enough to catch most editions of the morning papers. The *News Letter* account was fairly detailed. A strapline above the main heading read, VIGILANTE lEADER IS GUNNED DOWN AS 'CEASEFIRE' BEGINS, and there was a subhead: RUC HUNT TWO REBEL IRA KILLERS.

'Partington's price,' Finn repeated numbly.

'I don't understand.'

Caragh had come round to the driver's door and stood staring at him, her face empty with shock.

'The rifles were given to Sullivan in exchange for two things,' he said. 'Not just the ceasefire, but the death of Kilshaw. Timed to coincide, so that neither Sullivan nor the British could be held responsible.'

'Instead...?'

'Yes. The blame falls squarely on your brother and Billy McGarry. Have you read this? There's no doubt they're the two. This was the special job Sullivan had lined them up for. He must have convinced them that it would serve some revolutionary purpose. The minute it was done he turned on them, denounced them. They weren't warned about the truce. Someone had to take the blame, you see. The movement will reject them. Safe houses will be closed to them.'

Caragh said blankly, 'That bastard!'

He read the first paragraphs of the main story again:

Loyalist Vigilante leader James Kilshaw was shot dead by IRA gunmen as he drove into Belfast at 12:30 this morning – half an hour after the ceasefire called by

Colin Sullivan, leader of the militant Sullivan's Volunteer faction of the IRA, was due to begin.

Mr Kilshaw was shot twice in the head with a high-velocity rifle in a carefully planned ambush at Rose Cottage corner on the Ligoniel Road. He was on his way home from a Vigilante rally at Crumlin.

His car was in a convoy of three vehicles containing Vigilante bodyguards as well as Special Branch men. As the car slowed to less than 10 miles an hour to negotiate a hairpin bend, one terrorist shone a powerful floodlight in Mr Kilshaw's eyes and the other opened fire. He died instantly.

It seemed that the bodyguards had returned the fire but had not been able to prevent the killers escaping in a Land Rover. They had fled down the Glencairn Road. A search party later discovered a deserted farmhouse and barn nearby which had apparently been used recently as a headquarters for Sullivan's movement.

There was one paragraph of special significance:

In Dublin Sullivan immediately denounced the assassination, saying it was the work of dissidents acting against orders. They would be punished, he added. Mr Kilshaw's deputies in the ruling council of the Vigilante movement described the murder as a 'barbaric outrage.' But they added in a statement: 'Sullivan has declared a ceasefire and we must put his good faith to the test. Plans for the invasion of rebel strongholds will be suspended until the killers are captured and their action can be shown to be unauthorized.'

The Vigilantes would help in the search for the assassins, they said, adding ominously that they would not be held responsible for acts of retaliation provoked by the outrage.

The text of Sullivan's statement was at the bottom of the front page. He understood the killers to be a former high-ranking officer and a former volunteer in his movement. They were automatically expelled. The movement, too, would throw all its energies into capturing and punishing them. It had never been the policy of socialist Republicans to make sectarian war against their fellow Irishmen. Mindless violence could achieve nothing...

Etcetera. The high-mindedness was nauseating. As Finn lowered the paper his eye caught a paragraph in the Stop Press column. Mobs – or 'crowds,' as the *News Letter* preferred – of angry Vigilantes were out on the Shankill Road. Extra troops were rushing in to protect Catholic homes.

Caragh sat next to him now, looking as though she would like to cry if she could.

'Now we know who the ambush was for,' Finn said. 'Where will he go?'

'Oh, God, I don't know. Nowhere's safe. Here if the police don't get him the Vigilantes will. Down South it'll be Sullivan. England, perhaps? He's friends in London who might help him, if it's not too late already. The wee fool! If I could just have kept a closer watch on him...'

'London's no safer than anywhere,' he said. 'The IRA has too many friends there. He could give himself up and tell the truth, only nobody will want to listen. A temporary peace may come out of this; the more precarious peace is, the more severely the ones who threaten it are punished. Society becomes self-righteous. In Belfast he'll have nowhere unless it's your own house, and he won't last long there.'

'Jesus, Finn, don't talk, let's get there.'

The tears did not come but she had begun to shiver. Finn took the wheel, and in a little while they had picked up the M1 motorway and were heading for Belfast at eighty miles an hour. Incongruously, the day was splendid; the sun was in his eyes.

Sullivan and Partington. His mind could still hardly embrace the meaning of what they had agreed to do: to alter history slightly, no more or less. Sullivan believed in history, or claimed to, while Partington was fascinated by its clockwork. Between them they had murdered Kilshaw as surely as if they had shared in squeezing the trigger of Billy McGarry's rifle. Unwittingly, Finn had helped too. Now he understood why he had been meant to die as well – because as Partington's front man, shielding him from too blatant a connection with the IRA, he had also been the only witness to his involvement. While Finn had patiently traced the worthless documents, events had moved ahead of him. The ultimatum had been issued; somewhere in the labyrinth of committees and ministries, the drastic remedy had been chosen.

The timing had been crucial. Coming at the same time as the announcement of a ceasefire, it reduced the Vigilantes to confusion. Coming a day before their ultimatum was due to expire, it set off their reaction at half cock. Hatred of the IRA was their driving force, Kilshaw their mainspring. By the time they had re-formed round a new leader their *raison d'être* would have gone.

Curving in from the south-west, the motorway entered Belfast through the neck of low ground that lay between the hills and the river. Shortly before debouching its traffic into the streets, the road offered a sudden wide view of the city, a carpet of grey rooftops sloping down to the shipyards and the Lough. There was smoke, at least a dozen pillars of dark smoke, rising in the still air above Andersonstown, the Falls, and the city centre to dissolve in a haze high up in the brilliant blue sky.

'Catholic houses,' Caragh said dully. 'They're burning Catholic houses. For once I can't say I blame them.'

'Tomorrow they'd have burned anyway – a lot more of them, a lot more fiercely. That's the calculated risk Partington is taking.'

They came off the motorway approach road and drove through Andersonstown. The atmosphere in the streets was a shock, perceptible even from within the car, the tangible sense of an ugly and degrading fear. It was there in the way people scurried along the pavements and gathered in aimless, fidgety groups, as if waiting for a pronouncement of some kind. They talked little but their eyes were sharp with an anxiety they had lived with for three years, that one day the Protestant beast would be provoked too far. Some families were getting out altogether: rickety vans and trailers were being piled with mattresses, prams, hire-purchase washing machines, children, dogs, budgerigars. There were a lot of troops about, for once moving freely without having bricks thrown at them. Suddenly they were the best friends a Catholic could have.

'This could be the start,' Caragh said. They both knew what she meant.

'Civil war? No, I don't think so.'

'The thing that's always in the back of people's minds here. You live with it, like the knowledge of your own death.'

'The Vigilantes have had the wind knocked right out of them,' he said. 'Suddenly there's nothing left to fight against and they've lost the one man who would have led them into a fight anyway. Of course they'll be on the rampage a couple of days before they quieten down.'

In Roger Casement Park, the scene of many a rally of IRA sympathizers, an army bivouac had been hastily set up. The red berets of the hated paratroopers moved among vehicles parked on the lawns, surrounded by children who yesterday would have stoned them as readily as they now gathered to watch.

'Revenge is what they want,' Finn said. 'The culprits have been clearly singled out. Con Michael and Billy between them make a good composite scapegoat – everything the famous silent majority dislikes and distrusts, a long-haired radical teamed up with a working-class lout. Rejected even by their own people. Well, where do we start looking?'

'Our house. At least to eliminate it. After that it's all guesswork.'

Somehow it was tacitly agreed that they would search for Con Michael together, that they must do everything they could to find him. Not that if they did there was anything much they could do for him. Finn was helping partly for Caragh's sake and partly for more personal reasons. Con Michael had been a bloody little fool, the victim of his own arrogance and naïvete; he had also, like Finn, been the victim of a conspiracy that was not of his own making. Finn knew that if he were destroyed a lot of people would get an inexplicable pleasure out of it; it seemed important to deny them that pleasure. Nothing united people like the primal urge to defend, destroy. He was reminded of Partington's analogy about a pack of dogs. Maybe there was a way to stop them fighting – by making a couple of rabbits run past.

They had turned into Coolnasilla Park. Finn discovered, absently, that one of the plumes of smoke to which they had been drawing closer was now right in front of them. But he was more immediately aware of a wedge of men blocking the street fifty yards ahead. There might have been a hundred of them, facing the other way, some making quick violent gestures which, through the film of blue smoke that hung across the road, Finn failed to recognize until he saw the line of troops in riot gear formed up beyond them. Then he heard the clatter of stones and the ragged jeers.

'Love of God,' Caragh said. 'It's our house!'

The house must have been on fire several minutes and was just beginning to burn really fiercely. Flames licked at the paint on doors and window frames, thick coils of smoke rose from beneath the eaves, and, even as Caragh spoke, the heat shattered the glass in an upstairs window and smoke came gushing out.

'What if he's in there?' she said, aghast.

Finn punched the car into reverse to make a three-point turn. From down the street came a couple of bangs from Very pistols, and the crowd fell back towards them from the blossoming white vapour of CS nausea gas. Some of them, men and teenage boys in army surplus gear, were close enough now for Finn to see the Vigilante armbands; they carried sticks, bottles, lengths of chain. He reversed across the street and slammed into first gear.

'He may be inside,' Caragh said. Before he could stop her she had opened the door and leaped out.

'Come back!' he yelled. She was going at a stumbling run towards the front gate. He scrambled out after her, glancing at the Vigilantes. Those who had caught sight of Caragh watched her curiously. Then came recognition, with a howl like the baying of bloodhounds.

'It's his sister!'

'Get the bitch!'

Till now she seemed barely to have noticed them but she hesitated at the gate, held back by a solid wall of heat from the house, and looked round. Finn caught up with her. Perhaps twenty men had turned from stoning the troops and were running towards them; they were no more than thirty yards away. Through the confusion of smoke and CS gas and noise Finn saw the soldiers break through the line, riot clubs swinging. Beyond them was a flash of red: a fire engine.

Caragh stood bewildered. 'Move!' Finn said, seizing her arm.

A stone flung from twenty yards grazed her shoulder and decided her. Together they turned to run up the street.

It was already too late. Another crowd of men was surging across the unfenced lawns from the right. They were trapped between the two groups.

His mind reeled in confusion before settling on the only possibility: somehow to barge through to the advancing soldiers. He turned Caragh round again. The nearest of the Vigilantes was ten yards away, bounding towards them, raising his club.

Something hit Finn square between the shoulder-blades. He fell to one knee, groped for the half brick, and stood up just in time to smash it into the face of the Vigilante. He was a boy of about sixteen. He squealed, clutched at his face, and dropped the pickaxe handle. Finn seized it and rammed it into the stomach of the next man. But now the rest were on top of him, driven forward by the troops and the gas, a punching, panting, cursing sprawl of men who wrenched the club out of his grasp and kicked his feet from under him. Falling, he glimpsed Caragh held from behind by one man and tigerishly fighting off another who had ripped open her coat and the front of her dress. The crunch of breaking glass told him the car was being wrecked.

He was kicked twice in the ribs before he managed to seize the foot and bring the man toppling down onto him. Three or four others piled on to punch and gouge at whatever they could see. The next CS cartridge landed right in the middle of them.

It was a windless day; the gas billowed up in a wide, even mushroom. Before anyone had time to grab the cartridge and fling it away they were retching, coughing, blinded. Finn's stomach heaved as he thrashed his way out from under the heap of struggling men. His eyes streamed; his throat and lungs shrieked with the agony of the fumes.

He rolled clear, still retching. There was nothing for his stomach to throw up, and only a pool of sour saliva formed on the tarred roadway beneath his face. Between spasms he looked up, blinking through his tears. The dissolving gas drifted slowly up the street, together with the stragglers from the Vigilante mob; those who had been affected by it crawled, vomited, and stumbled, harried by the troops who were now in control of the street. Firemen hurried about and the flames crackled angrily as the first jet of water hit the burning house. Two soldiers, faceless behind gas masks and plastic visors, were taking turns thumping a teenager's head against a lamppost. A sharp word of command came from just over Finn's shoulder; the men let go of the boy and moved away. Finn recognized the voice.

He had to retch again before he could turn his head. Major Howarth stood looking down at him with an unpleasant smile.

'You're damned lucky, Finn. It was sheer luck that I spotted you among this lot.'

'I'm grateful,' Finn said, but still had to swallow his resentment of the man.

'What the devil brought you here? Don't you know better than to stay off the streets today?'

Once more Finn had to strain emptily, his face a few inches from the ground. His eyes were like hot coals, his head pounding, his throat raw. He said, 'What are *you* doing fire-brigading? I thought you'd be hunting assassins.'

'That too,' Howarth said. He was unamused and tired. 'We're all stretched to the limit. Ah,' he exclaimed knowingly, looking up as Caragh approached on the arm of a sergeant. 'Now I begin to understand. I take it you're Miss Hughes.'

She had not suffered from the gas as badly as Finn, but she was pale with shock. She clutched the lapels of her coat together to cover the tear in her dress.

'Yes...?' Her voice faltered. Involuntarily she glanced back at the flames still raging through the house.

'You're looking for your brother, aren't you?' For a malicious moment Howarth enjoyed the suspense. 'No, he's not in there,' he said brusquely. 'We haven't found him yet, but it's only a matter of time. For his own sake I hope we get there before the Vigilantes or the IRA do.'

Five minutes later they stood beside Howarth's Saracen armoured personnel carrier, drinking hot, sweet tea from enamel mugs. The troops squatted on neighbouring lawns taking a smoke break. The firemen had beaten down the flames and the house was a smoking shell, with walls still intact but everything inside destroyed. Bricks and glass littered the road. Caragh's car had had all its windows smashed; the Vigilantes had had no time to inflict further damage.

'Yes, they're disorganized, leaderless,' Howarth said. 'There's no direction from the top. The only thing they're doing systematically is burning down houses. Every place they can lay their hands on where IRA sympathizers are thought to live is going up. Understandable, perhaps. I suppose they reckon on flushing out Hughes and McGarry sooner or later.'

'What do you think?' Caragh asked. 'Will they?'

Howarth looked at her dubiously. The question had been mechanical yet deliberate; she was still in a state of shock. Finally he shrugged, deciding she couldn't know anything. If she did, she would hardly have let herself be drawn into this mess.

'Well,' he said, 'we've been raiding all the so-called safe houses we know since early this morning. Nothing. Cooperation from the people too – a rare phenomenon. It's obvious that the movement isn't sheltering them, which means either they've slipped out of the country or they've found a hiding place of their own – somewhere private, perhaps, unconnected with the movement. It can only be temporary, of course.' Again he enjoyed a moment's pause. 'You'd better face it, Miss Hughes. Without the IRA behind them, without people to shelter them, they can't survive. Arrest is the best they can hope for. Well, we must away. Give you a lift somewhere?'

'We'll manage with the car,' said Finn coldly.

'You'd be best off in an hotel keeping your heads down,' Howarth said. 'Nowhere out of doors is safe.'

They walked back to the Mini. Caragh sat in what seemed a numb silence while Finn plucked the remaining slabs of crazed glass out of the windscreen and the rear window. Then he got into the car. Howarth and the riot squad were moving off in their vehicles.

'Tactful bastard, that one,' said Finn.

She turned towards him, her look still remote and uncomprehending.

'I've an idea I know where we may find them,' she said.

37

It was a hunch, no more than that, but it was better than any-thing else they had to go on. The trouble was that it involved crossing from one side of the city to the other, over the River Lagan to the Short Strand area, a small Catholic enclave adjoining the shipyards and surrounded on three sides by Protestant streets.

In the normal way, with the religious boundaries drawn as clearly as they were, one chose one's route to avoid potentially hostile territory. Today the demarcations were meaningless. The Vigilantes swarmed everywhere; the army confronted them wherever it could afford the manpower. Finn drove cautiously down the Falls and the Grosvenor Road towards the city centre, making wide detours whenever the sight of smoke or the sounds of stone-throwing ahead indicated Vigilantes on the rampage. Apart from such noises these Catholic streets were unnaturally hushed. There was little traffic other than army vehicles; the few people out on the streets stood, as they had in Andersonstown, in small, self-preserving groups.

Cold air whistled through the car, numbing their cheeks.

'It was what he told us there about a hiding place that reminded me,' Caragh said. 'Somewhere they could be on their own and not be dependent on other people.'

'They couldn't last like that,' Finn pointed out. 'Soon they'd need food, money.'

'All they'd think of at first would be to hide. There was a place they and a few other Republican lads used to go until a year ago, a jazz club.'

'Billy mentioned it to me,' he said.

'It wasn't a real club at all, just an old empty house in the Short Strand that they kind of took over. They brought me there once. Billy had installed a bit of a stereo. He and Con Michael were the only ones who went there regularly, and once they had to go on the run the club just went out of existence. But I'll bet the house is still there and still empty. It had nothing to do with the movement at all, so Sullivan's people oughtn't to know about it.'

Finn nodded. 'Sounds like a prospect.'

Though he was still willing to help find Con Michael, he did not welcome the idea of further effort. He ached with weariness; every muscle felt bruised. The nausea gas still brought a clutching to his throat from time to time, and its stink clung to his clothes. He drove in a daze through the main shopping centre and round the white Christmas-cake City Hall; here there was less evidence of the day's violence, but these streets too were half deserted. The air seemed heavy with menace.

Just east of the city centre in the Markets area, another Catholic enclave, two or three houses and a couple of vehicles were burning. Turning into a side street when a barricade of wrecked cars blocked his way, he had to reverse hastily to avoid a prowling gang of Vigilantes. But in a minute he had found his way back to the street leading to the Lagan and to the Albert Bridge which crossed it.

Across the river the Short Strand came into sight. It was a street of uninspired dun-coloured brick terraces that ran for a quarter of a mile parallel to the Lagan. Most of the small identical houses were on the far side of the street, the river frontage being taken up by warehouses and wharves. Finn noticed these things in the moment before he saw something else. The Albert Bridge was blocked. A line of troops was drawn up behind portable barbed-wire barricades against a crowd of several hundred Vigilantes clearly determined to get from this side of the river across to the Short Strand. There was a bit of jostling but no fighting yet. The officer in charge seemed to be trying to persuade the men to go away, but as Finn slowed the car on the approach to the bridge a jeer went up.

'Try the other bridge,' Caragh said. 'Lower down.'

The Queens Bridge was sealed off too, but the Vigilantes had ignored this barricade to concentrate their forces in one spot. Cars were not being allowed across. Finn parked the battered Mini in an adjoining side street and they walked to the barrier.

Caragh did the talking. Only her accent got them through. 'Live over there, do you?' said the cockney sergeant. 'I was you, I'd keep clear. Things'll be getting naughty soon. Up to you. Hop it then, if you're going.'

They moved across the bridge. Ahead and slightly to the left were the shipyards, strangely silent; the enormous Goliath building crane which dominated the head of the Lough was immobile. Finn recalled reading that the Loyalists who formed a large majority of the work force in the yards were striking for the day to protest over the assassination. Just as they reached the east bank of the river the familiar sounds of conflict began on the Albert Bridge upstream – stones thudding into riot shields, yells, bottles breaking, the popping of Very pistols. The Vigilantes were trying to storm the barricade; it looked as though the Short Strand was the one Catholic area they had not yet managed to invade. Finn and Caragh hurried on. The time was just after ten.

The dilapidated little street awaited its fate. Families who had not been able to move out seemed to have locked themselves into their houses, the windows shut, the curtains drawn. The small corner shops were closed too. Not a child or a cat was out of doors. There was an incongruous bravado about the pro-IRA graffiti on the warehouse walls opposite. Caragh stopped as they were about to enter the street.

'I thought I knew exactly where the house was. Now I'm not

sure at all. It was fifteen months ago I was here, and at night. By day it looks different.'

'We'll have to work our way up it,' Finn said wearily. 'Let's get a move on.'

They began walking, looking over each house as they went. All of them were deceptively quiet and it was sometimes difficult to tell which were empty and which occupied, but within a couple of minutes they had found three that were definitely derelict, with windows boarded up and paint peeling from the front doors that led straight out onto the pavement. People were gradually being moved out under a slum clearance programme. None of the three, Caragh thought, had housed the jazz club.

As they drew nearer the Albert Bridge the ragged sounds of fighting between the troops and the Vigilantes grew louder and clearer. They could see white puffs of CS gas rising steadily through the still air. By the time they were three quarters of the way up the Short Strand they had passed seven abandoned houses. At the eighth Caragh paused, studying it.

'It could be this one. If only I could be sure...'

'If only,' said Finn, a trifle acidly.

'This door was painted cream, wasn't it? The club had a light-coloured door, I know that.'

The place looked little different from the others, mortar crumbling from between the bricks, the single ground-floor window broken and boarded up from inside with an uneven row of planks. Caragh took a hesitant step forward, put her face close to a gap between the planks, and peered inside. She called softly, 'Con Michael?'

No reply came. Finn tried the door impatiently; it did not budge. If the fugitives had entered the house they'd have had to force the lock.

'Nothing there,' he said. 'Either you've got the wrong place or they didn't come here anyway.'

From the bridge there came a sudden desperate volley of Very shots, drowned almost at once by the triumphant roar of the crowd. Finn looked up, startled. Above the balustrade and silhouetted against the clouds of gas he saw the heads of dozens of running men, the swinging of clubs, a length of barricade being bodily lifted and flung down into the river. The Vigilantes had broken through; they were invading the Short Strand.

'That's it,' he said. 'Let's get out.'

There were some houses they had still not checked, but this time she needed no persuading. Death had seemed very close in Coolnasilla that morning; if they were caught this time it was almost certain.

They turned away. Over the swelling tumult from the approaching Vigilantes they both heard another noise, quite distinctly: the breaking of glass. It came from deep inside the house.

They looked at each other incredulously. Someone *was* inside. Someone was breaking out through a back window.

'It's them!' Caragh said. 'It's got to be!'

'We're too late to do anything.'

'We can't abandon them. Don't you see, they're trying to get away from *those*.'

Desperately glancing up the street he saw the Vigilantes pouring off the end of the bridge. A straggling soldier who had tried to stop them was down on his knees, helmet off, being beaten insensible. They were less than two hundred yards away. Finn flung himself shoulder first at the door.

It gave more easily than he had expected. It burst open to send him tumbling several feet down the hallway. A length of staircase banister that had been used to wedge the door rolled away. So they had broken the lock. He stood up, covered in dust, and strode down the cramped little hall to the kitchen.

Whoever had been there was gone. Whoever had smashed the

window above the sink with its swollen and jammed wooden frame had cut himself badly in the process. Blood clung to the jagged edge of glass along the bottom and had trickled down the wall into the sink. Finn knelt on the stone draining-board and looked out through the hole. Behind the house was a tiny yard, an outside lavatory, a gate hanging on one hinge and opening into an alley.

'We'll follow,' he said to Caragh, who had come in after him. 'It's safer this way anyhow.'

As he stripped off his leather coat he heard the sounds of destruction from up the street – windows breaking, women screaming abuse. Soon there would be fires. He folded the coat over the broken glass and slid feet first out of the window. Caragh followed. Across the yard, through the gate and down the alley to the left, drops of blood a few inches apart formed a trail that gleamed in the sunshine. They went the way fleeing men would go instinctively, away from the Vigilante onslaught, towards the Queens Bridge and the shipyards. But what then? Where was there left for Con Michael and Billy to go?

They followed the trail, walking and trotting alternately as Finn tried to conserve the little strength he had left. They turned right and then left again down another alley running parallel to the first. The Vigilantes had not yet discovered this maze of grey brick walls and broken flagstones and overflowing dustbins, but they would not be far behind. The small blots of blood, sometimes separate, sometimes running together in a brief, bright flower chain, continued undiminished. Finn did not draw Caragh's attention to the obvious conclusion – that the injured man, whoever he was, had cut an artery. Not a critical injury in itself, but if he went on running and pumping out blood at this rate he would soon feel the effects.

He was feeling them already. A little way before the alley opened out on the Queens Bridge approach road opposite the shipyards, the trail ended behind the protruding wall of an outside lavatory. There were several patches of blood three or four inches across on the ground, and smudged red hand marks on the wall. Beyond this point there were no more drops.

'They've bound him up,' Finn said. 'They've stopped the flow with a tourniquet.'

The two of them came cautiously out into a wide intersection and looked around. A couple of hundred yards to the left the soldiers were still guarding the Queens Bridge. The fugitives would not have gone in that direction. To the right, three or four families who'd evacuated their houses were moving down the pavement carrying a pathetically ill-chosen collection of belongings – transistor radios, fishing rods, a reading lamp. Caragh and Finn followed; it seemed as good a way as any. At the next corner a jeep was parked and a group of refugees with their possessions piled in a handcart were arguing with a very angry and red-faced young Welsh Guards captain.

'We're bloody trying to save your bloody homes,' he was saying. 'What more do you want, for Christ's sake?'

'Yez should be chasin' them that started it all, that's what!' shouted a belligerent woman in a headscarf. 'I seen him with my own eyes, so I did, not two minutes ago. He's one of them ye're lookin' for, I swear it.'

'I assure you I've reported it. There's a whole company of men on their way to deal with him. I've less than half as many to fight off the Vigilantes –'

'A dozen of us seen him, yon feller with the gun. Run right over there to the shipyard, so he did. He'll be gone before yez dozy bastards do anythin'.'

The officer's reply was lost. Finn and Caragh walked past, mesmerized. Nobody spared them a second glance; they looked as much like refugees as the rest.

'Only one of them,' Caragh said quietly.

'With a rifle. Into the shipyards. It's obvious, isn't it?'

'Billy. Then where's Con Michael?'

'Only one person can tell us that. We've got just a few minutes to find him.'

Across the wide road and beyond the piers of the Sydenham Bypass flyover sprawled the enormous complex of the Harland and Wolff yards. Where in that maze of docks and buildings and half-built ships and machinery that Billy knew so well did one begin to look for him? Finn was too exhausted even to question the necessity of looking. Their search for Con Michael, their paltry attempt to do something for him – God alone knew what – had acquired a momentum of its own. Together they crossed the road.

The shipyards were surrounded by a concrete fence made of prefabricated sections about eight feet high and two wide. Could Billy, weakened from loss of blood, have climbed it? After walking along the fence for a minute they had the answer. One of the sections had fallen out. On the edge of the adjoining one was a smudge of blood.

Finn looked at Caragh. 'He may be planning to hole up in here. He'll be dangerous. You'd better not come in.'

'He trusts me,' she said. 'He'll talk to me sooner than you. Besides, I can't go back there.'

He glanced back. The familiar pillars of smoke rose from three or four places in the Short Strand, and a steady stream of Catholic refugees now moved out of the area. The Vigilantes would ignore the shipyards but the army wouldn't – not now that they knew Billy McGarry was in there. There was no way of telling how soon the reinforcements would arrive.

Nobody was within a hundred yards of where they stood. No one saw them slip through the gap in the fence, and at the moment no one would care anyway. They slithered down a grassy bank, crossed two railway lines, and went through an empty car park. They had no idea where to begin looking for Billy but they headed naturally for the focal point, the main building dock where, visible above the rooftops of storage sheds and office buildings, an oil tanker was under construction. On a normal day the yards would be clangorous with activity; now their enormousness only emphasized the silence.

Keeping close to whatever cover they could find and avoiding open spaces, they came within a couple of minutes to the block assembly area, from which prefabricated sections would be lifted by the travelling Goliath crane that straddled the dock, carried to the ship, and lowered into position. Crouching in the shadow of some elephantine steel structure, Caragh caught her breath.

'Look!'

A splash of blood, bigger than the earlier ones, lay on the concrete apron ahead of them. It was wet and bright. Billy had been that way not five minutes before.

Finn and Caragh now faced the stern of the tanker, a couple of hundred yards away. With a flash of insight he looked at the ship more closely. Soon, at something like a quarter million tons deadweight, she'd be ready for floating out of the dock. Now she was still a land-bound monster trapped in a meshwork of scaffolding. The only access to her upper deck, a hundred feet above the floor of the dock, was by a single stairway tower that rose from the sill on the starboard side.

'Up there,' Finn said, 'is the ideal place for a sniper to hole up.'

'Does he really mean to fight?'

'What else can he do? There's nowhere left to run. He won't surrender.'

'Let me go up,' Caragh said, 'and try to talk to him.'

'We'll go together.'

'He won't harm me. For all he knows you might have helped betray him.'

'How badly to you want to find your brother?'

'Not badly enough to want you killed.'

He shook his head. 'He's got to be asked the right questions. We've very little time.'

She shrugged. Cautiously, footsteps echoing, they approached the ship. Perhaps because of his exhaustion, Finn was oddly unperturbed by the idea that Billy might shoot him. He did want to speak to Billy anyway. He wanted to explore the possibilities of a half-formed idea that might even be to his own benefit.

His need for rest had become desperate. He could still taste the nausea gas in his throat. When he reached the foot of the stairway tower he wondered whether he had taken on too much. There were seven flights of stairs; the whole structure, erected to give workmen access to the upper deck, was of openwork steel and would afford little cover from the ground.

They saw another smudge of blood on the handrail. They began to climb.

After two flights they rested for half a minute. They climbed two more, paused again, and then plodded grimly on up the last three flights. The army would descend on the place any minute now. They must find Billy, talk to him, and get clear.

The top platform rose a few feet above the level of the upper deck, to which it was connected by a short ramp. They found themselves facing the half-built deckhouse. Forward of it, the acres of raw steel were covered with an incredible jumble of cables, drums, piping, bollards, and ventilation cowls waiting to be fitted. They stood at the foot of the ramp. Caragh called, 'Billy?'

Her voice echoed. She went to walk forward but Finn stopped her, guessing that from somewhere among the chaos they were being watched. Then came the same sound he had heard on the night he first met Billy, the compelling click of the rifle bolt being released. Heart thumping, he took Caragh's arm and they walked towards it.

Billy stood waiting for them in a narrow recess between two upright cable drums. He still wore the black track suit he must have used in the ambush last night, and there were traces of blacking grease which emphasized the dreadful pallor of his face. The rifle was cradled in his left arm. The right one hung by his side, dripping blood steadily from the wrist. A wide pool of it was growing tacky beneath the soles of his black sneakers. The tourniquet had been made with a sleeve torn off his shirt; since he'd had to tie it onehanded and in haste it had worked its way loose and was sodden with blood. They stared at each other for several seconds.

'Well, Billy.' Finn spoke to break the silence. Whatever he said would sound banal. 'You really did it this time, didn't you?'

'How'd you find me at all?'

'Followed your blood from the jazz club. You've left plenty behind.'

'So quick? Is others comin'?

'The army will be here soon.'

Billy nodded and leaned weakly against one of the cable drums. The flat grey eyes were misty. He glanced at the head of the stairway twenty yards off. 'I'll be ready for them, any road. That's the only way up.'

'You won't be ready for anything if you go on bleeding like that.'

Finn stepped forward and took his wrist. Billy, caught between surprise and suspicion, let him strip off the soaking rag. The gash was just deep enough to have snicked the radial artery without sending it into spasm, and blood welled rhythmically out. Finn gave a moment's thought to a fresh binding, then pulled off his tie and wound it tightly round the wrist, knotting it two inches above the wound. The flow was reduced again to a trickle. Billy nodded once more; it was the nearest he could get to thanks.

'We didn't know what had happened till we saw the morning papers,' Caragh told him. 'We came looking for you at once.'

'You came lookin' for Con Michael, you mean.' Billy gave the hint of a sardonic smile. 'Never mind, it's natural enough. I'll put you out of your misery. He's in England by now.'

Caragh's mouth opened in surprise.

'He stowed away on the ferry to Heysham,' Billy said. 'There was a wee steward he knew who'd help him. Only him, mind. I insisted we split up and take our chances separately. He must be safe over there by this time.'

'What do you mean, safe?' Finn asked.

Billy stared at him, surprised that his meaning should be questioned.

'Safer than you are, perhaps, but not much. You're trying to make Caragh feel better, aren't you, Billy?' Finn turned to her. 'He knows as well as I do that your brother is still in danger in England. Maybe the Vigilantes can't get to him but the movement certainly can. So can the police.'

Billy watched him for a few moments more and then shrugged. 'All right. Work it out for yourselves. I've my own problems.'

'Are you staying up here?'

'Sure I am.'

'They'll be here soon. They'll try and talk you into surrendering. After that there'll be no second chances.'

'Lookit,' Billy said, 'I'm after killin' eight men. Eight. I did it because I believed in the man I was doin' it for. Now there's none of that left. I've done time and I always swore I'd never go back inside. If I can kill any more today I will, and this time it'll be for me. For Billy.'

The words, softly uttered, sounded oddly vehement in the empty resonance of the ship. Billy's eyes moved restlessly. In his weakened state his manner was wilder, showing hints of his instability, that synthesis of cunning and bitterness and deprivation that had made him what he was. He was having one of his talkative patches.

'We listened to the news flashes on the radio last night. After it was all over, like, and us hidden somewhere we thought was safe. When we heard what Sullivan was sayin' there we just couldn't believe it, we thought it must be a mistake altogether. Then we heard they was out lookin' for us. We'd nowhere else to go. Con Michael had his pal on the ferry. Me, I went lookin' for someone, just one friend, who'd maybe bring me out into the country somewhere. Nothing. When the movement turns against you people get afraid. I'd nowhere but the old jazz club there.'

Finn, feeling suddenly dizzy, sat down on a paper sack full of welding flux. Billy stayed in his recess, leaning against the drum, his left hand round the pistol grip of the rifle. He looked as if he, too, could hardly stand upright.

'We were all meant to die,' Finn said. 'You, me, Con Michael. You knew too much, like me. I want to help Con Michael, Billy. Where will I find him?'

'No idea. He's a couple of friends in the Smoke, that's all I know.'

'What friends? Where?'

'He didn't say. D'you think we had time to talk about it? Friends from the days when he worked over there.'

'Has he ever mentioned names?'

'Never at all.'

'Spain,' said Caragh suddenly.

'What?'

'Frank Spain. I've been trying to remember it. That was the name of his best friend in London, a Limerick man. He talked about him once or twice. I'd have no idea where to go looking for him, though.'

'Places,' Finn said to Billy. 'Has he ever talked about places he used to frequent?'

'No. Wait a bit now,' said Billy, hesitating. 'You really do want to help him, don't you?'

'Yes. There's no time to explain why.'

Billy rubbed his jaw, considering. Finn glanced at his watch. It was twenty to eleven; they'd been on the deck of the tanker for ten minutes. In the same moment that his mind registered the fact his ears picked up an ominous sound, a deep, insistent drone. He looked round. Three helicopters were approaching in line-ahead formation over the Lough. They'd be above the ship-yards in a minute or two.

He stood up. 'What do you know?' he demanded.

'All right,' Billy said quickly. 'If Caragh will trust you, so must I. Kilburn. They'd do a powerful bit of drinkin' at a pub in Kilburn, him and whoever his friends were. It was called Colleen Kavanagh's. He was always on about it.'

'Thanks, Billy.'

'You'd better go.' Again there was the suggestion of a smile. 'Sorry I never got to hear your King Oliver music.'

They scrambled for the stairway tower. Once off the top plat-form they were reasonably safe from being seen. Descending the stairs, Finn watched carefully as the helicopter spread out over the yards, flitting between the cantilever cranes, dipping and hovering curiously above the rooftops, the deck of the tanker, and other elevated positions. They were spotters; ground troops would soon be moving in.

From the foot of the tower Finn and Caragh scuttled through the ordered confusion of equipment on the dockside and then among bollards and crane legs at the edge of the apron. It was important not to be seen from the air, to get out the way they had come before the troops on the ground closed their perimeter and trapped them.

They hadn't too much to worry about. Within a couple of minutes the helicopter crews had spotted Billy and were circling the deckhouse of the tanker, relaying information to the company of paratroopers being driven through the main gate of the yards. Finn and Caragh were crossing the railway tracks and scrambling up the grassy bank to the gap in the fence before the soldiers had closed in to surround the ship.

Things did not happen as Billy had expected them to.

He had guessed, correctly, that the deck of the tanker was too cluttered to allow a helicopter to land an assault party on it. He had assumed that the only other way they could come was up the narrow stairway tower, and he had the top platform well covered. He could have killed half a dozen of them before they got near him. Billy had overlooked a third alternative.

For almost half an hour after the paratroopers had moved into position, nothing happened except that he was twice invited through a loudhailer to surrender. He did not bother to reply. Sitting down now in the recess, harbouring his strength, he began to wonder whether they planned to starve him out or let him bleed to death. That wouldn't happen in a hurry, thanks to Finn's fancy tie. There was still some blood flowing, but not much. He had to flex the hand constantly to prevent it going to sleep.

Even when he heard the diesel generators of the Goliath crane start up, Billy did not realize quite what was happening. The crane was parked over the block assembly area, well astern. He had not been in a position to see the assault party of hand-picked marksmen enter its pier leg and travel up to the bridge girders, three hundred feet from the ground, where they were stationed at intervals along the open walkway. Only when the crane began to move, beginning a journey of a quarter of a mile to the ship, did he understand.

A fear possessed him unlike anything he had known before, a feeling that had nothing directly to do with the prospect of dying. He knew what everyone who had worked in the shipyards knew, that the Goliath was the biggest crane in the world. It straddled the hundred-yard width of the dock and moved along its twin tracks at something less than a walking pace, titanically unstoppable, warning sirens yelping like attendant dogs at its feet. What frightened him was that this awesome progress was on account of him.

As the crane approached he summoned up his strength and moved, picking his way forward among the debris, hoping for a clear line of sight to the men on the walkway. But the sun was now high and obliquely behind them and they were lying down, offering the smallest possible targets.

The crane overarched the stern of the ship. Its shadow fell over him. He began to hurry, as if movement itself had become important, darting from cowl to cable drum to pipe joint. The helicopters followed. He had thought there was plenty of cover; now he knew that from directly above there was little chance of concealment.

He paused, crouching behind a packing case. The nearer the bow he got, the more the debris on the deck thinned out. He had never been panicky or impetuous but something was urging him on; something unnerved him about the sheer size of the machine they were using to destroy him. It was as if an understanding of his own infamy had suddenly come home to him. The crane had almost drawn level. He moved forward.

A shot splintered the corner of the packing case, six inches from his face. He flung himself down behind it, trembling. Then he squirmed round the case and suddenly two more bullets had screamed off the steel plate of the deck. They could see him. He must keep moving.

He darted to a bollard, then to a stack of pipe sections. The crane rumbled on. In front of him now was open deck for the length of a cricket pitch. Cables were strewn across it, but there was no cover of any kind. He must cross it. He discovered that his tourniquet had worked its way loose and blood was dripping again. The bridge of the crane was directly above him now.

He ran, zigzagging. The deck all around him rang with the impact of flattening bullets. On the walkway the paratroopers had stood up and were firing almost vertically down on him.

He got within five yards of the nearest cover, a heap of scaffold tubing. Then he tripped on a cable and sprawled on the deck, letting go of his rifle. The next bullet took him between the shoulder-blades.

The paratroopers did not stop shooting until they were very sure that Billy was dead. By then he was barely recognizable.

By then, too, Finn was driving to Aldergrove airport.

Using the crane had been the idea of some Protestant workmen. For the chance of sharing in the destruction of Kilshaw's murderer they had broken their strike.

38

Colleen Kavanagh's was what you would expect it to be, an Irish fortress in the alien wastes of north London. It was cavernous, gloomy, and bare, with Guinness beer mats on the tables and handbills advertising Gaelic dances taped to the front of a glass cabinet containing stale sausage rolls. On a Wednesday evening it was quiet, a low point between pay packets. Finn ordered a Scotch and asked the curly-haired young barman casually if Frank Spain had been in.

'Not yet, no.'

'You're expecting him, then?'

The barman picked up his English accent; it caused a moment's hesitation. 'He's in some evenings,' he said, back-pedalling.

'Midweek evenings?'

'Sometimes.'

It was promising enough. Frank Spain was still a regular; he hoped the man, if he did have something to hide, was intelligent enough not to change his routine.

'I'll wait,' Finn said. 'Tell him I'm here when he arrives, would you?'

He sat down on a hard bench across from the counter. The other customers had noticed the accent too; they watched him with guarded interest. There were about a dozen of them, mostly solitary men hunched over their pint glasses, expatriates contemplating the emptiness of the evening. One, a man with amazingly soft blue eyes, wore a scab in the middle of his forehead distinctively shaped by the rim of a broken glass.

He'd had an hour's sleep on the plane from Belfast – enough

to keep him going for a couple more. His head had cleared sufficiently to allow him to form a plan for the next few days. He no longer wondered quite so much why he was doing it. Partly it was for Con Michael's own sake, though he still couldn't pretend any liking for the young man; partly for Caragh's sake; and very definitely, now that he'd had a chance to weigh things up, in the interests of his own safety.

Instinctively he recognized Frank Spain the moment he entered the pub, even before the barman began a whispered conversation with him. Frank Spain looked Spanish, with eyes like black olives and a bold, full, sensuous mouth that had never originated in Limerick. Almost certainly he was one of those west coast Irishmen descended from the survivors of the Armada who had limped ashore there to leave their genetic stamp on the community.

The barman was pointing. Spain stared at Finn and then walked over slowly. He was about thirty, with straight, greasy black hair that fell across the shoulders of a stained pullover. His fingernails were cracked and grimed with builders' dirt. The other customers watched, but they were out of earshot.

'Is it me you're wanting?'

'Yes. The name is Finn. We have a mutual friend who may have mentioned me.'

He watched the other's face for a reaction; Spain's hostile stare continued.

'I can't think who you mean.'

'Do you want me naming names?'

'I don't know what you're on about, feller.'

'You ought to know who's hiding him even if you aren't.'

'Now lookit...' The big navvy fists clenched; behind him the drinkers stirred, sensing the welcome rarity of a midweek punch-up. 'What do you want in here talkin' nonsense? You're not welcome at all. You'd best get out damned quick.'

Finn watched him coldly. 'Do you want me to say his name out loud? In front of them? The movement has a lot of friends in this part of London.'

The aggressive stance was suddenly abandoned. 'I can't tell you nothing,' Spain muttered. 'I've not seen him in three years.'

'I didn't say you had. Just listen. I want a message delivered. I don't care how it reaches him. I can get him out. But I must be put in touch with him now, tonight. Yes, out of the country. I can get him off the hands of whoever's hiding him.'

Spain hesitated, gulped, succumbed slightly. 'What'd be in it for you?' he asked.

'Never mind. Just tell him Finn wants to see him.'

'How do I know you're not a copper?'

'You don't,' said Finn maliciously.

'What d'ye expect me to do then?'

'Go away and speak to the right people. Be back within an hour. I won't stay longer than an hour.'

'No. Wait till I make a phone call.'

He was away ten minutes. When he returned the look he gave Finn was a very strange one indeed.

'Come on with me now,' he said.

39

For some reason, people who had stayed once at Finn's hotel in Belfast would usually be given the same room the next time. Rumour said it was to make life easier for the army telephone tappers. But Caragh had checked in under her own name while Finn was flying to London; when he returned he found they had been given a room two doors down from his old one on the fifth floor.

He slept for twelve hours. It was midday on Thursday when Caragh pulled open the curtains and he sat up, blinking, to look out across the city. Several fires had been visible during the night, but now only two or three columns of thin smoke rose above the outlying reaches. As he had expected, the Vigilantes were running out of steam.

'Will I come back over with you?' Caragh asked.

'That's the worst thing you could do. You'll be watched. Go back to Dublin and wait. When things look safe I'll send for you. You'll be putting him at risk otherwise.'

'I know him so well,' she said. 'He's not built to survive in these conditions, no matter what he tells himself. Are you sure this idea of yours will work?'

'I'm not guaranteeing it. If he does exactly what I tell him he'll stand a good chance.'

She'd been trying to hide her anxiety about her brother but it kept breaking through. He got up, went to the window, squeezed her arm, and kissed her reassuringly. Affection turned to a languid desire and he led her back to the bed again.

Later, when they were dressed and thinking about lunch, she said, 'You're the strangest man, do you know that?'

'Oh?'

'Gentle. And yet ruthless too. You can be as ruthless as Sullivan when you've a mind to.'

'I've got an interest in survival, that's all. I've learned not to take it for grant –'

The room seemed to give a jerk; the whole building shuddered. There came a thick, compressed crump from somewhere through the walls and, a second later, the tinkle of blown-out glass in the forecourt below.

'Jesus Christ!' Finn breathed. He caught a glimpse of his face, drained suddenly of colour, in the dressing-table mirror as he ran for the door. He flung it open and turned down the corridor.

Frightened faces were appearing at other doors but he was the first one there. Smoke poured from what would have been his room. The door hung outwards on one twisted hinge. As he wrenched it open the reek of bitter almonds caught at the back of his throat.

The room still swirled with dirty grey smoke. Chemical slime clung to the walls. The bomb had been planted – perhaps in a cardboard box, shreds of which could still be identified – and primed to go off as the bathroom doer was opened. It had blown the wall of the bathroom through the built-in cupboard opposite. Blood was sprayed everywhere, as if a bag full of the stuff had burst, and among the bricks and broken white tiles lay several things recognizable but grotesquely disembodied: half a rib cage, a hand, a pair of tights with one pale leg still inside. One stained and lumpy shape was wrapped in part of the green overall of a chambermaid.

The shocked faces had formed a semicircle behind him. Then others were pushing them aside, a security guard, an assistant manager, the house doctor. At the end of the corridor someone was screaming hysterically. Finn turned away.

'*Who?*' demanded Caragh in a fierce whisper. She had

followed him out; they stepped back now into the doorway of their own room. 'Who'd do that to you?'

'You name it. The Vigilantes? The IRA? Quite a few people would prefer me dead. I can think of one who would take some trouble to kill me, but I didn't expect it so soon. All I'm sure about is that it's time to get out.'

'Back to London? Already?'

'I'm not waiting to give them another chance. I can't wait till the police start asking questions about the recent occupants of that room either. I'll send for you when it's safe.'

'You mean that, Finn?'

'I mean it,' he said. And he did, but had no time to consider its implications. He pecked her on the cheek and walked away, back through the throng of people outside the bombed room towards the lift.

In the lobby he had a moment of panic. It was already filling with policemen; people trying to check out were being questioned and their baggage was being searched. Finn had no baggage. He walked out of the door just as an ambulance crew came in, matter-of-factly unfolding the plastic bags in which the remains of the dead chambermaid would be collected.

There was only one cab at the rank outside Great Victoria Street station, and it was pulling away with a fare just as Finn approached. He stood fuming with nervous impatience for two minutes until another arrived.

'Aldergrove,' he said. 'As quick as you can.'

There must be a flight to somewhere in the next hour or so – London, Glasgow, Birmingham, it didn't matter which. This country, North and South, grew unhealthier for him by the minute. He wouldn't even have returned from London last night except to reassure Caragh. Well, to see Caragh; perhaps that was nearer the truth. He knew now that he would send for her, and he knew she would come.

The journey took twenty minutes. The other taxi from the station rank had come to the airport too and was dropping its passenger in front of the terminal building. Finn's driver pulled in behind. He got out, reached for his wallet, and then recognized the other arrival, now entering the building.

It was Partington.

Even from the rear, in a velvet-collared overcoat and an astrakhan hat, he was unmistakable, a dumpy figure hurrying self-importantly past the policemen on guard at the door towards the BEA reservations counter. In one gloved hand he carried a bulky briefcase.

Finn stared in a stupor for a few seconds before thrusting three pound notes into the driver's hand and following. A growing certainty now possessed him, and a growing anger. Suddenly he was channelling all the pain and fear and outrage into a consuming hatred of Partington. His hands twitched; he longed to hurt, scar, humiliate – physically, because no other way was possible. He stopped a few feet short of the counter, where the fat man had presented his ticket.

'There's one to London in forty minutes,' the girl was saying. 'Will that do?'

Finn stepped forward. 'Can you get me on that flight as well?' he asked.

'If you'll wait just a moment, sir...'

Partington looked round – with no surprise, with no expression but the oily stare that Englishmen reserve for strangers who speak out of turn. Beneath the ridiculous hat, with his neck hidden under heavy clothing, his face looked fuller and flabbier than before, his features smaller. He said nothing and turned away, drumming with gloved fingers on the counter as the return portion of his ticket was filled in.

Someone else attended to Finn. Anger made it difficult to control his speech, explain what he wanted. They had a seat for him on the London flight, but he had to buy a ticket and was still waiting for it when Partington left the counter. Finn watched him stop at the check-in desk and then mount the stairs to the departure lounge. A minute later he followed.

Standing at the head of the stairs he looked across from the cafeteria at one end to the bar at the other. The lounge was un-crowded. He saw Partington walking towards the door of the men's lavatory at one side of the bar. He was making it easy – perhaps too easy, Finn might have thought if he had been clearer-headed. He was obsessed with the urge to punish, to inflict on Partington some of the responsibility for what he had done. He did not care about the consequences. He walked towards the door, pausing at a vacant table near the bar to pick up an empty lager bottle. A minute alone with him was all he wanted, a minute in which to see fear and pain distort the self-indulgent features.

He pushed the door open and rounded the screening wall. Partington stood at a corner of the urinal, his back towards him. The briefcase was on the floor behind him. They were alone.

'Partington!'

He turned.

Finn stepped forward, raising the bottle, ready to smash off its base on the edge of a washbasin.

'I shouldn't come any closer, Finn.'

He stopped. Partington held something which he had raised to shoulder height, ready to be thrown but kept well clear of his face. It was a wide-mouthed glass jar half full of colourless liquid. The lid was off; across the space of six or seven feet between them Finn could smell bitter almonds.

'Nitrobenzene,' Partington said. 'Dangerous stuff.'

Finn stood where he was. If he'd needed proof of what Partington had done, there it was. 'I noticed it makes a good bang,' he said.

'With other constituents. On its own it's poisonous. A faceful of this, Finn, and you'll very likely die. Not at *once*, so I'm told. The skin absorbs it; it attacks the nervous system. Slowly. Just imagine – I was about to flush it down the drain.' He gave what was meant to be a puckish smile; the inner coldness had never been more evident. 'Were you hoping to teach me a lesson? You can't, you know, certainly not by behaving like a soccer hooligan. If you've got something to say be quick about it. Get rid of that first.'

Finn's anger had given way suddenly to weariness. Resignedly he tossed the bottle into a wastebin full of paper towels. In the event he might not have been able to use it anyway. 'You've tried to kill me twice,' he said. 'Once in Dublin, once today. Is it that important, what I know? Are you that afraid I'll embarrass you? Will you try again?'

'Perhaps.' Partington lowered the jar of nitrobenzene but did not let go of it. 'I don't *expect* you to become an embarrassment, Finn. I'd simply rather guard against the possibility. It's *tidier*. It would allow a number of quite important people to sleep more easily.'

'Because I know that they arranged to have Kilshaw murdered? And supplied guns to the IRA?'

'Quite so. Sometime, for some reason, the occasion might arise, you see, where it suited you to reveal it. I don't say that many people would *believe* you; you've not a shred of proof and there are no other witnesses. But if you went about it the right way you could cause something of a stir. We'd rather you didn't have the opportunity.'

'There is one other witness,' Finn said. 'Con Michael Hughes. You expected him to die too, didn't you? To be killed by his own people or the Vigilantes in the first few hours after Kilshaw's murder. It didn't happen.'

'He'll be found soon,' Partington said. 'He'll go to jail

protesting that Sullivan double-crossed him. Nobody will listen. He knows very little.'

'He knows more than you think.' Finn paused. 'He and I had a long talk last night. We exchanged all the information we had. We agreed on a sort of mutual insurance policy.'

'You −?' The automatic flush in the urinal suddenly came to life, preventing Partington from speaking for several seconds. When he did his tone was sceptical. 'Are you trying to tell me *you* know where he is, when his own people can't Find him?'

'I was sent in the right direction by Billy McGarry. Yesterday. Before he was killed. Don't you believe that either? Why don't you ask to see the clothes he was wearing when they brought him out of the shipyards? There was a tourniquet made out of a silk tie. You'll remember the tie — the one I was wearing on Tuesday. If you still need convincing, look at the maker's address on the tag. Jermyn Street.'

Partington watched him without expression. But for the first time since Finn had known him he seemed lost for a rejoinder.

'Con Michael and I agreed on this,' Finn went on. 'If you have him killed to shut him up, then I will ensure that the whole story is aired in the most damaging possible way. And vice versa. We both have the facts at our fingertips. We'll use the Opposition, the radical press, any other means we can. The only way you can stop it happening is by killing us both together, and we'll make damned sure you never find us together.'

'What if...? I can't stop the *police* looking for him.'

'We think we can handle that end of things. All we want from you, your committee, the IRA, is to be left alone. For you it's the only guarantee of silence.'

Partington nodded very slowly for perhaps half a minute. Then he seemed to notice the nitrobenzene in his hand. He held the jar out at arm's length and emptied it carefully down the pissoir. He threw the jar into the wastebin.

'Very well, Finn. Stalemate in preference to *defeat*, hm? I always thought you weren't to be trusted. Come along, we'll miss our plane at this rate.'

40

On Saturday morning Finn travelled by four different tube trains, two buses, and a taxi and finished up less than two miles from his own flat. He didn't think there'd been anyone tailing him. If there had, he was certain by now that he'd shaken them off.

The house was a few minutes' walk from Colleen Kavanagh's pub, a run-down Victorian semi in a street already half fallen to the council demolishers. Daylight accentuated some of the squalor which darkness, on Finn's last visit, had managed to conceal: the overflowing dustbins, the leaking drain which had nourished green slime on the steps, the sheet of hardboard covering a broken window. The building had been gradually subdivided as it drifted down the social scale, from a family house into three flats, then into a dozen rooms, most of them now occupied by Irish labourers and their families.

The ground floor smelt of babies and boiled cabbage. Finn gave two light knocks on a door on the first-floor landing. Frank Spain's black eyeball appeared at a hole burned with a cigarette end through one of the upper panels. A key rattled in the lock and he was allowed in.

The bed-sitter was small and cramped and smelt vaguely, as it had before, of unwashed clothing. Con Michael, sitting on the end of the bed, had visibly lost weight in three days. His face was sallow and shadowed by a fuzz of black beard, the eyes feverish. But more than ever Finn was reassured by that superficial resemblance on which a great deal now depended.

Con Michael greeted him apprehensively. He was subdued and a bit dreamy, like a man who has suffered a recent bereavement. Finn sat down on the only chair.

'It's fixed for tomorrow,' he said.

'Not a minute too soon neither,' said Frank Spain, locking the door behind them. 'We'd have had to move himself. We've heard rumours, like. Questions are bein' asked hereabouts.'

Finn produced two documents, showing them in turn to Con Michael.

'These are what I was telling you about. This one is called an MOD Ninety. It's a travel identity and movement card. Every British serviceman has one. There's all the bumf on it: number, rank, name, photograph. The important thing to remember is that it takes the place of a passport; it's the only form of identification a serviceman needs when he travels abroad. This one is my own, of course.'

'And the other?'

'A reservation on an RAF Transport Command flight leaving Northolt in Middlesex at fourteen hundred hours tomorrow for Germany. Also mine.'

Con Michael looked at him gloomily. 'I don't know at all. D'you reckon I can really pull it off?'

'Yes. Impersonating a British officer isn't that difficult. Just look at that photograph. It was taken nine years ago when these cards were first issued. The similarity is there, even if only on the surface. What passport photograph ever really looks like the bearer? Nobody is going to check the date of issue because the card remains valid indefinitely. And the rank that's embossed on the back is captain because I never bothered to get it changed when I was last promoted. You're just old enough to pass for a bright young captain. The point is that there'll be no suspicion unless you do something incredibly stupid. They're looking for you at docks and airports; they'll never conceive of you flying out with a crowd of servicemen going back from leave to the Rhine Army.'

'It would never occur to them,' Con Michael said, 'that an officer would lend himself to the arrangement.'

'Quite,' said Finn. 'Belonging to a stereotyped class has its advantages.'

'I'm not too confident, I can tell you.'

'You'll feel better when you've smartened up. Shave and haircut, of course – officer's length, mind, don't make the mistake of having a short-back-and-sides. And you've got to dress the part. A check sports jacket is about right for a Sunday, and twill trousers, no cuffs, no flares. Can you find those somewhere?' he asked Frank Spain, who nodded.

'A shirt with a soft collar,' Finn continued, 'any style *except button-down* – that would be in shocking taste, seen only in American films. Tie, a bit trendy but nothing psychedelic. You must remember I'm atypical on every count. Soft shoes, probably rough suede. You'd better carry something in the way of hand baggage. Get yourself to Northolt in good time. Once on board, bury yourself in the *Sunday Telegraph*. And I mean the *Sunday Telegraph*. Try not to talk; they'll find your accent odd. Above all, once you've passed the control point don't use my name. You might be talking to someone who knows me.'

'And then? In Germany?'

'The plane lands at Wildenrath, a couple of miles from Rhine Army HQ. Refuse transport to Rheindalen. Get out on the road, and once you're clear of the military complex start hitching rides south, to Bonn and then to Adenau. From Adenau find your way to a village called Bischoff. The landlord of the inn has the key to my cottage, and he'll direct you there. He won't think it odd; I sometimes lend the place to close friends. There's plenty of food. I'll be in Germany by Monday, but it'll be a few days before I can safely come down to you. Then we can talk about your future. I reckon you'll need a couple of months there before the immediate heat is off.'

'What do you do for a travel document?' Con Michael asked.

'What I normally do. Use my passport. Fly on a civilian plane.

You're entitled to an Irish passport, of course. Perhaps later we'll get Caragh to apply for one on your behalf and you can move on.'

'Are you in love with my sister?' Con Michael asked suddenly.

'I don't know,' Finn said, and paused. 'As soon as I have the chance, I hope to find out.'

'Thanks for all this, Finn.'

He walked downstairs and out into the raw December morning. Children were brawling in the grounds of a high-rise council estate opposite the house, and on a wall behind them someone had chalked IS THERE LIFE BEFORE DEATH?

He hoped the idiot would remember about the button-down collar.